Sebastian. My first, my only love.

I'm coming back, I tried to tell him. *I'm coming back to Wyldcliffe.* And I seemed to hear an echo in my head: *Come back, come back, come back....*

I touched the silver necklace that was hanging on a slender new chain under my shirt. The necklace had been a gift from Frankie before she died, a pretty trinket with a sparkling crystal at its center. It had always been in our family, but if anyone had told me a few months ago that it was known as the Talisman, and that it was an heirloom of the Mystic Way, sealed with elemental forces, I would have laughed. Great joke. I didn't do weird stuff, paranormal, Wicca, magic—whatever you wanted to call it. I had been the last person on earth who fancied the idea of chanting around a bonfire under the moon.

I wasn't laughing now, though. Everything that had happened in my first term at Wyldcliffe had changed me forever. I had a new reality, however incredible it seemed.

ALSO BY
Gillian Shields

The Actual Real Reality of Jennifer James

Immortal

GILLIAN SHIELDS

Betrayal

KATHERINE TEGEN BOOKS
An Imprint of HarperCollins Publishers

*With thanks to Henry Elliott at the Romany
Life Centre, Cranbrook, Kent, England*

Katherine Tegen Books is an imprint of HarperCollins Publishers.

Library of Congress Cataloging-in-Publication Data
Shields, Gillian.
    Betrayal / by Gillian Shields. — 1st ed.
        p.   cm.
    Summary: Prompted by her love for the seemingly doomed
Sebastian, sixteen-year-old Evie Johnson returns for another term at
the strangely sinister Wyldcliffe Abbey School, where she and two close
friends try to develop and combine their newly discovered powers to save
Sebastian and themselves from the encroaching forces of evil.
    ISBN 978-0-06-137586-6
    [1. Boarding schools—Fiction.   2. Supernatural—Fiction.
3. Witches—Fiction.   4. Love—Fiction.   5. Schools—Fiction.
6. England—Fiction.]   I. Title.
PZ7.S55478Bet   2010   2009023430
[Fic]—dc22   CIP
                                                              AC

Typography by Amy Ryan
11 12 13 14 15 LP/BV   10 9 8 7 6 5 4 3 2 1
❖
First paperback edition, 2011

For my parents,
Pat and Bob Davison, with love

When you walk through the fire, you will not be burned, and the flames will not harm you.

—*Isaiah 43:2*

Prologue

My name is Evie Johnson. I am sixteen and a scholarship student at Wyldcliffe Abbey School for Young Ladies. Yes, the famous school hidden away on the bleak moors, where the wind sighs over the hills and the heather blooms under the wide, restless sky. Everyone's heard of Wyldcliffe. Everyone says how lucky I am.

What else do you want to know? Favorite subjects—history and English. Best sport—swimming. I adore Italian food, and hot chocolate, and the sound of the waves on the shore. All perfectly ordinary. Except that my boyfriend, Sebastian, is dead.

Sebastian James Fairfax. Nineteen years old, dark hair, blue eyes, a smile like an angel; poet; philosopher; my first, my only love . . . beautiful, beautiful Sebastian.

When I say *dead*, I don't mean because of a tragic car accident or some cruel illness. I mean something so different, so off-the-scale different that you can't imagine it. Sebastian is dead, and yet Sebastian is alive. Sebastian loves me, yet Sebastian is my enemy. I am alone, but I have my friends—my sisters.

Sometimes I have to remind myself that everything that happened to me last term was true, and that my story isn't over yet. I have to keep on, right to the end, whatever that might be. I have to believe that Sebastian won't betray me.

There are many kinds of betrayals. There are the small ones: the unkind word, the laughter behind someone's back, the petty lies. And there are the betrayals that break hearts, destroy worlds, and turn the strong, sweet light of day into bitter dust.

One

The holidays were over. Outside the window of the cottage, the winter dawn was cold and gray. The bare tips of the straggling rosebushes in Frankie's garden were nipped by frost. Tomorrow I wouldn't wake up in this familiar room, to the cry of seagulls wheeling out over the bay. Tomorrow everything would be different. I was going back to school. I was going back to Wyldcliffe.

My suitcase was stuffed with presents that Dad had awkwardly, tenderly forced on me. I hadn't wanted anything, but he had insisted. And so, apart from my school uniform and my textbooks and gym clothes, my luggage also contained a new camera and a whole lot of expensive gear for the riding lessons he had persuaded me to take when I got back to school.

It was as though he had been trying to make up for the pain of the first Christmas without Frankie. The only mother I had ever known, Frankie had been my darling grandmother, who had looked after me since I was a baby. Now she was gone, and Dad was trying to buy me some comfort to cushion the loss. Only a year ago, Frankie's death would have been overwhelming. But Wyldcliffe had changed me. I was stronger now, not simply a schoolkid anymore. Wyldcliffe had taught me about fear and danger and death.

It had taught me about love.

Frankie's funeral had been a few days before Christmas, in the church on the headland, with the sound of the sea sighing below the cliffs. I didn't cry. I just felt quieter than I ever had before, cut off in a circle of silence, as though the little gathering of well-wishers and neighbors, and the vicar and the hymns and the flowers, were nothing to do with me or Frankie. She had gone, like a bird flying into the dawn, and all the rest was a soothing ritual for the people left behind. But Dad was really upset. Afterward, when everyone had drifted away murmuring clichés and condolences, he blew his nose and wiped his red eyes like the gruff soldier he pretended to be, and said, "Sorry, Evie, it brought back everything

about Clara . . . your mom . . . sorry . . ."

He was remembering my mother's funeral, fifteen years ago. I had no memory of it, of course. I was only a baby when she died. *Sorry*, Dad said, *so sorry*, and loaded me up with presents that I didn't really want. Then the days had slipped past, tender with grief, until it was time for me to return to school and leave the gulls and the cliffs and the sea behind me once again.

Now my bags were packed and ready, and the holidays were over. I was going back.

I glanced at my little clock near the bed. The day was only just beginning, but I could already hear that Dad was up, getting ready to start the long journey to London. It was time for me to get up too, though there was someone I had to talk to before I did anything else. I pulled on a pair of jeans and a sweater and crept out of the cottage, heading down the rocky path to the beach.

As I hurried along, the pale sun rose from behind the clouds, spilling a wash of light on the waves. I took a deep breath. Those powerful waters gave me strength. *Well, she's always loved the sea, poor girl*, the kind neighbors had said when they saw me hanging about the beach every morning, but they couldn't guess the truth. I actually needed to be near the water, like I needed to breathe. Waking or sleeping, I heard its voice calling me, I felt it quicken my body, and I felt its restless pull. *Water for Evie*, Helen had said. *I thought it would be like that.*

I went down to the edge of the sea and closed my eyes, giving my mind to my mystical, beautiful element. I reached out for its power, asking for what I wanted most in the whole world. The waves beating on the shore echoed in my heart and pulsed through my veins. And then he was there.

Sebastian walked over the pebbles and came up behind me, dropping a kiss onto the back of my neck.

"Poor Evie," he said. "You're sad today, my girl from the sea."

"Not when I'm with you." I sighed and leaned back against his chest and nestled in his arms. Just to be close to Sebastian was happiness itself, enough to wipe out every other sorrow. "Don't move," I said. "I want to watch the sun on the waves."

We stood and watched together as the light grew stronger and the gulls swooped low.

"I shall always think of you at sunrise after this," Sebastian said. "You're my sunrise, Evie, my new beginning. My life was nothing before I found you. And it would be worth nothing if I ever lost you."

"You'll never lose me, Sebastian," I replied, and for some reason I shivered. "Don't even say it. We'll always be together."

"Always," he said quietly. "Forever."

I wanted to stay like that, not moving, overwhelmed by the miracle of finding each other in all the million chances of the world. But Sebastian's mood changed in an instant and he laughed teasingly. "Aren't you going to swim?" he asked. "I've heard that mermaids swim in all weather."

"Only if you'll swim with me." I laughed in reply, knowing that the water was freezing and all we could do on a cold January morning was skim stones and scramble over the rocks and hold each other for warmth, clinging together like the roses clung to the old walls of the cottage.

"We'll come back here in the summer to swim, Evie. And we'll feel the sun on our faces all day long, then stay up late and make a campfire on the beach, and watch the stars wheel across the sky."

"It sounds perfect."

"Everything's going to be perfect for us. You can tell me stories about when you were a child, and I'll make up bad poems in praise of your beauty, and we'll talk and wonder and laugh and put the whole world right. We'll have this summer together, and the next, and the next . . . a thousand golden days, just you and me." He held me close, and the sound of the sea seemed to hypnotize me. I no longer felt cold.

A gull cried harshly in the white winter sky. "Come on. Let's walk to the headland," Sebastian said. "I want to tell you something. Something important." He pulled my hand gently to follow him, but as I started to walk by his side, he was gone. I was alone.

Had it been a dream, a fantasy, or a vision? I didn't know. I only knew the pain when the dream ended, and I had to face the truth. Sebastian wasn't there. Oh, he came to me in snatches like this, but it wasn't enough. Before I could stop myself, I cried out, "Come back . . . where are you . . . where are you?" But there was no reply.

I was alone, and the wind was icy, like tears falling on snow. Sebastian was far away and I didn't know whether I would ever see him again.

Two

Dad and I traveled together as far as London, where we had decided to say our good-byes on the platform of King's Cross station.

"Take these to share with your friends," Dad said, handing over an expensive box of chocolates. I was going to make the journey north to Wyldcliffe on my own, and Dad was returning to his duties in the army. He was still young and fit—well, not so young now, but definitely attractive—and as we waited together in those limbo moments, I wondered why he had never married again. The answer flashed into my head: *Because of you, Evie, because of you.* . . . I felt a quick pain in my heart when I thought of everything he had done for me, and I hugged him tight.

"Have a good term." He smiled. "And write to me."

"Of course. Every week."

"Evie . . ." Dad hesitated. "Promise me you'll look after yourself. I worry about you. You're growing up so quickly."

"I'm fine, Dad. Honestly." I climbed aboard and the train began to pull away. I leaned out of the window and waved as the platform was left behind and Dad got smaller, looking somehow diminished and gray in the distance. "I'm fine," I whispered, then dropped onto a seat, stuffing the chocolates into my bag. At least this time I had friends to share them with: two solitary friends out of the massed ranks of snobby, unwelcoming Wyldcliffe students. When I had taken this train back in September I had been a new girl going into the unknown, but now Sarah and Helen would be waiting for me when I arrived at school.

I was longing to see them both. They were more than my friends; they were my family—my sisters. The three of us were bound by mysterious ties that still astonished me. We had been drawn into a world of beauty and danger, and each of us had a powerful elemental connection. *Water for Evie, earth for Sarah, air for Helen . . .* There was nothing we couldn't do, I told myself, if we stayed true to

one another and to our secret sister, Lady Agnes Templeton. She was my distant ancestor, the fourth member of
our Circle and the servant of the sacred fire. As the train
gathered speed through the dreary suburbs, everything
that had happened last term churned around my head like
an endless mantra: *Agnes, Sebastian . . . Fire, water, earth,
air . . . Agnes . . . Sebastian . . . Sebastian . . .*

Sebastian. My first, my only love.

I'm coming back, I tried to tell him. *I'm coming back to
Wyldcliffe.* And I seemed to hear an echo in my head: *Come
back, come back, come back. . . .*

I touched the silver necklace that was hanging on a
slender new chain under my shirt. The necklace had been
a gift from Frankie before she died, a pretty trinket with
a sparkling crystal at its center. It had always been in our
family, but if anyone had told me a few months ago that
it was known as the Talisman, and that it was an heirloom of the Mystic Way, sealed with elemental forces, I
would have laughed. Great joke. I didn't do weird stuff,
paranormal, Wicca, magic—whatever you wanted to call
it. I had been the last person on earth who fancied the idea
of chanting around a bonfire under the moon.

I wasn't laughing now, though. Everything that had
happened in my first term at Wyldcliffe had changed

me forever. I had a new reality, however incredible it seemed.

Sebastian James Fairfax, it said on his gravestone. *Born in 1865. It is thought he departed this Life in 1884, by his own hand. God rest his soul.* Sebastian hadn't died, though. Young, impetuous, and restless, he had been loved by Agnes all those years ago. When they had stumbled across the ancient teachings of the Mystic Way, Sebastian had ignored her warnings and searched too far and too deep, corrupting its sacred powers in a doomed quest for immortality. He had learned to prolong his existence, but ultimately he had only half fulfilled his tormented search for everlasting life. Now he was bound by the terrible masters he had served, the Unconquered, who had cheated death and lived forever in the shadows. They would ensure that Sebastian would pay the price for his failure to join their ranks.

The ugly buildings and sparse trees that flashed past the train looked so real and solid and normal. But my world was not like that anymore. I had left normal behind when I had first met Sebastian in the September twilight. Now I lived in a world of unseen powers and impossibilities.

My dreadful, unimaginable reality was that Sebastian

was doomed to fade, to wither in body and spirit until he was a demon, a slave of the Unconquered, not their equal. His only hope—the one desperate option left to him—was to take the Talisman and use its mystical powers to become one of the Unconquered himself. And the only way he could possess the Talisman was to kill me.

Sometimes, reality was too painful to bear.

I shifted in my seat and rested my aching head on the cool glass of the window. A memory forced itself into my mind; I saw an underground crypt lit by flickering torches and a crowd of hooded women, the coven of Dark Sisters who had once served Sebastian. They were chanting in a wild frenzy, desperate for Sebastian to claim the Talisman and lead them to eternal life. Sarah and Helen and I had been trapped there, and yet—and yet—when it seemed that we were beaten and that Sebastian would tear the Talisman from me, he had refused to hurt me. *I love you . . . I love you, girl from the sea.* His love had given me the courage to reach out to my elemental powers, and I had raised a storm that had swept the coven away. But when it was all over, Sebastian had disappeared. His black horse had been found wandering over the moors, and all trace of its rider had vanished.

I had to see him again, though. Dreams weren't enough.

Memories weren't enough. I was going back to Wyld-cliffe to find Sebastian, but I didn't know what would be waiting for me. All I could do was ask myself the same unanswerable questions for the hundredth time. What was Sebastian's reality—his love for me or his need for the Talisman? Would he stay true to his brief words of love? Or would he, in the end, betray me in order to save himself?

"Come on, come on, hurry up," I muttered under my breath to the train. I had to get to Wyldcliffe. I had to know the truth.

Three

FROM THE PRIVATE PAPERS OF
SEBASTIAN JAMES FAIRFAX

It's because I love you that I had to tell you the truth.

You know everything now, Evie. You know that these were my failings: greed, ambition, selfishness, madness, destruction.

I did not mean to do wrong. I wanted to stride across the world like a great explorer, flying near the sun, soaring in thought and time and space.

I wanted to live forever.

Now my grave lies empty and I shall never find rest there. That is the inescapable fact, the dreadful truth. That is my reality.

But there is another truth, even here in the darkness.

This memory is true. I must hold on to it and not let go.

This is what happened. I was in the crypt under the ruins at Wyldcliffe. You were there too—I saw your bright hair and your pale face—and there were women baying for your blood, screaming with fear and hatred. The coven. The Dark Sisters. They were trying to hurt you, trying to turn me against you. You were afraid. And then, beyond my own fear and my own need, I remembered something. I remembered that I loved you.

I called to you, my girl from the sea. I called out my love for you. I remember it so clearly.

You were transformed, like an angel. You summoned your powers against the High Mistress and her women: I saw the waters rise; I saw a vision of Agnes. I remember that you were close to me, and I wanted you so much, and then you were gone. Then there was only darkness and pain, and I forced myself to crawl to this hiding place.

Here, in this secret corner, I am surrounded by the tattered remnants of my former studies. I have no need of food or companionship, or light or warmth. I have pen and ink and my memories of you. I scratch out these words in order to try to reach you.

It is because I love you that I have to tell you the truth.

I am leaving this world, Evie.

Soon I will close my eyes and awake not in your arms but into everlasting night. And then there will be no waking from that deepest, darkest dream.

Four

I woke suddenly from a deep dream. Someone was talking to me.

"Um, excuse me—are you going to Wyldcliffe?"

A girl, about eleven or twelve years old, was hovering nervously near my seat on the train. She was dressed in the dark gray and red Wyldcliffe uniform, all new and stiff and slightly too big for her. I was still in jeans and casual clothes.

"I hope I didn't wake you up," she said apologetically.

"No—um, of course not, it's okay." I shook myself from sleep. "I'd just drifted off. Silly of me."

"So you are going to Wyldcliffe?" The girl pointed at my luggage on the rack over my head. My suitcase had an address label tied on the handle, printed in Dad's firm handwriting: *Wyldcliffe Abbey School.*

"I guess that gives me away." I smiled up at her, trying to be friendly. "Yes, I am."

"Can I sit with you?" She had a nasal kind of voice, as though she had a permanent head cold. "I've been wandering up and down the train, trying to find another Wyldcliffe girl."

"Sure. Of course you can." I moved some magazines from where I had chucked them on the opposite seat and she sat down. "Is this your first term?"

"I was supposed to start in September, but I was ill," the girl said with a kind of suppressed excitement—or was it fear? She was dark and thin, with a sickly complexion and dull black eyes that seemed to fix themselves onto my face. "Do you like Wyldcliffe?"

I hesitated. I wasn't going to tell her what I really felt about Wyldcliffe, or what I really knew about the place. "It's an amazing building," I began brightly. "Like a castle in the middle of the moors. The teachers are, well, a bit old-fashioned, but they know their stuff. There's a choir and orchestra, if you like music. And most girls ride on the weekend. Even I'm going to learn."

It sounded like something I was parroting from the school's prospectus:

Wyldcliffe is England's premier traditional boarding school for girls. Located in the stunningly beautiful Wylde Valley, we pride ourselves on the highest academic and social standards. . . .

What the prospectus didn't say was that Celia Hartle, the High Mistress of Wyldcliffe, had disappeared in strange circumstances at the end of last term. It didn't say that she was High Mistress not only of the school, but of the deadly coven of Dark Sisters. The authorities had been baffled by Mrs. Hartle's disappearance, but Sarah, Helen, and I knew that she had vanished after the battle in the crypt. Part of me hoped that she was dead, and yet part of me was sickened by the idea. Either way, whatever had happened to Celia Hartle, the coven would be waiting for me and my Talisman when I got back.

"But horses are unpredictable, aren't they? It must be really frightening."

"Oh . . . um . . ." I hadn't really been listening, lost in my own thoughts. "Sorry?"

"Horses," the girl repeated, looking more scared than ever. "You can get hurt. You know, thrown off and all that. It's dangerous."

I laughed shortly. After everything I had faced at Wyldcliffe I wasn't going to get too worked up about sitting on the back of a well-fed pony. "I don't suppose I'll be going very fast," I said. "So you're not going to ride then?"

"My mom can't afford to pay for extras like that."

"Oh, yeah, of course . . ." I tried to cover my blunder. "Anyway, Wyldcliffe is a good place to study, though I expect you'll be a bit homesick to start with—"

"I won't," she said abruptly. "There's nothing for me at home. My dad lives in America and my mom is always working."

Poor kid, I thought, *poor sad kid*. She looked so young to be going off to boarding school all on her own. "Couldn't your mother have traveled with you to Wyldcliffe, you know, on your first day?" I asked.

The girl flushed scarlet and I immediately wished that I hadn't said anything. It was none of my business if her mother couldn't be bothered with her, and now I had put my foot in it again. "Mom came to the station, but she couldn't spare the time to come all the way with me. She said I'd be okay, that there would be other Wyldcliffe students on the train." The girl frowned for a moment before looking up at me with her disconcerting, hungry eyes. "Anyway, she was right. I've got you now, haven't I?"

I smiled uncomfortably, feeling sorry for her, yet somehow repelled at the same time. There was something needy about this girl, something that would condemn

21

her to being a bit of a misfit. Well, I knew all about that. The Wyldcliffe students had made it clear that I didn't fit in. I wasn't a blond, carefree English rose with a nice little trust fund and a pedigree going back to William the Conqueror. I didn't belong, and I had a funny feeling she wouldn't either.

Silence fell between us. I didn't know what else to say, so I took a book from my bag and pretended to read. After a few minutes, she interrupted me with another question.

"Is there a teacher called Miss Scratton?"

"Yes. Why?"

"She taught my mother at Wyldcliffe, years ago. Mom says she was a good teacher but a bit weird. Always on about the past."

"Well, Miss Scratton's a history teacher, so I guess that's natural."

The past. *I can never get away from the past, wherever I go.* . . . Sebastian had said that, and now it was true for me too.

"What are the other teachers like?" the girl asked nervously. "Are they all like her?"

The faces of the Wyldcliffe teachers, or mistresses, flashed in front of my eyes. I let the book fall onto my lap. There were plenty who were a whole lot weirder than

Miss Scratton. Miss Dalrymple, for instance, the plump geography mistress, with her bright blond curls and little-girl laugh. Or Miss Raglan, stiff and awkward and angry, who taught math. It wasn't the love of teaching that kept those two at Wyldcliffe; I was sure of that.

"Well, they tend to be kind of strict," I said. "There are lots of rules at Wyldcliffe, so you have to be careful, or you'll end up with a pile of demerits and detentions."

The girl rummaged in her bag and pulled out a faded booklet. "Have you seen this before?"

My heart thudded as I recognized it. Of course I had seen it before. I had devoured every word of that little book a hundred times over, searching for clues, searching for the truth. . . .

"Yeah, I think so," I said evasively, taking it from her. The title was printed in gold letters on the blue cover: *A Short History of Wyldcliffe Abbey School, by Rev. A. J. Flowerdew.* "There's a copy in the library at school," I said. "Where did you get this?"

"I told you that my mother was at the school. She's into all this kind of thing, and I've read tons of stuff about Wyldcliffe." The girl snatched the book back from me, flipping through its pages, searching for something. "Have you seen this picture? Do you know who it is?"

As I looked down at the page, my heart seemed to explode in my chest. Yes, I knew who was in that painting.

"It's Lady Agnes Templeton," the girl went on. "Her family owned the Abbey before it became a school. It says here that Lady Agnes died in a riding accident." She looked up and added confidentially, "But it's not true. She ran away."

"What?" I stared at her, utterly astonished.

"All I know is that she went off to London and that it wasn't her parents who went looking for her. It was a young neighbor of hers, a distant relation. Have you heard about him? His name was Sebastian Fairfax."

"Um . . . no . . ." I lied. But the blood was racing in my head: *Sebastian . . . Sebastian . . . Sebastian . . .* I switched the girl's voice off and plunged back into my own private world.

Right now, at this very minute, Sebastian would be fading. The frightening, supernatural process had already begun last term. I remembered his pale face, his weakened voice, his reddened eyes, and his horror at the idea of becoming a demon spirit. Second by second, drop by drop, Sebastian's existence was draining into the shadow world. Time was running out. Perhaps—the thought tormented me—perhaps it had already happened. Perhaps when I got back to Wyldcliffe I would discover that he had already left this world and vanished into the darkness.

I wouldn't think that. I wouldn't let that be true.

There was a way out of this nightmare, and I was going to make it happen. Somehow, I had vowed, I would master every secret of the Talisman that Agnes had bequeathed me and wrench Sebastian's destiny into my hands. I would not let him fade in torment for my sake. I had to find him, before it was too late. The train rattled out an endless, grinding song: *Come back . . . too late . . . come back . . . too late . . . too late. . . .*

"Sebastian Fairfax was crazy." The girl leaned closer and touched my arm to get my attention. "They say Wyldcliffe is cursed because of him."

I recoiled from her touch, suddenly furiously angry. This girl knew nothing about the reality behind her stupid tittle-tattle. How dared she drag Sebastian's life out to be picked over like some cheap newspaper gossip?

"I don't believe in all that nonsense," I said coldly.

"Well, everybody says Wyldcliffe is haunted." The girl slumped against her seat again, looking small and skinny in her badly fitting uniform. "And my mom said that when she was at Wyldcliffe the students were always daring one another to look for Agnes's ghost after dark. Mom never saw her, though. Have you?"

I stood up abruptly. "I'm going to get some coffee in the buffet car." As I dug my purse out of my bag, I tried to calm down. After all, she was just a kid going to boarding school for the first time, excited by what she had heard about the old Abbey and its long history. It wasn't her fault she was awkward and plain and tactless. I tried to force myself to sound friendly, even if I didn't feel it. "Well, I won't be long then . . . um . . . what is your name?"

"Harriet." She smiled faintly. "Harriet Templeton. Enjoy your coffee."

I jumped, as though someone had fired a pistol.

Templeton. Harriet Templeton. Could she . . . Was she related to Agnes in some way? If so, was she related to me? And why was she so interested in Sebastian?

The train swerved on the track and I stumbled along to the next carriage, where the drinks and snacks were served, my head whirling. I paid for my drink, but I didn't go back to my seat. I found an empty corner in the corridor and stared out of the window, letting my coffee grow cold as we sped farther and farther from London, and into the far, wild north.

Five

FROM THE PRIVATE PAPERS OF
SEBASTIAN JAMES FAIRFAX

In the far wild north I watch and wait,
For the girl from the restless sea.
Oh, far wild wind, please find my love
And send her back to me.

In the far wild north my heart will break
For the girl with the sea-gray eyes.
Oh, my love—my love—

*Evie—my words die, my body trembles, my heart is
cursed.*

I tried to write a poem for you once before and I failed then, just as I am failing now.

The effort of using pen and ink is almost too great for me, but somehow it brings you before me so clearly. I long to be with you, to hear your voice and see your face, and in these desperate moments when I try to find the words to tell you how I feel, I can fool myself that you are close.

But it is all for nothing. My words are empty and meaningless. The ravings of a madman, people would say, if anyone ever chanced to read them.

They called me mad, long ago—more than a hundred winters ago, in another life. Another reality.

I had returned from London, fired by every possibility of the Mystic Way, both permitted and forbidden. I was obsessed with the dark secrets I had discovered and determined to pursue my selfish dreams of eternal life, whatever price I would have to pay. I studied, plotted, and schemed until my brain was fevered and my body was weak. My family and friends thought I was crazy. Back then it was Agnes who watched and prayed for me from a distance, as I believe and trust that you do now.

Dear Agnes.

Dearest, darling Evie.

How clearly I can recall every detail of that other

life—my mother weeping and my father cold and angry and the servants lingering in corners and the doctor making his pompous pronouncements that so enraged me. Everything that happened then stands out sharp and clear like a picture, and yet the things that happened only recently seem to be fading in my troubled mind.

Fading, blurred and confused, like water clouded with ink.

Everything is fading.

I must remember. I must rouse myself to fight. I must find you.

And yet what can I bring you but more danger and sorrow? It is best that I hide here, like a wounded animal waiting for the end. Here I can but hope to die, thinking of you with my last strength.

No, that will not be the way—my fate is not to know death. There will be no end to my pain and degradation. No end. Life without end. Darkness without end, enslaved.

Is this what I worked so hard for? Is this what Agnes died for? Yet even now I feel my masters hovering, ready to suck me into their black world of demons and shadows.

Evie, I am so afraid. I, who thought I was destined to

know and conquer everything! I dreamed that I would be a master amongst men, a conjurer, a magician, a lord of the Mystic Way. I was fated to be a worker of marvels, to triumph over death itself, and yet now I am afraid.

I have one fear greater than all the rest—that you were never there at all. Perhaps, like my fatal vision of eternal youth and knowledge, you were simply another crazy dream. The raving of a lunatic.

A dream girl.

A dream life.

A dream love.

In my dream we were by the wild sea. It was cold, as cold as the first day of winter, yet my heart was warm and alive, because you were there. I saw you standing by the shore, shrouded in thought, your head bowed. Then I stole up behind you and wrapped my arms around you, kissing your neck, and breathing in the scent of your beautiful hair. I remember your hair, as bright as a living flame. I wanted to tell you something.

I want to tell you—

Do not come back. She is still near, the High Mistress. She is waiting, getting ready to tangle you in her evil webs once again. You must not come back. Never come back. It is better that way.

Oh, Evie, I am not strong enough to mean that! If you are no more than a dream, then come to me, as quick as a bird flying home. I love you, girl from the sea.

Come back, come back, come back.

Six

I was back at Wyldcliffe, and it was all about to begin again.

"Is this the school?" Harriet asked. "Are we there?"

The cabdriver from the station had dropped us at the wrought-iron gates that led into the school's private grounds. It was almost dark. Picking up our bags, we turned down the curving drive. The gothic towers and turrets of Wyldcliffe Abbey loomed up in the dusk, frozen in time by the whirling snow. I couldn't decide whether it resembled a palace or a prison, but either way there was no escape.

"This is it," I said softly. "This is Wyldcliffe."

That cursed place, some of the locals called it. Harriet had been right about one thing—people said that the place was haunted. The stories about Agnes had become legends: old tales that her ghost walked near the Abbey; that she would come back to Wyldcliffe again one day to put right a great wrong; that she could heal the sick; that Sebastian had committed suicide using an ancient silver dagger. Oh, they said all sorts of wild things, but nothing could come close to the truth.

Tall trees stood black and bare on either side of the drive, and drifts of snow glimmered in the dusk. Night was falling over the rugged hills that marched around the Abbey like brooding guardians. Sebastian was out there, somewhere, I was sure. For a moment I allowed myself to imagine that he would be waiting for me by the lake on the Abbey's grounds, eager to tell me that he had been healed by some amazing miracle. I would hear his laughter and see the flash of his mocking blue eyes. I would taste his kisses, which made my heart dance and my blood turn to fire in my veins. We would be like any other teenagers who had stumbled across their first love. . . .

I hurried forward and Harriet trotted next to me like a faithful dog.

"Gosh, it's so big. And so old."

"You'll get used to it."

As we drew nearer to the massive building, I thought

I heard something in the trees away to my left. I paused and looked around uneasily. Deep in the distant shadows, I thought I caught a glimpse of someone moving silently behind the trees. "Who's there?" I called, but my voice sounded thin in the frosty air. Everything was still, like a stage set before the play begins, waiting for something to happen. I was being watched. For an instant I wondered if I should turn and run. Had I been crazy to come back at all? But the Talisman lay cool and quiet against my skin, giving me courage, giving me hope. I could do this, I told myself. I could face it. I had to. Sebastian would be waiting.

"Come on, Harriet, let's get inside. It's cold."

We dragged our suitcases up to the great oak front door and stepped into the large entrance hall, where a fire was blazing in an old-fashioned stone hearth. The paneled walls and the gilt-framed paintings and the cabinets full of silver school trophies were just as I had remembered. There was the smell of flowers and beeswax and wood smoke, mixed with a subtle scent of money and tradition. Students in school uniform were lingering by the fire, or hurrying down the corridors that led from the hallway, full of first-day errands and importance. As I stood there, taking it all in, a girl with curly hair and warm brown eyes threw herself at me.

"Evie! You're back! Oh, it's so good to see you."

"Sarah!"

We hugged each other and smiled, though there was a lump in my throat.

"How are you?" Sarah asked quietly. "It must have been hard, having the funeral to deal with."

"I'm okay, honestly." I remembered that Harriet was still hanging on to my shadow like an unwanted party guest. "Um, Sarah, this is Harriet. We came on the train together."

"Hi." Sarah smiled. "Shall I take you to see Miss Barnard, Harriet? She's in charge of the younger girls. Dinner will be served soon, so you don't want to be late."

"Yes, please," said Harriet gratefully, and I was grateful too, to be free of her at last. Sarah swept Harriet away with a motherly air, saying over her shoulder, "But we need to talk, Evie. As soon as we can."

I headed for the dorm to unpack, hauling my suitcase up the grand marble stairs that wound their way to the upper floors. I paused for breath near the top and glanced down over the edge of the elaborate iron banister. The black-and-white tiles of the hallway looked far below, and the height and space around the magnificent staircase were almost dizzying. For a second, my mind slipped, and the rest of the school didn't exist, only a terrible sheer drop, with those bright tiles swirling below me like a crazy giant chessboard. I seemed to see the figure of a girl lying on the floor like a broken toy, her eyes staring up into mine, a ribbon of crimson blood spreading over the endless black and white. . . .

A bell rang out shrilly. It was the warning bell, telling the last few parents lingering over their farewells that it was time to leave their daughters behind. I took a deep breath and looked again. There was no one lying on the tiled floor. What had it been? A memory? A prophecy? Or merely one of the tricks that the brooding atmosphere of Wyldcliffe played on my imagination?

It was nothing. I wouldn't allow myself to be distracted from what I had to do. Find Sebastian. Awaken the Talisman. It was as simple—and as difficult—as that.

Climbing the last few steps, I reached the third floor. Long, door-lined corridors stretched out on either side of the staircase. This was the top of the building; only the disused attic lay above. I headed quickly for my dorm, hoping to find Helen there. But the high-ceilinged, cold white room was empty.

There were five beds, each with thin drapes that could be pulled around for a little privacy. The only relief from the room's clinical whiteness was a framed photograph of a teenage girl that was fixed over my bed, and an elaborately carved window seat that gave a view of the grounds and the surrounding hills.

I opened my suitcase and hurriedly changed my jeans and sweater for my school clothes. The old-fashioned tie hid any sign of the Talisman hanging under my shirt. I knew, though, that I would have to find somewhere to hide my precious heirloom. I couldn't trust anyone except Sarah and Helen, and I couldn't risk the necklace falling into the wrong hands. I had to keep the Talisman safe, as safe as a dying man's secret.

Twisting my long curls into a neat ponytail, I checked myself in the mirror. Red hair and pale skin and sea-gray eyes, just like Agnes. In my crisp uniform, I looked like the perfect Wyldcliffe student. It was only the expression in my eyes that gave me away. . . .

I was about to leave when I caught sight of something in the mirror that made me turn around. Looking carefully on the opposite wall, I noticed that a scrap of paper had been left in the frame of the photo over my bed. I went over and eased it out, but before I had a chance to look at it, a familiar voice rang out.

"Oh, God, look who's turned up. Couldn't you

find somewhere else to take you in, Johnson? Like an orphanage?"

The door had swung open and a pretty blond girl in designer clothes was standing there, flanked by two other students. "Sorry, Celeste," I replied, slipping the paper into my pocket. "I couldn't resist coming back just to annoy you."

Celeste scowled. "Well, keep out of my way."

"Oh, I intend to. I'm not exactly longing to get to know you better."

Celeste had done everything she could to make my first term at Wyldcliffe as difficult as possible, burning up with resentment over the fact that I had taken the place of her cousin Laura in the dorm. Poor Laura; it was her photo that hung over my bed. Poor, dead Laura, destroyed by Wyldcliffe. Drowned in the lake, the official story went, but the horrible truth was that she had been killed by the coven.

Another grim reality. Another Wyldcliffe secret.

"Hi, Sophie," I said to one of the girls hanging behind Celeste. I actually almost liked Sophie. It wasn't her fault that she was stupid and scared and bossed around by Celeste. I smiled at her and she glanced at Celeste anxiously before replying in a stilted voice, "Hello, Evie. Did you have a good holiday?"

"Why are you bothering to talk to her?" snapped India. There was nothing soft or helpless about India. Everything about her was expensive and polished, but she never laughed or fooled around or seemed really happy. Wyldcliffe was littered with girls like India, each one of them a tiny betrayal of too much money and not enough love. She pushed past me rudely. "We only came up here to get changed for supper. Why don't you leave us alone?"

"Willingly," I replied. "Well, see you around, Sophie. I'm going to look for Helen. Don't let these two suck all the blood out of you."

I strode out into the corridor. Students were making their way to the stairs in little groups. I caught snatches of conversation around me: "The police still don't know what happened . . ." "My mother wasn't very keen on sending me back here . . ." "I hope they find out soon . . ."

They were talking about the High Mistress. I realized that ever since stepping over Wyldcliffe's threshold, I had been expecting Mrs. Hartle to swoop down on me, tall, elegant, and cold, as she had on my very first day. It was difficult to remember that she was no longer there, watching over the school like a malevolent queen bee. Even though she was gone, I had to admit to myself that I was still afraid of her.

I bent down and pretended to fiddle with my shoe so that I could hear what the other girls were saying. Wild rumors had circulated among the Wyldcliffe students about Mrs. Hartle's disappearance the term before: that she had stolen money from the school and had fled the country; that she had run away with a secret lover; that she had been abducted by a crazed killer. It wouldn't be long before someone blamed alien invaders. None of them could imagine that the truth was even weirder than any rumor.

The gossiping girls passed by: ". . . I hope they tell us what's going on . . ." "It's creepy not knowing . . ." They ignored me. To them, I was just dumb old Evie Johnson, a scholarship student, an outsider who had nearly been expelled last term for wrecking the memorial procession in honor of Lady Agnes Templeton. I was no one.

After they were gone, I stood up and remembered the piece of paper. I pulled it out of my pocket. In small black letters someone had written:

AGNES IS DEAD. LAURA IS DEAD.
YOU WILL BE NEXT.

Whoever had written the note had wasted no time. This was a declaration of war.

Seven

I reached the gloomy dining hall with its rows of wooden tables and benches. The high table where the mistresses sat was on a raised platform at the top of the room. The place was slowly filling up with girls wearing identical red-and-gray clothes. I scanned their faces quickly, then walked over to where a tall, fair girl was sitting alone, her pale beauty dimmed by the air of sadness that clung to her.

"Helen," I said quietly, slipping into a seat next to her. "I've missed you so much."

Helen looked up and I could tell that she had been crying. Any ideas I'd had of telling her about the note I'd just found evaporated. It looked as though she already had enough to deal with.

"I'm sorry, Evie," she said in a low voice. "I should have come with Sarah to look for you, but I just couldn't. I've been walking around the grounds all afternoon, hiding from Celeste and her gang, trying to summon up the courage to face the rest of the school."

"You must be frozen, staying out there in that snow! Besides, you can't hide from Celeste all term, Helen. You mustn't let her get to you."

"I know, I know. It's going to be so hard, though, listening to all the talk about Mrs. Hartle." Her voice dropped so low that it was almost inaudible. "About my mother . . ."

None of the other Wyldcliffe students knew that Helen was Celia Hartle's daughter. Mrs. Hartle had abandoned Helen in a children's home as a baby, then had secretly gotten in touch with her a year ago and brought her to Wyldcliffe. She had urged Helen to join the coven, cruelly rejecting her when Helen had refused.

"Now that she has gone, it hurts not being able to let anyone know that she was my . . . well, my family," Helen went on. "Does that sound weird? When she was around, I was so angry with her for hiding the truth about me. I've had to hide so much, all my life. I'm still hiding. It makes me feel as though I don't exist." She picked nervously at the cuff of her sweater. "I hated her for being in the coven and for what she did to Laura, and for what she tried to do to you, but she was still my mother. I suppose I hoped that one day she would remember that. And now it's probably too late."

"But do you really think Mrs. Hartle is gone?" I asked quietly. "Is she . . . is she dead?"

"Shhh!" Helen frowned warningly. The room was filling up with girls and it was impossible to talk any longer. Sarah came in and sat opposite us.

"Sorry I've been so long," she said. "I had to take care of Harriet, then go down to the stable to check the ponies." Sarah was crazy about horses and kept two in the Wyldcliffe stables.

"Did I tell you Dad has signed me up for riding lessons?" I asked lightly, unable to speak about anything more serious.

"Excellent. Mrs. Parker is a good teacher. Much better than me." Sarah had tried to teach me to ride the term before on her pony Bonny, but although I could just about cling to Bonny's back, I wasn't what you'd call an elegant horsewoman. Helen fell silent as Sarah and I talked about the chances of riding over the hills in the snow; then another bell rang. The girls sprang to their feet as the staff filed in and took their places. The carved chair where the

High Mistress had always sat was left empty, like a hollow throne.

Miss Scratton, the mistress in charge of the older students, stood in front of the whole school and said the usual grace in her quiet, scholarly voice. She reminded me of a nun, with her black academic gown and her severe hairstyle and her Latin prayers . . . *Benedic, Domine, nos et dona tua.* . . . In my first term at Wyldcliffe Miss Scratton had been the only one of the mistresses I had felt I could trust. I wasn't sure why exactly, but her clear mind and scrupulously fair methods seemed to make it impossible for her to be one of those howling, grasping women that we had encountered in the crypt.

The prayer came to an end. Miss Scratton indicated that we should sit down. There was the scraping of chairs and benches and a quick rush of excitement: "She's going to tell us something . . ." "I told you so . . ." "Some news at last . . ."

"Before we begin our meal, I would like to welcome you back to school," Miss Scratton announced. "These are not easy circumstances in which to begin a new term. Sadly, our High Mistress, Mrs. Hartle, is still missing. The police are doing everything they can, and we have to carry on as normal, despite the uncertainty, despite the loss we feel." For a fraction of a second she seemed to look straight at Helen, who was sitting silent and stiff beside me. "In Mrs. Hartle's absence, we must continue to strive for the high standards she always set. The school governors have put certain arrangements in place to ensure that your education will continue uninterrupted. Miss Raglan, our math mistress, has been appointed as Deputy High Mistress, and will lead the school until further notice."

There was an intake of breath, a gasp so loud that it sounded like a fist banging on a drum. It seemed that everyone had expected Miss Scratton to be put in charge. I had certainly expected it, and when I saw the faint flush spreading over her thin face, I guessed that she had expected it too. "I am sure," she went on determinedly, "that we will all give Miss Raglan the support and loyalty that she deserves." She began to clap and a few people joined in, but the applause didn't last long.

Miss Raglan stepped forward. She was tall and gray haired, with a heavy, clumsy body and an angry red complexion.

"It is an honor, even in these sad circumstances, to be responsible for Wyldcliffe," she said. "I can assure you that everything will continue as it was under Mrs. Hartle's inspired leadership. There will be no loss of standards.

There will be no change at all."

She sat down abruptly in Mrs. Hartle's tall chair, looking awkward and out of place. Miss Scratton hesitated for a moment and then said, "Please enjoy your dinner now, girls. Afterward, the lights-out bell will ring early, as it is the first day and you must all be tired from traveling."

The women who worked in the kitchens brought out large platters of food and placed them on each table and the girls began to serve themselves obediently, their little moment of surprise over. Wyldcliffe students were used to doing as they were told. Everything would be the same; there would be no changes. . . . Wyldcliffe never changed. Tradition. Order. Discipline. It was the same now as it had been a hundred years ago.

I tried to eat too, but I wasn't hungry. Celia Hartle might have gone, but I knew that any of the teachers who were surveying the rows of girls could be one of her Dark Sisters. If Mrs. Hartle was indeed dead, then sooner or later another High Mistress would rise up, eager for revenge. I looked at each one of the mistresses in turn: Miss Raglan; Miss Schofield; Mrs. Richards, who taught biology; Madame Duchesne, the French mistress; Miss Dalrymple; and all the rest. My head buzzed with questions. Had one of them written that note? I wondered.

Which of them had been in the crypt on that night last term? I had never liked or trusted Miss Raglan, and now she was in charge of the school. Was she also in charge of the coven? Or was she simply a dry, cold teacher, obsessed with the rules and traditions of this elite academy?

As I picked at my food, I looked around at the other students. I noticed that Harriet was sitting hunched over her plate, not saying a word to the girls near her. I guess she'd been shown the true Wyldcliffe welcome. Not having looks or money or confidence to recommend her, Harriet had already been dumped to fend for herself. The rest of the girls—so rich, so well connected, so attractive— seemed to have been protected from every evil from the moment they were born. And yet Laura had been one of those golden girls and she had fallen victim to Wyldcliffe's secrets. I suddenly felt that I wanted to root out the sickness at the heart of the Abbey for all our sakes, not just for Sebastian.

Dinner was over. More prayers, more standing to attention as the staff filed out, followed by the rows of girls. As Sarah turned to leave, I grabbed her arm. "Meet me and Helen after lights-out," I whispered.

"Where?"

I mouthed two words: *the grotto.*

Sarah nodded in silent agreement and walked out after the others, heading for her dorm. I turned to Helen.

"Let's get this over with as quickly as possible," I said. As scholarship students, Helen and I both had to do various mindless chores to show our undying gratitude: tidying classrooms, sorting out music books for choir practice, stuff like that. Usually after supper we set trays with china cups and silver spoons, ready for the staff to take their coffee in the mistresses' common room. I went over to a cupboard at the side of the room where everything was kept and began to arrange the trays, while Helen knocked on the door to the kitchens to ask for some cream. A flustered woman in a rather greasy apron opened the door and peered at us.

"No, not tonight, she doesn't want you doing it anymore. She doesn't want students hanging around, she said."

"Who did?" I asked.

But the woman scuttled back into the hot kitchen. I felt that someone was watching me. When I turned around, I noticed that Miss Raglan was still sitting in her carved chair on the raised platform, slowly twisting her hands together.

"I gave the orders," she said, getting up and walking

toward us. "You are relieved of this duty."

"But you said there wouldn't be any changes," replied Helen. I was surprised. She usually kept quiet in front of the mistresses. "Mrs. Hartle always asked us to get the coffee trays ready. You said everything would continue just the same."

"I was not referring to such trivial matters."

"I don't think Mrs. Hartle's wishes should be seen as trivial."

"What? Are you questioning my authority?"

"Of course not," Helen replied. "You're the High Mistress now, aren't you?"

She stared fearlessly into Miss Raglan's heavy face, holding the older woman's gaze, until Miss Raglan seemed to stagger and step backward.

"I . . . I am the Deputy High Mistress; that is all. Naturally we hope that Mrs. Hartle will return shortly . . . naturally. . . . Well, carry on."

Miss Raglan stumped away, reminding me of a beaten dog. I looked at Helen in amazement. "What was all that about?"

"I don't really know." She shrugged. "I kind of felt the need to challenge her somehow. Sorry. I guess we shouldn't draw attention to ourselves." She looked down and started polishing a spoon, then sighed heavily. "Perhaps it's just me, but I feel so trapped. We'll have to be careful, Evie. I feel them hovering on every side, watching, waiting. . . ."

"Waiting for what?"

Helen sighed again. "Waiting for us to make a mistake."

Eight

FROM THE PRIVATE PAPERS OF
SEBASTIAN JAMES FAIRFAX

Waiting—waiting—waiting—

Waiting for the end.

I have lost count of the nights since I last saw you. But this night feels different. Something is going to happen. Something has changed.

This place is as cold as death. My limbs ache and my breath turns to clouds of ice. Winter, it must be, in the outside world where seasons still exist. When I was a boy I would wait for the first snows, as though waiting for a miracle—

Something is happening. The silence of this place is broken by the sound of the sea on a distant shore. I feel the waves breaking and beating in my heart. I sense you near.

Have you come back, my darling? Have you risked everything to return to this valley of secrets?

I will wait for you.

This night feels different.

A power has returned to Wyldcliffe, pulsing with life like the sun. The air is more alive. Everything is watching and waiting—

I am waiting for you. Do you still think of me?

What will be the next part of our story, Evie? Are you still hoping for a miracle? Do you dream that Agnes, the gentle healer, will reach across the void to touch me with her great gifts? I rejected her help long ago, and I fear she cannot help me now. But miracles do exist. This air. This darkness. The snow that lies all around this sleeping house. The stars overhead. How profoundly mysterious everything is! Not only the strange paths that we have walked, but the ordinary things that I took so much for granted. The earth under my feet. Every individual life: each tree, each bird, each child. Every precious soul—

They are all mysteries. We are surrounded by miracles.

You are my miracle.

So I will wait. I will hope. Here, in my darkness, I will lift my eyes to the sunrise.

I will wait for you.

Nine

I was waiting.

Tick . . . tock . . . tick . . .

The little alarm clock on my bedside table counted away the minutes, its metallic drone tempting me to close my eyes. I was used to this. Night after night the term before, I had lain in this narrow white bed, waiting to hear the regular breathing of Celeste and Sophie as they drifted off to sleep. I knew how India would sometimes mutter as she turned over in bed, and how Helen lay rigid on her back, staring up at the ceiling until her eyes grew too heavy for her to stay awake any longer. I knew every creak of every floorboard in that bare, white room. Night after night, I had slipped out of the dorm and crept down the old servants' staircase to meet Sebastian in secret. And tonight he might be waiting for me once again.... Perhaps the miracle would have happened.

Tick ... tock ... tick ...

When I felt the room settle into sleep around me, I groped on the floor for my shoes, pulled my robe on, and crept out. I didn't wait for Helen. She would get to our meeting with Sarah in her own way.

Gliding down the hushed corridor, I slipped through the curtained door that led to the old back stairs. As I closed the door behind me, I was plunged into blackness, shut off from the rest of the school. For an instant a stab of panic shot through me. I had always been stupidly scared of the dark, fearful of being trapped in a lightless, narrow place and left to suffocate. I grabbed a small flashlight that I had hidden in my pocket and flicked it on. That was better. *Breathe, Evie, don't forget to breathe. . . .* The little beam of light revealed the dusty wooden stairs that had once been used by the servants when Agnes had lived ay Wyldcliffe. Now this part of the building was out-of-bounds, but I didn't care. I didn't live by their rules anymore. Clutching my flashlight, I tiptoed down the steps. I wasn't going to let childish fears stop me now.

Thirty-two, thirty-three, thirty-four ... fifty-five, fifty-six ...

I counted the steps until I reached the bottom. To one side, a door led back into the main part of the school. In the other direction a musty passageway led to the old servants' wing, a warren of moldering storerooms and pantries. I forced myself to walk into the icy blackness, past a rusting row of old servants' bells, past the rustle of mice in the walls. At last I reached a faded green door that led out to the stables. I drew back the bolts and stepped outside.

The cobblestones of the stable yard were bright with frost, and the sky seemed high and clear and far away. A thin cloud passed across the moon, like a trail of silvery smoke. I paused for a second. How profoundly mysterious everything was, I thought. Not only the strange paths that Sebastian had taken me down, but the ordinary things that we all took so much for granted. The stars overhead. The earth under our feet. People. Friendship. Love. They were all mysteries, full of power and danger—especially love.

I had to hurry.

I crossed the yard, then ran lightly down the icy paths and across the snow-covered lawns. A few minutes later I reached the edge of a wide lake, its waters as black as the sky. Next to the lake, the famous ruins of Wyldcliffe's ancient chapel loomed up like a ghostly ship. I came to a halt, my legs suddenly trembling, my heart beating wildly.

Here the medieval nuns had once worshipped; here Agnes had lain in death on the cold earth. And it was here that Sebastian and I had met in secret, under the northern stars. It was here that we had talked, and laughed, and quarreled, and made up again. It was here that we had first kissed. . . .

Reality hit hard. Sebastian wasn't waiting for me under the ruined arches. There was going to be no quick-fix solution, no easy fairy-tale happy ending. If Sebastian couldn't work the miracle, I would have to do it myself.

But I couldn't do it alone. I needed the Talisman and I needed my sisters—Helen and Sarah and Agnes. I left the lake and the chapel behind and ran over the frozen earth, on and on into the dark.

Sarah lit a candle and stuck it in a niche in the wall and the cave sprang to glowing life. We were in the grotto, a weird underground folly built by Agnes's father at the far edge of the Abbey's grounds. Its walls were decorated with glinting mosaics of mythical creatures, and a stream trickled around a statue of Pan. The yellow light of the candle flickered over the grotesque images, bringing them briefly to life.

"Did anyone see you coming here?" I asked.

"No, I'm pretty sure we're safe—for the moment. But I wish Helen would get here. There's so much that we need to decide."

Just then a wind sprang up, sharp and cold and scented with wild heather. Our hair blew across our faces and the candle flame flickered. I caught hold of Sarah's hand as the wind whirled around us and a haze of silver light began to glow. I thought I could hear a distant sound, like birdsong in the middle of a storm. The next moment, the wind dropped and Helen seemed to step out of the silvery light, slightly flushed and out of breath.

"Sorry," she said, pulling a wry face. "It must look a bit freaky, turning up like that."

"It was amazing," said Sarah. "I've never seen you do that before."

I reached out to touch Helen's arm. She was really there, suddenly in front of us. Helen had told us about her extraordinary ability—what did she call it . . . dancing on the wind? She could get to any place she wanted by stepping through the air with the power of her thought, like a knife cutting through silk.

"You really can do it," I said in wonder. "That is incredible."

"No more incredible than what you did last term, Evie, making the lake rise up," Helen replied with a self-conscious smile. "We've all got powers. The question is, how are we going to use them?"

I suddenly felt cold. This wasn't about amazing feats to delight openmouthed spectators, like a circus act. This was deadly serious.

"I guess you both know what I want to do," I answered quickly. "I want to look for Sebastian and use the Talisman to help him. We know that I can't give him the Talisman of my own free will. I tried that last term and it didn't work. The only way Sebastian can use it is if he breaks the bond between me and the Talisman by killing me. And the only way I can use it is if I discover its secrets and find out for myself how to awaken it." I had rehearsed this speech over and over, but it didn't make it any easier, and I faltered. "I know—I know it all sounds crazy. And I know it could be dangerous. I need your help, but you're my best friends. I don't want you to get hurt."

"Where do you think Sebastian is now? And why hasn't he been in touch with you?" asked Helen.

"There are only three possibilities," I said, trying to

stay calm and unemotional. "Either Sebastian has already faded and gone beyond our reach forever. Or he is lying in hiding somewhere, getting weaker, hoping that I'm coming back to him. Or . . ." It was hard even to say it. "Or he has stopped loving me and is my enemy, with only one aim—to kill me and steal the Talisman."

"Sebastian hasn't faded completely, not yet," Sarah said slowly.

I looked up at Sarah. She sometimes had flashes of intuition about people, perhaps inherited from her long-ago Romany ancestors. I had learned to trust her when it happened. "What do you mean? Why do you think that?"

"There's such a strong connection between you that I'm sure you would know if that had happened. Besides, I sense him here in Wyldcliffe's valley, like a faint pulse of energy. Don't you?"

"Yes, it's exactly like that." Eagerly, I told her about the times he had appeared to me: on the beach, in my dreams, and in my head, like the murmur of the sea. "I think he's trying to reach me."

"But is it you that he wants, or the Talisman?" Helen's voice was low and sad. "Sebastian told you that as he faded further into the shadow world, he would forget all human ties. Once he's on the edge of existence he might not be able to control his desire to rip it from you, even if it means destroying you. He warned you what would happen."

"But he doesn't want the Talisman," I argued. "He didn't use it that night in the crypt. He would rather fade into a demon spirit than hurt me."

"But he had only just begun to fade then," Helen replied. "If it comes to a final choice between joining the Unconquered or becoming their eternal slave, can you really be sure what Sebastian would do?"

"And what about the coven?" said Sarah. "The Dark Sisters still want the Talisman. Sebastian promised them the secrets of everlasting life if they helped him to find it. They have waited, generation after generation, for him to give them what he promised. He might have changed his mind about the whole thing, but they haven't. The coven will do everything they can to take the Talisman from you, Evie, and force Sebastian to use it, before it's too late."

"But Mrs. Hartle's gone. Isn't the coven weaker without her? Have they had time to find another High Mistress?"

"I can't believe my mother's dead," Helen said. "That night last term she was damaged in some way. She took the biggest hit and had the biggest shock when we opposed her. But she hasn't gone, and neither has the coven."

Reluctantly, I showed them the scrap of paper with its stark warning. "I think this must be from one of the Dark Sisters. I found it in the dorm."

"So they're getting ready to attack you again," said Sarah grimly. "Like I said, the coven doesn't want to see Sebastian delivered into the hands of the Unconquered. They want to make use of him for their own ends."

The Unconquered . . . the coven . . . the shadows . . .

I suddenly felt hot and faint and I crumpled to the ground. A sheet of scarlet flame seemed to leap behind my eyes, and the smell of blood was sharp and sour in my nostrils. The light faded around me and I saw a man with a merciless, beautiful face, crowned with livid fire. It was one of the Unconquered lords and he was circling around Sebastian, who looked pitifully pale and ill. As the demon master came nearer, I felt my skin being scorched by his foul presence. Then I saw myself thrusting the Talisman into his crimson eyes, as I chanted a stream of unknown words and shielded Sebastian with my body.

"No!" I cried. "Leave him; don't touch him!"

"Evie, what's happening?" asked Helen.

"I saw him! I saw Sebastian!" I gasped and shuddered. "Sebastian's master—he's getting closer all the time. But Sebastian's still in this world and he's alone. I'm sure the coven doesn't know where he is." I sprang to my feet and faced my friends. "I've got to do something, now, before it's too late. Look, I've got something that they want—the Talisman. The Dark Sisters believe that the Talisman holds the key to immortality. If it's really that powerful, why be so afraid of them? Can't I use it myself to fight them? If I can work out how to use the Talisman, I can reach Agnes's powers—I'll wield the sacred fire, like she did. With such power I could stop Sebastian from fading, or reverse time . . . or . . . or . . . Oh, I don't know, but I've got to find a way out of this. I can't let him fade into some kind of demon, I just can't!"

"We know you can't," said Sarah softly. "And we can't let you face this alone. You don't have to ask for our help. We'll go anywhere you go, and do anything you need us to."

"Sarah's right," Helen said, her clear eyes gleaming in the candlelight. "It will be dangerous to try to help Sebastian, but it's just as dangerous to do nothing and wait for the coven to attack. I'm with you, Evie. When do we start?"

I hugged them both, unable to speak. "You're the best friends I could ever have," I mumbled incoherently.

"Friends?" Sarah smiled. "I thought we were sisters?"

I laughed suddenly, as though nothing could crush the feeling of strength and life that was rushing though me.

We were united. As we hugged and laughed and cried, an echo of Agnes's voice rang around the cave: *My sisters . . . my sisters . . .*

Four sisters, four elements, one purpose. And there was hope burning inside me, like a pure white flame.

Ten

So where do you want to begin?" asked Helen.

"I've been trying to understand my powers better," I said eagerly. "I don't know all the answers yet, but I spent hours at home in the holidays trying new things, up on the cliffs before anyone was around, or in my room late at night. I'm learning more; I want to show you. Look at this."

I held my hands out in front of me and closed my eyes. I went into myself, deeper and deeper. Everything fell silent around me, yet I could hear, as though a long way off, the sound of the waves crashing on the shore at home. My body began to tingle and I was aware of the blood rushing through my veins. *The water of life . . . the blood of my veins . . . awaken in me. . . .* I felt an invisible wave of energy flooding over me. I opened my eyes and knelt down to trail my fingers in the stream that gurgled around the base of the statue. The next second I heard the crack of ice. The stream had frozen, as still as the statue that stood above it. I clicked my fingers and the stream flowed once more.

"That's fantastic, Evie," said Sarah. We looked at each other and grinned excitedly, still totally awed by this new world we were discovering.

"What about you?" I asked her. "Have you done anything new?" Last term I had seen Sarah use her earth powers to make a seed spring into life before my eyes and to make the ground shake under our feet.

"Yes, I think so," she answered shyly. "Yes, I have." She searched around in the dim cave, then stooped to pick up a small chunk of rock that lay on the bed of the stream. Holding it cupped in the palm of her hand, Sarah covered the rock with her other hand and frowned with concentration. When she drew her hand away the rock had crumbled into dust.

"Wow! This proves that last term wasn't a fluke. Helen, let's see if we can awaken the Talisman. Let's do it now, straightaway," I begged. "At home I tried calling to it and chanting over it and anything else I could think of, but nothing happened. But here in Wyldcliffe, in Agnes's home, it might respond, if we all work together."

"I've got a feeling you have to do this on your own, Evie," Helen replied. "Didn't Lady Agnes say in her journal that she was leaving the Talisman to you? That she was sealing her powers in the necklace so that they would be guarded for you to use? I'm not sure if she meant us to be part of that."

"But we could try anyway, couldn't we?" said Sarah.

"Well, we've nothing to lose. Let's try." Helen gave me an encouraging smile and took some candle ends from the niche in the rock and arranged them on the ground. As she lit each one, she chanted, "May this light guide our steps, may it illuminate our minds, may it cleanse our hearts. . . ."

At last the candles were burning in a ring of quivering flames. A thrill of anticipation ran through me. In the Sacred Circle our powers would be united and magnified; we would be stronger, ready for anything. I stepped inside the ring of fire, undid the shining necklace, and laid it carefully on the rocky ground. Then Sarah and Helen stepped into the circle and we held hands. Helen began to speak in a low voice: "We call on you, our sisters of wind, earth, and sea. We call upon the fire of life. Bless our circle. Guide us." Then Sarah began to chant softly,

"The air of our breath, the water of our veins, the clay of our bodies . . ."

We raised our arms to the moon and the stars, which wheeled above us unseen.

"Sacred Powers," I called. "Permit me to use the gift that our sister Agnes bequeathed to me. Let me know its strength; let me understand its secrets. Open the Talisman to me, I beseech you." Then I knelt down and placed my hand over the crystal at the heart of the Talisman. A silver-blue light flared out from the jewel as I touched it, making the mosaics spring to life with a thousand reflections. My heart began to race. "Water of life, I call on your powers to open this path to me. Agnes, Sebastian, help me. . . ."

I tried to focus my mind on the great and boundless ocean, as deep as my love, as wild as my dreams, as powerful as my enemies. I heard the sigh and roar of the waves. I heard Sarah and Helen chanting and I joined in, summoning my secret self as I had when I had raised the lake from its quiet bed: "I think, I feel, I desire . . . I command the Talisman to hear my call. . . . Mystic Powers, come to our aid . . . help us now. . . ."

But the light from the crystal died away and nothing happened.

Reality.

The Talisman remained beautiful and lifeless in my hand. The moment had passed.

"It's no good." I sighed. "This isn't going to work."

I fastened the necklace around my neck again and stepped out of the circle. Helen blew out the candles on the ground. The grotto looked like a dank cave, not a place of wonder. All my excitement had evaporated.

"I'm sorry, Evie," said Helen said quietly. "But somehow I never felt it would be as easy as that."

"What are we going to do?" asked Sarah. "Every day, every hour and second is precious. We have to make some kind of progress."

"Perhaps that's the problem." A thought had struck me. "Maybe we haven't progressed far enough in the Mystic Way. When Agnes made the Talisman, she was at the height of her powers. I know Helen has been in tune with her gifts for a lot longer than we have, but you and me, Sarah—well, aren't we really just beginners? Perhaps I need to develop my powers more so that I have the same power over water as Agnes had over fire. She had all sorts of amazing abilities. Won't I need the same?"

Sarah seemed struck by what I had said. "It seems to make sense. But we've so little time—"

"Then we'll practice as much as we can," I interrupted. "We can come here every night if necessary, or find somewhere in the school where we won't be seen. What do you think? Is it worth trying?"

Helen and Sarah placed their hands over mine, as though they were taking an oath. "We won't stop until the Talisman opens itself to you, Evie. We'll make this happen; we promise."

And we didn't stop. The first week at Wyldcliffe went past in a blur as I threw myself into my studies, by both day and night. I was buzzing with adrenaline, hungry to learn, and it didn't seem to matter what. Whether I was in the grotto turning water into silver mist, or drawing liquid essences from the stones of the cave, or hunched in the cold classrooms studying Latin verbs or chemical reactions, I was on fire. Knowledge was power, I kept telling myself, and it seemed to me that the knowledge I sought might lie anywhere: in an obscure bit of poetry, in a scientific formula, or in an ancient spell. This term I was going to be at the top of every class and ahead of every idea.

All that week the snow lay around the Abbey, white and blank and cold. Any lingering hope that Sebastian would contact me had withered like a green shoot in the bitter frost. But I refused to despair. I was young and strong, I would outwit the coven; I would find Sebastian; I would soon know every secret of the Mystic Way.

Wherever there was darkness, I would bring light, and that light would never be overwhelmed.

Eleven

It is so dark here, Evie.

I light a candle but it does not seem to ease the darkness of my mind.

I said I would be patient and wait without complaint, but it is so hard, when every hour, every minute drains me of strength.

Have you forgotten me?

I should not blame you if you have. I have nothing to offer you. My powers are fading. I am a prisoner. I am trapped.

At times a faint gray gleam peeps through the cracks and crannies of this dusty room, and I guess that somewhere there is light and freedom. But that has nothing to do with me now. I have forgotten the outside world. I have forgotten yesterday. Only the old memories remain.

I remember the gray-haired parson at Wyldcliffe Church, when the world was younger and I was innocent of its dangers. What was that he said? "I go whence I shall not return, even to the land of darkness and the shadow of death . . . where the light is as darkness." It seems an eternity since I sat in the little stone church in the village, watching the sparks of dust dance in a shaft of sunlight, trying not to yawn as the parson droned on, whilst Agnes shook her head reprovingly at me, half frowning, half laughing.

If only I had not been so proud and stubborn all those years ago! If only I had listened to Agnes, and never meddled with forbidden knowledge! I have been so blind and crazy, from the beginning—

And yet, if I had not traveled this road I would have lived my life and died and passed from this world before you were ever born. I would never have met you, never have heard your voice, or touched your hand, or felt your lips on mine. That would have been the worst punishment of all.

There is something I must tell you.

I must warn you.

They are coming closer—

Oh, Evie, such fear! I see their pitiless, undead faces. I see their king, his iron crown flickering with red flames, as he reaches out to me with his fist of steel, pulling me closer into his trap. I hear the howling and gibbering of demons and I feel myself fading into that endless night—

Yet I will face this horror with open eyes rather than hurt one single strand of your bright hair.

They tried to make me betray you once before, but they couldn't. They shall never succeed. I may become a creature of darkness, but I will never, ever forget that I love you.

Twelve

I couldn't forget Sebastian, not for a single moment. He was in my thoughts and dreams and in the very air I breathed. Sometimes I seemed to feel the touch of his hand on mine, or hear the echo of his voice in Wyldcliffe's gloomy corridors. Part of me just wanted to skip my classes and go looking for him out on the moors, but I knew it would be a hopeless task. He could be anywhere, concealed by the remnants of his powers. But no, I had to stick to my plan to open the talisman. Once I could do that, I was sure it would lead me to him. I had to work without thinking, and the image of him, pale and sick and suffering, kept me going through the long hours of effort and study.

On Saturday afternoon, after lessons had finished for

the day, I picked my way down the snow-covered path from the stables, where I had been helping Sarah with her ponies. Checking that no one was watching, I summoned a surge of my thought and gave a flick of my wrist. A drift of snow in a flower bed melted instantly, revealing tight young spikes of green struggling up through the earth. A fierce wave of joy shot through me, then died away. I had proved that I had power over water, but how was I supposed to use it? Was this getting me closer to the heart of the Talisman?

"Isn't it c-cold?"

I looked around, startled. Harriet was stumbling down the path toward me. I hoped furiously that she hadn't seen anything. Since our ride on the train together she had latched onto me and seemed ready to bump into me at every corner, waiting to ask me something: "Evie, do you know where I can get a new notebook?" "Evie, how do I ask about joining the choir?" "Evie, can you help me with my math assignment?"

"What are you doing out here?" I asked. Her nose was tipped with pink and her teeth were chattering. "You'll catch your death of cold."

She shrugged. "Classes are over and I've nothing to do."

"Well, why don't you go and sit inside with your friends?"

Harriet looked awkward and said in a tight little voice, "I haven't really made any friends yet."

I felt sorry for her, but I simply didn't have time for this.

"Well, you won't make any friends wandering about on your own," I said briskly. "Some of the younger girls do arts and crafts in the dining hall on Saturday afternoons. Why don't you go and join them?"

"I'd rather talk to you."

"Don't be silly. You need to be with girls in your own form." I shooed her away as kindly as I could. "Off you go, Harriet. And next time you come outside at least put your scarf and gloves on!"

I watched her go, then hurried to join Helen in the main entrance hall. Quickly forgetting about Harriet, I stood for a moment warming myself at the fire that was burning low in the stone hearth. Helen had already started our Saturday chore of arranging hothouse flowers in the great bronze vase that stood on the table in the entrance hall—another dumb scholarship duty. The rich blooms contrasted with her gossamer hair, and even in her drab school clothes she looked like a wild young goddess surrounded by ivy and lilies and roses.

The art teacher, Miss Hetherington, walked across

the hallway, carrying a pile of sketchbooks.

"Lovely flowers, girls," she said approvingly. "We need some color in the middle of all this snow." For a moment I could imagine that I was in a regular school, where the teachers really were just teachers, and not women to be feared. But this was Wyldcliffe, where no one could be trusted. "I'm glad you're here, Evie," Miss Hetherington went on. "I was looking for you. This note was left by mistake with the staff mail. It's addressed to you." She handed me a small envelope and walked away. Suddenly apprehensive, I tore the note open.

HOPE YOU ENJOYED YOUR FIRST WEEK.
IT WILL BE YOUR LAST.

"It's another one," I said, handing it to Helen. "Another threat."

"What are you going to do?"

"There's nothing I can do. Just keep going. Try harder. Work quicker. What else can I do?"

And so that night I slipped out of bed once more and crept down the servants' staircase and into the yard. On the far side of the Abbey's sweeping lawns, dense thickets of snow-covered shrubs concealed a mound of rocks.

I pushed my way through the tangled undergrowth and twisted under an overhanging branch. The dark mouth of the grotto gaped like a secret tomb. I stepped inside and the steady beam from my flashlight met an answering gleam of candlelight. Sarah and Helen were already there, marking a circle on the damp, rocky ground.

While they were busy I stood by the statue, watching where the stream bubbled around its base, welling up from some underground source. The water flowed through a narrow channel in the cave floor, then disappeared again into some kind of cleverly hidden drainage culvert. Water . . . it had to hold the answer somehow . . . water, endless movement, source of all life. On an impulse, I knelt down and unfastened the Talisman and laid it in the icy stream. Its crystal heart shone deeply, glistening in the water like a bright eye. I felt Helen and Sarah watching me, and the gleaming shapes on the wall seemed to watch too; nymphs and centaurs and fauns and fantastical beasts, everyone was watching and waiting. I scooped up the water in my hands and let it fall back down in blessing, then leaned over the jewel in the stream.

"Speak to me now," I begged. "Show me the way." It seemed to glitter like a precious treasure tossed onto a piece of wasteland; then it grew dim and I saw instead my reflection in the running water. But it wasn't me; it was Agnes, looking up at me. She was going to tell me something. . . . She seemed to have a message for me in her gray eyes. . . . *Evie, follow my path.* . . . *They are getting closer.* . . . *Evie* . . . *Evie* . . .

"Evie!" Sarah was shaking me, dragging me back to the present moment.

"What is it?"

"I feel something. . . . Listen." Sarah silently crept over to the farthest depths of the little cave, where a projection in the rock wall concealed the mouth of a tunnel. We had used the tunnel to escape from the crypt under the chapel at the end of last term. She stretched her hands against the rough walls, a look of intense concentration on her face, as though she were listening through her fingertips.

"Can you hear that?" she said softly, but I shook my head. I could hear nothing except my own heart hammering away and the trickle of the icy stream. I picked the Talisman out of the water, half-annoyed with Sarah for disturbing me. Agnes had been trying to tell me something. To follow her . . . Well, I was trying to do that. What else? Something about someone coming closer . . .

"They're getting closer!" Sarah spun around, panic gleaming in her eyes. "The Dark Sisters! They are gathered down in the crypt. I can hear their voices through the rock and earth of the tunnel; I can feel the tread of their feet. They're coming this way!"

"Get back to the school!" I cried. "Helen, you get out of here in your own way. We'll hold them off and get back through the gardens. Hurry!"

Helen hesitated. "I can't leave you here."

"You must! Go!"

The next moment, Helen seemed to pull the air around her like a thick cloak, and she disappeared. Sarah spoke under her breath and made signs over the mouth of the tunnel. It began to cave in, and rocks tumbled heavily to block the entrance. "Get back, Evie," Sarah shouted. "Let's go!"

We blew out the candles and I followed Sarah as she led us unerringly out of the lightless cavern. I could hear the water swirling around the statue behind us, and now I thought I heard the echo of pounding feet as the Dark Sisters made their way up the long, twisting tunnels from the crypt to the grotto. But they wouldn't be able to get through, at least not straightaway. Sarah had given us a chance to escape.

The next moment we were outside, scrambling through the undergrowth of the shrubbery and heading for the school. We ran across the lawns, trying to stay under the cover of the weeping willows that bordered them. The ruins looked like fantastical silhouettes against the snow, but we didn't stop to admire them. We raced to the stable yard, where the old green door would lead us back into the servants' quarters. Panting, we pushed the door open, then stopped for breath.

"The coven must be meeting," I said with a gasp.

"But I wonder why they were moving from the crypt up to the grotto? It's not going to be safe now if they are trampling all over it."

I knew why the coven was on the move. "They must have known we were meeting down there."

"How?"

I shrugged. "Who knows who is spying on us for them? Or perhaps they can sense the Talisman, get drawn to it somehow. And that note I got, it must have been meant for an attack tonight." I should have been afraid, but I wasn't. I suddenly began to laugh softly. "Whoever wrote it is going to be disappointed. They won't get rid of me that easily. You were too clever for them, Sarah. They'll never catch us."

"I still don't want to be found out of bed by Miss Scratton, though. Come on. Helen should be safe in your dorm by now. Let's get back as quickly as we can."

I switched on my flashlight and we padded swiftly down the dusty passages, then crept up the back stairs to the third floor. "You go first," I said. "I'll give you ten minutes to get to your dorm; then I'll go to mine. We don't want to be seen together. If you bump into one of the staff you can say you had to go to the bathroom, and I'll do the same."

Sarah slipped out into the main corridor and shut the door softly behind her. I had once panicked here, last term, when I had been trapped on the deserted stairs, but now I hoped I was braver. I tried to pass the time by imagining the lives of the young servants who had actually used these steps, running up and down to do their chores when Agnes was alive. Hadn't she mentioned them in her journal? I was trying to remember their names when something caught my eye.

On the wall opposite the door to the corridor, a rough panel seemed to have been nailed into place long ago. It was covered with cobwebs and grime, and I had never noticed it before. I tried to pry off a corner of the panel with my fingers, and it simply crumbled away to dust, leaving a jagged gap in the wall. Holding up the flashlight, I peered through this hole and caught a glimpse of more narrow steps, rising up to the abandoned attic floor.

I was tempted to pull the whole panel away and explore, but something stopped me. *Sane, sensible Evie.* Sarah would have gotten back to her dorm, and I needed to do the same, I told myself. With the coven on the move, this was no time to indulge in adventures. I would be sensible. I would get back to bed.

I cautiously opened the door to the corridor and stepped into the main part of the school. A lamp outside the bathroom glowed dully. As I crept back to my dorm, I heard a soft noise. Standing at the other end of the long passage, at the top of the marble staircase, was the slight figure of a girl. Moonlight from the arched window over the stairs shone on her white nightgown and she stood unnaturally still, staring down over the edge of the banister, like a statue.

Like a ghost.

Thirteen

gnes?" As I stepped closer, I realized that this girl was not as tall as Agnes and that her hair was dark, not auburn. "Who's there?"

The girl ignored me. She leaned farther over the wrought-iron balustrade that was keeping her from plunging like a doll to the ground floor fifty feet below.

"Be careful!"

She slowly turned her face in my direction. Her dull eyes stared at me glassily, empty of any life or recognition. I had recognized her, though. "Harriet?" I called out in a low voice. "What on earth are you doing? You might fall."

Harriet didn't reply, but just kept on staring and staring. She began to walk toward me, moving straight ahead with that ghastly, dead expression on her face.

"Harriet!" I grasped her by her shoulders and something clicked in my head. *She is not dead, but sleeping. . . .*

Of course, Harriet was sleepwalking, that was all. She was still staring at me, blank eyed and unresponsive. Her hand twitched; then her head began to droop. I steered her toward a carved bench that stood near the top of the staircase and forced her to sit on it. As Harriet's head lolled down and touched her chest she woke up.

"Harriet, what are you doing out here?"

"What?" she said, looking around vaguely.

"Did you know that you sleepwalk?"

"No . . . I mean . . . yes, sometimes, but not for years, not for ages." Her eyes seemed to focus on me properly for the first time. "Please don't tell anyone, Evie."

"Why not? Can't the nurse give you something to stop you from doing it? You could hurt yourself wandering around in the dark. I think the staff should know."

"No, please don't say anything! I don't want anyone to know. I'm sure I won't do it again."

"So what brought it on?" I asked.

"It's being in a new place, that's all." She looked at me pleadingly. "Please don't say anything. They already think I'm . . . Anyway, what are you doing out of bed?"

"Um . . . I was kind of half-asleep and I thought I heard

someone in the corridor, so I came to look. That's all. And we'll get about a hundred demerits if the mistresses wake up and catch us. I guess we'd better get back to bed and get some sleep."

Harriet blinked fearfully. "I wish my mom were here."

I wanted to be kind, but she made me feel cold somehow, as though I couldn't really be natural with her.

"Look, Harriet, it takes time to get used to boarding school. You need to give yourself a chance to settle down and make friends. Then you'll feel more at home."

The old clichés sounded so stilted and patronizing. She looked up at me with her dark, frightened eyes. "Do you really think I'll make friends? I feel that no one likes me."

"Don't be silly." I tried to laugh. "I like you." But I wasn't really sure whether it was true.

"Do you? Do you really?" Harriet stared at me, then smiled gratefully. "So I've got one friend, haven't I? I'll go to bed now. It's funny," she said as she stood up. "One of these rooms must have been Lady Agnes's bedroom. It's like we're in her shadow. . . . Well, good night."

"Wait, Harriet, stay a second!" There was something I needed to ask her. "I've been kind of wondering whether your family has anything to do with Lady Agnes— you know, with the Templetons who lived here? Are you . . . um, connected at all?"

She looked down, suddenly sullen again. "Aren't we all connected, if you go back far enough? What does it matter, anyway?"

"Please, Harriet, I—I need to know; it might be important."

The silence around us seemed to grow deeper.

Harriet's sallow cheeks flushed pink. "Templeton is my mother's name. My parents are divorced and I hardly see my dad; he's not really interested. . . . I mean, he's really busy. Anyway, after they split up she wanted me to be called Templeton too."

"You said your mother was a student at the Abbey. Was that because she was related to the Wyldcliffe Templetons?"

She looked embarrassed again. "That's not very likely. My mother was here on a scholarship. I don't think she really fit in. But she got this dumb idea that she must be related to them because of her name, and started to think that maybe she should really have been a lady with a big house and horses and money. She was obsessed with anything to do with Lady Agnes. She said I should act like I was Lady Harriet Templeton, and went on and on about Agnes as if she were some kind of family relative." Harriet looked away with a bitter expression on her face. "That's why Mom sent me here," she added. "Since Dad left she's never had time for anything but her job, so that she can earn enough money for me to come to this place and be a proper Wyldcliffe lady. But it was all a kind of dream. I didn't really want to come. I—I miss her."

My heart sank. Poor Harriet. Poor sad Harriet.

I watched her pad back to her dorm, then fled to my own bed. There was no rest for me that night. But it wasn't Sebastian or the coven that kept me awake. It was the small, everyday tragedy of one plain, awkward girl, who was quietly suffering under the roof of this great house. As I tossed and turned I heard the village clock strike three. I groaned and buried my head under my pillow. I couldn't cope with any more problems. All I wanted to do was to go to sleep, and dream of Sebastian.

Fourteen

FROM THE PRIVATE PAPERS OF
SEBASTIAN JAMES FAIRFAX

I hear the clock strike three. There is no rest for me this night.

They are looking for me. The women who were once my servants now pursue me with deadly hate. And you, my darling girl, they hate you too.

When I remember them, and my past dealings with them, my heart sickens. But these women, these Dark Sisters, whose hearts and minds I once controlled, have moved beyond my influence now. My powers have faded.

Even so, I must rise from this sickbed; I must venture out and try to warn you—to stop them—I must.

I can't—

I can't—

Oh, Evie, Evie, where are you? All I want is to hold you again, to protect you from what I have done to you. I would give anything to be able to walk and ride and run as I once did. Perhaps this is a punishment, this weakness, for my being so arrogant as not to realize my good fortune in the days of my strength.

My body is weak. My mind is fading. But my love is strong, even now.

I must tell you—I know what they want, those deadly women.

Oh, it looks so harmless, so innocent! A pretty trinket around a pretty throat, that is all. A simple necklace, to be admired and then forgotten.

How it burned me when I tried to touch it, the night you first showed it to me.

The pain seared my mind but opened my eyes to the truth of who you were and what your necklace was. Then I knew how Agnes had contrived to keep her greatest secret from me.

Oh, hide it, hide it from me! The Dark Sisters are not the only creatures who desire the Talisman. I also long for its silver tracings. I long for the depths of its crystal heart;

I long for its powers that could set me free. Let no one see it. Let no one touch it. Keep it from them.

Keep it from me.

Hide it, Evie, hide it, before it is too late—

Fifteen

It was getting late. The short winter day was coming to an end. I was climbing the marble stairs to the dorm, my legs aching after a long and weary game of lacrosse. I hated the stupid game, all mud and sweat and bruises, and it was always made worse by the sneers of Celeste and her cronies. *Come on, Johnson, can't you do better than that? Why are you so useless, Johnson?* I wanted to lie down and close my eyes and sink into oblivion. The walls of the corridor seemed to swirl around me and the light from the lamps shattered into a hundred colors. . . .

Stumbling forward, I opened the door of the dormitory. The window was banging and the thin drapes around the beds flapped like sails in the icy wind. I shut the window, then knelt on the seat and looked out over the frozen hills.

The sun was dipping low and red in the clear winter sky, and the snow was stained crimson, as if the whole world were on fire.

"Isn't it beautiful, Evie?" someone said behind me.

I turned and there he was, an angel in the shadows, with his long dark hair and his deep blue eyes, and that smile that was only for me.

"Sebastian!"

I flew across the room and his arms were waiting. He caught me close and pressed me to him and I knew that the nightmare was over, at last.

We clung to each other; then I broke away, torn between tears and laughter.

"I didn't know where you were. . . . Oh, Sebastian, I was desperate to see you. Where have you been?" A hundred other questions jostled against one another in my mind, but I couldn't stop smiling, because I was happier than I had ever been in my whole life.

"There's something you need to know," Sebastian said quietly, and the look in his eyes made me afraid. Now I saw how ill he looked, and how his clothes hung loose and crumpled on his lean frame.

"Sebastian—what's wrong?"

"I'm running out of time."

So this wasn't the miracle I had been hoping for. The church bell began to strike and the sound echoed crazily around the room. *Time . . . time . . . there's no time left. . . .* The walls seemed to shake. . . . I grasped hold of Sebastian's hand and he pulled me gently to him.

"Evie, I've been sick and weary for so long, but I had to find you. I have to tell you something."

"What is it?" I asked, afraid to hear his reply.

"That you're the most beautiful girl I ever saw." He smiled and my heart flipped over, but the clock was striking, calling to Sebastian from far away. But I couldn't be sad, not now, not yet. I would be sad later, when the bell stopped ringing. Right now, at this moment, Sebastian was there, next to me, and I could smell the sweet warmth of his body as he leaned over to kiss me. . . .

There was a crash, a knocking at the door, and Miss Scratton entered the room, dressed in a long black robe. She held out her hand and said coldly, "Your necklace, Evie, give me your necklace."

The lights swirled again and I felt Sebastian slip out of my arms. "No," I cried. "No, no, no . . ."

"The necklace, Evie," he shouted. "I have to tell you . . . hide it . . . don't let them see it . . . they're coming. . . ."

He seemed to vanish into the red glare of the dying

sun, and all I could hear was Miss Scratton's harsh voice: "Your necklace . . . your necklace . . . your necklace . . ."

I woke up, sobbing under my breath. "No, no, no . . ." The sound of the church bell was drifting clear and high across the frozen valley. Three . . . four . . . five . . . six . . .

Another day was dawning without Sebastian. I sat up, then dragged myself out of the dorm and down the corridor to the bathroom. Tugging open the door of one of the cubicles I retched violently into the basin. To be with Sebastian in my dreams, to hear him and touch him and hold him, and then to be flung back into the empty waking world was more than I could bear. I was sick again, spilling out my guts instead of my heart. Sebastian was out there somewhere, slowly fading from this world and sinking into the abyss, and I was still hadn't found out how to stop it.

I washed myself with cold water, trying to freshen my body and my mind. Water—my beautiful, translucent element: as quick as fire, as smooth as air, as weighty as earth . . .

Hide the Talisman, Sebastian had said. Had it really been him, or was it my jumbled thoughts trying to make sense of things while I slept? Perhaps I had been too flippant about our escape from the coven the night before.

The confidence I had felt then began to drain away. After all, if Sarah hadn't been able to sense their movement through the layers of earth and rock they would have been upon us. The Talisman could have been taken. I could have been taken. It could have been my last week, my last day, as the note had threatened.

As I dried myself, my hand brushed against the necklace, cool against my skin, hanging on its silver chain under my nightclothes. Although my high-buttoned school shirt and tie usually covered it up, there were times when I had to change into my gym clothes, take showers, lie in bed asleep. At any moment, one of the mistresses, whether she served the coven or not, might see it and demand it from me. *Give me your necklace . . . give me your necklace. . . .*

I had made a decision.

I would trust my dream Sebastian. He had told me to hide the Talisman, and I would, until I was ready to use it. Pulling my robe tight, I hurried out of the bathroom and went back to the dorm. I crept over to Helen's bed and shook her gently awake.

"Shhhh!" I warned her. "It's only me."

Helen sat up and yawned, pushing her hair out of her sleepy eyes. I knelt at the edge of her bed and tried to explain everything in a hurried whisper, before the other girls woke up.

"After this weird dream and what happened last night, I think we definitely need to hide it somewhere safe," I said in a low voice.

"I think you're right. Wearing it is like an invitation for them to come and get it. But where would be really safe?"

I had already decided. There was only one place it could be.

"Uppercliffe. No one will find it there."

"Okay. When?"

Fortunately it was Sunday. We would be allowed out that afternoon.

"We'll go today, as soon as we can," I said.

Celeste turned over lazily in her bed and opened her wide, innocent eyes. "Go where?"

I ignored her. The sooner the Talisman was buried out of sight, the safer it would be.

Sixteen

FROM THE PRIVATE PAPERS OF
SEBASTIAN JAMES FAIRFAX

I have been buried out of sight, here in this narrow, light-less place. But now, at last, I will get out. I will be free.

I saw you.

Perhaps it was an hour since, or a lifetime ago. I can no longer reckon such things. But I saw you, Evie. I touched you. I felt alive again. You always made me feel alive.

Life, breath, strength—all because of you.

I was waiting for you in the chamber in the Abbey that had once belonged to Agnes, though all was bare and altered. It was sunset. The earth was alive with fire and ice. Fire and water.

Agnes and Evie.

Agnes was like my sister, but you are my whole world.

I waited for you. I heard your footsteps and the next moment you were in my arms. If I close my eyes, I can still recall the softness of your skin and the scent of your hair—I can feel the flutter of your heart, the sigh of your breath . . .

Oh, God! How can I stand to be away from you for one single moment when I have so little time left?

Seeing you has given me strength.

I will reach you again, and not just in my mind. It was a dream, and yet not a dream. Now I need to make it a reality. You have awoken me, and I no longer feel so drained of life.

I will get out of here.

Evie, I will come to you, I will find a way.

A light shines on my face. The darkness has receded slightly. The frost in me is thawing, and all because of you.

Seventeen

The snow had thawed overnight and the country lanes had turned into mud-spattered slush. Most of the girls in my class complained about wet feet and cold fingers during the long morning walk to the village church and back, but I had other things on my mind.

Sarah and I were going to ride to Uppercliffe Farm that afternoon, and before our visit to the farm, I was going to have the first of the riding lessons that Dad had arranged. To be truthful, I wasn't crazy about being on horseback again. *Horses are unpredictable, aren't they? It's dangerous. . . .* I had tried to shrug off Harriet's silly comments, but my stomach had begun to flutter with nerves. Although I could sit on a pony and jog over the moors, I didn't really know how to ride properly. I hoped the teacher wouldn't expect me to gallop, or jump, or do anything fancy. I wasn't afraid of swimming in the roughest seas, but I hadn't been brought up around horses and I would never be entirely comfortable with them.

After lunch, I went up to the dorm to change, pulling on the smooth new jodhpurs and shiny riding boots that Dad had given me at Christmas. I felt for my necklace under my sweatshirt.

"Agnes?" I hesitated. "Agnes, tell me, am I doing the right thing? Should I take it to Uppercliffe?" The thin curtains around my bed stirred, as though blown by a breeze from the moors, and I heard the echo of a sigh. Then there was silence, except for the urgent beating of my heart.

Sarah would be waiting. I had to go.

I swung out of the dorm and clattered down the marble steps and reached the second floor, where the staff quarters were. Miss Scratton was locking the door to one of the rooms. She looked up and saw me, then beckoned me over.

"I hear you are going out riding with Sarah? She made a request last night for you to ride over the moors together this afternoon."

"Um, yes . . ."

"Be careful that you don't stay out too long. It's getting colder again, and I believe that more snow is on its way."

"I'm sure we'll be fine, Miss Scratton."

"I understand that your grandmother's funeral took place over the holidays," she said, quiet and grave as usual. "Death is very hard for the young. Let me know if there is anything we can do."

She seemed to look at me with genuine pity in her cool, intelligent eyes. For a moment, her kindness threatened to unnerve me. Part of me wanted to talk to her, tell her all about Frankie, and to be soothed and comforted. I felt confused by the image I'd had of Miss Scratton in my dream, reaching out to grasp the Talisman. It didn't fit with this apparently concerned teacher who stood in front of me. I forced myself to smile calmly.

"Thank you. But I'm okay."

"I have no doubt of it," she replied softly. "There is an ancient saying: 'The heart grieves, but the wise man does not seek out the dead.' Remember that, Evie. Don't—"

Just then, Miss Dalrymple emerged from one of the second-floor rooms, smiling and nodding and dabbing the corner of her mouth with a tiny lace handkerchief. "Going riding, Evie? Splendid! I'm sure Miss Scratton here could give you some good advice. She's a marvelous horsewoman, quite marvelous." The fussy, overbearing teacher smirked as she bestowed her compliment. "Indeed, Miss Scratton's advice on any subject would be invaluable."

A flash of irritation seemed to play across Miss Scratton's narrow features, but she smoothed it away. "What nonsense! I haven't ridden for years. You'd better get along, Evie. And as I was going to say, don't run on the stairs."

I made my way out of the building and across the stable yard. What had Miss Scratton been about to say? Don't what? It had nothing to do with running on the stairs, I could have sworn. And how much had Miss Dalrymple overheard? *The wise man does not seek out the dead. . . .* Had Miss Scratton been talking about Frankie—or about Sebastian? But that would be impossible, unless— unless what? If she were one of the Dark Sisters and knew about Sebastian she would hardly want to give me advice. I kicked a pebble across the cobbles and shoved my hands in my pockets, deep in thought.

"Hey!"

"Oh! I'm so sorry!" I had walked straight into a tall, athletic-looking boy. He was about eighteen years old, with corn-colored hair and an amused expression. I stepped back and drew breath. "I'm really sorry. I didn't see you."

"It's okay, no worries." The boy smiled. "I love being

treated as though I don't exist. Invisible man, that's me."

"No, it wasn't that. I mean, I know who you are," I babbled. "You're . . . um . . . Josh, aren't you? And you—"

"Help out in the stables, yeah. Don't worry; you can walk into me anytime."

I blushed, though I didn't quite know why. Josh, on the other hand, seemed to be entirely at his ease.

"Well, I'd better go," I said idiotically. "Mustn't be late for my riding lesson."

"No," he said, smiling again. "Well, I hope you enjoy it."

"Yeah, thanks."

I hurried over to Bonny's stall and saddled her up with fumbling, inexpert hands. I was surprised that Sarah hadn't come to help me, but I guessed she would be along soon. Struggling with the last buckle, I finally got the saddle and bridle on and led Bonny out through the yard to the practice paddock that lay beyond it. Sarah was already there, fussing over a quiet gray horse that was tethered to the rails, and talking to Josh.

Sarah looked happy and animated, and I felt that I had never really seen her so clearly before. I hadn't realized how pretty she was. With a stab of surprise, I saw that the glow in her eyes was because of Josh, and the next moment blamed myself for having been so stupid as to not notice something so important about my best friend.

At the far side of the paddock Harriet was shivering alone in the cold, looking like a kid who had no one to play with. She had evidently ignored my advice about trying to get to know her classmates. I sighed. I really didn't want her watching my first efforts with the riding instructor. And although Sarah might be delighted to see Josh, I wasn't that keen on his seeing me making a fool of myself with my beginner's efforts. Why had I ever agreed to these lessons?

Sarah turned and waved to me. "Hey, Evie, are you all ready?"

"I guess so. Where's this Mrs. Parker, or whatever her name is?" I grumbled. "She's supposed to be here right now."

Josh straightened up. "I'm Mrs. Parker," he said with a grin. "At least, I am for the moment."

I must have looked confused, as he explained, "Judith Parker is my mom. She gives the horse riding lessons here at Wyldcliffe, but she sprained her wrist a couple of days ago. So you'll have to put up with me."

"I'm not sure—"

"Don't worry; I've got my basic teaching certificates. I won't let you break your neck."

"Oh, okay then," I said ungraciously. I led Bonny into the practice ring and scrambled up onto her back.

"No, not like that. Let's start right from the beginning." Very patiently, he showed me how to mount properly, how to sit up straight but relaxed, and how to grip the pony's sides with my knees.

The hour flew by. Josh was a good teacher, and when he got up onto his gray horse to demonstrate something, I couldn't help noticing the grace and confidence of his supple body. At one point he had to correct my posture and I felt his hand, warm and strong in the small of my back. And all the time I sensed Sarah watching Josh with her steady gaze, and Harriet watching all of us like a starving child. . . .

I was glad when the lesson ended.

"You've done well," said Josh. "I think we'll make a horsewoman of you eventually."

"I just want to stay on and not make a complete idiot of myself."

"Oh, I think you can do better than that." He smiled as I dismounted. "Much better."

"Josh! Where have you been?" An angry voice cut across the damp, cold air. "I've been waiting for you to saddle Sapphire for me forever!"

Celeste was staring at us indignantly from the path that led to the stables.

"You could try saddling her yourself, you know," snapped Sarah. "It wouldn't kill you."

"My father pays full livery fees," Celeste fumed, "and I expect—"

"It's okay; I'll come and do it," Josh said. "Evie's lesson ran over a bit, that's all." He turned to me and said, "Same time next week?"

"Mmm, yes, I mean, if your mom's arm isn't better."

He gave me an amused look, a gleam of admiration in his eyes. "Oh, I think she might have to rest it for quite a while." Then he began to stride away after Celeste, throwing a quick glance over his shoulder to Sarah. "See you around, Sarah."

For a fraction of a second Sarah looked disappointed by his casual manner, but she hid it almost instantly with a cheerful smile. "Yeah, see you."

We set off for Uppercliffe Farm, both lost in our thoughts. I trotted cautiously on Bonny, while Sarah rode confidently on her other pony, Starlight.

"So have you known Josh long?" I asked, as we left the school gates behind and began to climb a narrow path that wound over the moors.

"Three or four years, since I started at Wyldcliffe. Josh was always hanging around the stables, doing jobs for the old groom who used to be here. He still thinks of me as a pony-mad kid." She flashed me an odd look. "I'm not the kind of girl guys notice. I'm not like you."

I felt uncomfortable, as though I had trespassed on something private. I tried to think of something to say. "He seems a really good rider."

"One of the best," Sarah replied, her face lighting up again. "He's done tons of shows and competitions, but you need money to take it seriously. So he helps his mom with her riding school and works at Wyldcliffe. I think if he can't do riding professionally he wants to study to be a veterinarian. He's . . . well, he's a nice guy." She stopped herself, then frowned. "I don't know how he can put up with the attitude he gets from people like Celeste. He's not a servant, and she's not a princess, whatever she might think. He's worth a million times more than she is."

She suddenly urged Starlight on and went ahead over the wet ground. I hadn't heard Sarah talk like that before. Why hadn't I noticed before the warmth in her eyes and the light in her face when she spoke to him? I tried to remember the times I had seen her and Josh together last term. He had been down at the stables, I remembered, always with that same laid-back smile and athletic grace under his scruffy riding clothes, but I hadn't seen him showing any special attention to Sarah. Perhaps he did still think of her as a kid, or perhaps he felt that the Wyldcliffe students were off-limits, too stuck-up and snobby to be interested in a stable boy. Whatever the reason, I could see clearly now that Sarah liked him, and was suffering over it.

I hoped I had been mistaken about the admiration in his eyes when he had looked at me. I wasn't interested in Josh and I would hate to upset Sarah. It probably hadn't meant anything, I told myself. *Forget it.* Getting to Uppercliffe was all that mattered. I urged my pony to keep up with Sarah, and as I jogged over the wintry hills, the Talisman knocked against my heart.

Eighteen

ppercliffe Farm. It was hardly more than a ruined cottage, tucked away on the lonely hillside and overgrown with rough grass and nettles. The wind swirled over the drifts of snow that still lay here and there. It was easy to imagine what it must have been like in the old days: miles away from anywhere, the only sounds coming from the birds and the bleating of sheep. Here at Uppercliffe, Lady Agnes had concealed her greatest treasure— little Effie with the auburn curls, Agnes's daughter, and my great-great-grandmother.

Sarah and I slipped off our ponies and walked up to the tumbled remains of the house. The sign of the Talisman, the precious heirloom, had been scratched in the stone above the door many years ago. This seemed a fitting place to hide it. I prayed that the coven wouldn't think of searching for it there. I was pretty sure they didn't know of Agnes's connection with the old farm.

"We'll find a good hiding place inside," I said.

"Okay, but be careful; the ceiling has mostly fallen in and there are still some timbers that look a bit dangerous."

"I'll be careful," I promised. I walked under the door's stone archway and into the ruined house. All at once a halo of blinding light dazzled me and my stomach heaved as though I were falling from a great height. I blinked and when I opened my eyes again, I was standing in a low parlor. A stout woman in a long skirt was bending over a smoky fire. I knew who she was. It was Martha, Agnes's old nurse, who had lived at the farm long ago. She wiped her face with her apron and turned to rock a wooden cradle, where a baby with a wisp of bright hair was fast asleep, wrapped in a homespun blanket. Martha sang softly as she rocked the baby; then she looked across to the corner of the simple room, where Agnes was sitting at a small table, writing in a black, leather-bound book. It was her journal. I had read every word of it under Sebastian's anxious gaze as he had tried to explain the tangled web that connected all of us: Agnes, Sebastian, Effie, and Evie.

Agnes broke off from her writing and looked straight up at me, and I saw recognition in her eyes.

"I'm here!" I tried to call out, but the words wouldn't come. "I'm here!" Then I woke from the spell, moaning, "Here, here, here . . ."

"Is this where you want to hide it?" Sarah asked in a worried voice. "Do you mean here?"

Without realizing it, I had crouched down in the far corner of the crumbling house, where Agnes had been sitting at the table. I was clawing at the cold earth with my bare hands.

"Yes, here," I said, panting. "Here, this is the place. . . ."

"Wait, Evie; Helen will be here soon," Sarah urged. She moved closer to me and put her hand on my arm. "Did you see her just now? Did you see Agnes? Does she think we're doing the right thing?"

"I don't know. I only know I have to dig here, in this corner. . . ."

Outside, one of the ponies neighed in alarm, and I thought I heard the sound of hoofbeats. I got up shakily and went out to see what was happening, hoping to see Helen. But it wasn't her. I immediately tensed up, on the alert. This wasn't supposed to happen right now.

On the far side of a dip in the moors a couple of Wyldcliffe girls on horseback were talking to two other riders. The strangers weren't wearing proper riding clothes, just sweaters and torn jeans. One of them looked like a young girl of about eight or nine on a shaggy pony. An older teenage boy, maybe her brother, was riding bareback on a piebald horse. He slithered down to the ground and stood protectively by the girl. He looked sullen, as though the conversation had turned into an argument. Sarah came and stood next to me as I watched them.

"That looks like Celeste and India. I hope they don't come poking around here."

"But who are they talking to?" I asked.

"They might be local kids." Sarah frowned. "Or maybe . . . Yes, Josh said that some families had arrived at the travelers' camp on the other side of the village, that patch of waste ground beside the road. I think these two must be from there."

"You mean they're . . ." I hesitated. "Travelers, you said. Do you mean Gypsies?"

"I guess so. I'd love to talk to them if we get the chance one day."

Sarah was very proud of her Romany blood and kept a precious photograph of her long-ago ancestors next to her bed. But Celeste didn't seem very friendly toward the two young strangers.

Just then she spoke to them angrily and then jerked her horse's head around and cantered away, followed by India on her leggy, nervous-looking chestnut. The boy shrugged and spoke to the girl, then jumped up on his own horse with amazing quickness and strength. They didn't look anything like the romantic notions I had of Gypsies, but they seemed . . . I don't know, tough somehow, part of the landscape, less groomed and polished than the Wyldcliffe students with their expensive gear, but more at ease. They began to move off.

"Come on," I said, "let's get out of sight." I pulled Sarah back into the ruined cottage. "We can't waste any more time. If Helen has been held up, we'll have to start without her."

I went back to the spot in the corner where I had been digging and tried to scrape away more of the earth. A few moments later, the air swirled and grew bright, and Helen seemed to step out in front of me, as if blown there like a leaf on the wind. I was getting used to her appearing from nowhere like that.

"Are you okay?" Helen asked. "You look kind of upset."

"It's nothing; don't worry," I said. "But there are other riders out on the hills. We think we've found the right place, but we mustn't be seen."

"I've brought a spade and some other stuff," she said, showing me the rough canvas bag she had slung over her shoulder. "I took it from the gardener's shed. I'll keep watch if you want to do the digging."

But I was still shaking too much to be of any real help. I had seen Agnes, here in this abandoned house, and I couldn't brush off the sense that something bad was going to happen. The words I had heard her speak in the grotto came rushing back to me, and I felt sick and dizzy. *Follow my way . . . they are coming. . . .*

"I'll do it if you like," said Sarah. I nodded gratefully and tried to get my breath back as Sarah crouched on her knees in the corner and explored the ground. The old floorboards had rotted away, and she was feeling the bare earth as though caressing something precious. *Earth for Sarah . . .*

"There's something under here," she said excitedly. "I can feel it in the earth, calling to us. Pass me that spade."

Deftly, Sarah began to remove the top layer of soil; then she threw the spade to one side and began to scrape the earth carefully with her fingers. Something broke away from the mud and she lifted it out.

"It's an old box," Sarah said, rubbing the dirt from its sides. "You open it, Evie. It must have belonged to the people at Uppercliffe once."

She passed the black box to me. It was made of tin and rusted over. There was no lock, only a crude clasp to fasten it. I pulled it open with a jerk.

"Wow," breathed Sarah. A scent of rose petals rose from the little box, dry and dusty, but still sweet.

"They must be so old," said Helen. "And what's that?"

I lifted out a soft linen pouch and felt inside it. My fingers closed on something hard and cold. It was a small, battered gold locket, strung on a bit of ribbon. I fumbled to open the locket. Tucked inside was a single curl of red-bronze hair, soft and fine like a child's. *A little girl with bright curls, sitting on the doorstep at Uppercliffe . . .*

"It must be hers—Effie's," I said in amazement.

"Martha must have kept it in this box, in a safe place under the floorboards," said Helen. "But why was it left here for all this time?"

"Perhaps when Martha died it was forgotten about," Sarah replied, examining the locket carefully. "We'll never really know."

"Don't you think it's odd," I asked eagerly, "that we've

come here to hide one necklace and we find another one? Is that just a coincidence?"

"I'm not sure I believe in coincidence," Sarah said quietly. "Perhaps Agnes wants you to wear it. Why don't you put it on?"

I unclasped the Talisman and tied the locket in its place. For a moment I stayed quite still, waiting.

Nothing happened.

What had I really expected? Visions? Omens of disaster? An apparition of Agnes telling me that I mustn't let go of the Talisman, even for a minute? But there was nothing. Nothing bad was going to happen.

"So, are you ready. Evie?"

"Yes, I'm ready."

Slipping the Talisman into the linen pouch, I laid it on the papery rose petals and shut the box with a snap. Then I pushed the box back into the ground and covered it with the black soil. Sarah smoothed the place where the earth had been disturbed and replaced the stones.

"There," she said. "Let the earth hide it well."

"Let the Talisman lie in peace," said Helen, and she made a sign in the air with her hands. "Let the earth hold it and our memories guard it and the winds blow lightly over it. Let it sleep quietly until it is needed."

I said nothing. Soon, I vowed, I would come back to claim it, when I was powerful enough to wield the Talisman and work a miracle. Until then, the battered little locket hanging around my neck was some kind of comfort.

Helen left us, in the same strange way as she had arrived. Sarah and I rode quietly back to the school. By the time we reached the stable yard and dismounted, my legs were stiff with cold. I took Bonny back to her stall while Sarah went to look after Starlight. My body ached after the long ride. I began to brush the mud from the pony's wiry coat.

"Hi, there," said a voice behind me. I turned and saw Josh, a harness slung over his shoulder and a piece of straw stuck in his hair. "I thought I'd see how you made out riding over the moors, as you're officially my student. Not too exhausted?"

"I'll survive." I smiled at him, yet felt strangely self-conscious. "My muscles are complaining a bit."

Josh stepped closer, letting Bonny nuzzle his hand as he offered her a bit of broken carrot. He looked at me curiously. "I get the feeling you're not that wild about learning to ride," he said. "Do you mind if I ask why you're having lessons?"

"It was my dad's idea," I said. "I think he felt it was the proper Wyldcliffe thing to do."

"You don't seem like the typical Wyldcliffe girl."

"I'm not," I said. "I'm here on a scholarship. If Celeste and her friends had their way, I'd be doing chores in the kitchen."

"Oh, Celeste." He shrugged and laughed. "I wouldn't take much notice of her. So where did you go this afternoon?"

"Across the moor," I said, reluctant to tell anyone where I had been, but Josh didn't seem easily discouraged.

"Did you get as far as Uppercliffe? There are some good rides up there."

"You know Uppercliffe?" I asked in surprise.

"Of course," he answered. "My family has lived around here forever. We used to own the farm at Uppercliffe years and years ago."

My heart jumped. Another connection. Nothing was simple at Wyldcliffe; nothing was quite what it seemed. I didn't know what to say, but before I had time to decide, a girl called Julia Symons burst into the stables. "We've all got to go to the dining hall right away," she said importantly. "Miss Raglan wants everyone there immediately." She hurried off and I could hear her calling, "Everyone to the dining hall!" A bell started to ring in the distance.

"You'd better go," Josh said. "I'll finish this for you." He gently took hold of the brush I had been using on Bonny's coat and our hands touched for an instant. "See you next week?"

"Um, yeah . . . thanks . . ."

I turned and fled. Was this the news we had been waiting for? Was Mrs. Hartle alive or dead?

Nineteen

We stood in silent rows in the dining hall and waited for Miss Raglan, the Deputy High Mistress, to speak. Harriet Templeton and Julia Symons were standing next to her. They both looked upset.

"We have some bad news, girls," said Miss Raglan. "This afternoon, while you were enjoying your recreation time, one person has shown no regard for the comfort or happiness of our community." Her words were somber, but she seemed agitated, excited even. "There has been a series of thefts. These two girls have lost something valuable this afternoon, items of jewelry that were in their dormitories. While this is very distressing, I must remind you that jewelry is not allowed, and all items of value should be handed in to the staff at the beginning of term. In that way we can avoid these unpleasant incidents."

She paused and looked around. Did I imagine that her gaze lingered on me for a moment? I felt my newly acquired locket burn against my skin under my sweater, but I stared back at her unblinkingly. I wasn't going to give up this memento of Effie so easily. As for the Talisman, it lay in its bed of cold clay, and Miss Raglan would never find it.

"The staff is searching the dormitories at this moment for the missing articles, and any other valuables found there will be taken for safekeeping. Any girl who is still wearing an item of jewelry must hand it in now and nothing further will be said. However, any girl who continues to flout this rule will face the consequences."

There was a pause; then a few girls fumbled to unfasten the chains that they had been wearing under their shirts. Miss Scratton walked down the rows with a basket and, one by one, the necklaces were dropped into it. She passed me by without a glance.

"I need hardly say that any girl who has any information about this incident must come to see me afterward," Miss Raglan announced. "The missing items are a Tiffany diamond pendant and a small silver heart on a chain."

"That was mine," Harriet burst out. "My mother gave it to me. It's mine and I want it back."

A few girls sniggered at her red face and blinking eyes, but not many. If there was one thing the Wyldcliffe students understood it was the importance of possessions.

"And I am sure we will soon get it back," said Miss Raglan smoothly. "We cannot tolerate thieves at Wyldcliffe."

Miss Raglan dismissed us. Harriet burst into tears and dashed out. The students broke into little groups, gossiping over the latest drama.

"I felt sorry for Julia, but I don't know why anyone would bother to steal that piece of junk from that Harriet kid," India sneered as she linked arms with Celeste. "It's not as if it were really valuable. My God, a tacky little heart on a cheap chain. Harriet probably got it out of a packet of cornflakes."

She and Celeste laughed their cruel, braying laughs.

"You don't know what's valuable to other people," Sarah retorted. "Not everything beautiful comes with a big price tag."

"Yeah," I added, sick of India and her snobby friends. "Harriet was fond of the necklace because her mom gave it to her. Isn't that enough for you?"

India looked furious, but she twisted her mouth into

an insincere smile. "Like you'd recognize what's beautiful or valuable, Johnson. I don't suppose you're hiding a precious jewel in your locker, are you? Have you got any family heirlooms tucked away with your spare socks?" Her words were mocking, but I felt flustered.

"Of course not . . ."

"Come on, Indy, don't waste any more time on these losers," said Celeste. "I want to make sure that Josh has groomed Sapphire properly." She dragged India away.

"We'd better go too," said Helen. "Let's go and see if Harriet is okay."

We walked down the corridor toward the marble steps. Sarah lowered her voice. "This can't be a coincidence, all this stuff about handing in jewelry. I wonder if it was some kind of setup. I'm sure Raglan is onto something. She must be searching for the—" She broke off and glanced around cautiously.

"Well, at least it's safe now," I said. "And we've got work to do tonight."

"What, down in the grotto? But we can't; the coven was trampling all over it last night."

"No, not there," I whispered. "Meet me on the servants' stairs at midnight."

Midnight. It couldn't come quickly enough. There was

something I had remembered, something that I desperately wanted to do.

We carefully shut the door to the corridor behind us and stood on the landing of the servants' staircase.

I pointed the flashlight at the broken panel that I had noticed earlier. Sarah and Helen glanced at each other in surprise at my discovery, then helped me pull away the rest of the rotten wood. We worked as quietly as we could, and soon we had made a gaping black hole, big enough for us to climb through to the hidden steps to the attic. The stairs were narrow, and the air smelled of mold and damp. I hesitated for a moment, but Sarah gently butted me from behind, so I led the way, clutching my flashlight and ducking to avoid the trailing cobwebs.

We climbed the crumbling steps and emerged onto a wide area, like a wooden platform. At one end, a tower-like gable contained a grimy window that let in a smudge of moonlight. In the other direction, rather than one big attic, as I had expected, a tangle of deserted rooms seemed to sprawl under the very eaves of the house, spreading farther than we could tell. Dust lay thick as a carpet on the bare floor, and there was a profound silence. It almost seemed wrong to break the spell of the place. Once, the Victorian maids—young girls like us—had slept up here after their work in the big house was done. They had worked and dreamed and had secrets, and now there was no trace of them left behind.

I tried the handle of the nearest door and opened it. A small room was crammed with old trunks and battered suitcases, perhaps abandoned over the years by long-gone Wyldcliffe students. There was no room for us to work there, so we crept farther on and tried another door. It was locked.

"I hope they're not all locked like this," I said impatiently, rattling the handle. Then I noticed something. There was no keyhole, and yet the door was firmly shut.

"Perhaps it's stuck with age," suggested Helen.

I tried to push the door open, leaning my shoulder heavily against it, but I couldn't. "It's bolted," I said. "From the inside."

"Let me see," said Sarah. She laid her hands on the door and felt all over it, quiet and intent, as though she were listening to the wood that had once grown from the earth as a young tree. "There are two metal bolts on the inside. And something else—a peculiar vibration, something I can't quite make out."

"But how can it be locked from the inside?" I puzzled. "And why?"

"To keep everyone out, of course," Helen said. "I'm going to get in there and have a look."

"Are you sure, Helen?"

"Of course. And if it's only full of old suitcases or mattresses you can laugh at me afterward."

"Be careful." I squeezed her hand quickly as she gathered her thoughts and powers. The next moment she had veiled herself in the familiar swirl of air and had vanished through the ether to the other side of the door.

Silence.

"Helen?" I called. There was still no answer. Sarah tapped more urgently on the door. Then we heard a muffled scraping of metal bolts and the door was flung open by Helen, looking triumphant.

We saw a tiny room, its walls sloping under the roof. It was draped with faded purple silk, like a tent, and on the floor was a rich Persian carpet. A carved wooden desk stood in the middle of the room, and the shelves behind it were crowded with thick glass bottles of what seemed to be dried herbs and plants. They had faded labels: *Mallow, Hyssop,* and *Rue.*

"But that's Agnes's handwriting." I gasped.

"This must have been her secret study before she ran away to London," said Sarah excitedly. "Where she came to do experiments and study the Mystic Way."

"She must have sealed it with her powers," added Helen, "so that no one could get in."

"No one except us," I said in wonder.

Under the shelves, great earthenware jars stood in a row. "There's oil here," said Sarah. "And water and sand, and all sorts of other things. And bundles of candles—all different colors—white and purple and green and red."

"It's perfect!"

"And look!" Helen had scuffed aside the moth-eaten carpet with her foot. Half-hidden by the rug, painted on the floor, there was an intricate silver circle, decorated with stars and moons and flowers and elaborate symbols. The whole room and everything in it seemed to be alive with endless possibilities.

"This is a sign," I said, looking around in amazement. "Agnes wants us to come here to learn more, like she did. We can start straightaway. There's something I'm longing to try."

"What is it?" asked Helen.

"Don't you remember how Agnes described in her journal that she conjured a flame when she was in London, and it showed her an image of Sebastian far away in Wyld-cliffe? Why shouldn't I be able to channel my water powers to do something similar and see Sebastian now, wherever he is? It might give us a clue as to where he's hiding, and what's happening to him."

"Okay, let's try it," Sarah replied. "What do you need?"

We looked through the array of equipment that was crammed into the little room and found a shallow bronze bowl. I filled it with water from the jars under the shelves and placed it in the middle of the circle. Helen lit some candles and began the chanting. I sat cross-legged by the bowl, lightly resting my fingertips on the surface of the water. Then I closed my eyes and allowed myself to drift on the sound of Helen's voice, letting my mind wander wherever it wanted to go. Memories started to rise up behind my eyes.

I was sitting with Sebastian by the edge of the lake, watching the reflection of the moon as it wavered on the surface of the water. *The water of life . . . the blood of our veins . . .* My mind drifted back further. *I know what I want to do. . . . I want to swim with you, girl from the sea. . . .*

We were side by side, swimming in the lake; then I was panicking, being pulled under. I was drowning . . . falling into the deep black waters of memory. *Sebastian!* I called in my mind. *Where are you? Tell me where you are!*

I opened my eyes with a start and found myself crouching over the bowl, still holding on to the rim. As I peered at my reflection in the water it changed, and the next moment it was Sebastian's face that I saw on the glassy surface. He was lying down, so pale and still that for a moment I was terrified that he was dead. *No, that's not right,* I thought. *He can't die; he never died. . . .*

Sebastian opened his eyes. I saw him heave himself onto his elbow and pass his hand across his face. He had a litter of papers and letters next to him, which he suddenly swept to one side. Then he got unsteadily to his feet and began to walk away, as though every step hurt. He staggered on farther and the image began to fade. He was leaving me.

"Don't go, don't go!"

I hurled the bowl to the other side of the room and burst into tears. Sarah held me quietly, like a mother soothing a child, as I cried and cried and couldn't stop.

Afterward, I was ashamed. Nothing would be achieved by tears. Action and strength and knowledge were needed, not weak emotions. At least I had seen Sebastian, I told myself. He hadn't passed from my sight yet, though I still didn't know where he was hiding. I had to work faster and harder. I had to be more focused. There was no more time for weeping.

I would have to throw myself with even greater determination into our experiments. I promised myself that I would sneak up the hidden stairs every night to work in Agnes's secret room, pushing myself further and further to unlock the mysteries that would set Sebastian free and bring him back to me at last.

Twenty

The days raced by in a dream and the nights were a blur, as we worked so hard, missing sleep and constantly worrying about being caught. No one seemed to know about the staircase up to the attic, though, and we were safe for the moment. French, biology, math, music—they jostled in my mind side by side with our experiments in the Mystic Way. One night Helen made a pile of books rise into the air and float across the room. The next it was Sarah's turn, as she held a lump of clay in her hands and it shaped itself into a delicate model of a tree, all by the power of her thought and will. We were special, I told myself feverishly; we would soon be able to do anything we wanted; we were gifted, chosen, special. . . . But as each day passed I became more and more tired. My limbs ached and my head buzzed. I was kept going by love—and fear—for Sebastian.

It was hard to believe that Celeste and the others knew nothing of what we were going through. They could still care about who got an expensive package from an indulgent parent, and who had been given a solo in the school choir, and who had made the lacrosse team. The life of the school rolled on its usual course, but we were not quite part of it. I tried to avoid any contact with the other students. It was easier not to trust anyone, except Helen and Sarah. I didn't want to give myself away by a careless comment or an overheard conversation. But I couldn't totally avoid Harriet.

She was always popping up like a lost puppy, ready to run and fetch me a glass of water at lunch, or to pick up my pen if I dropped it, or to help me with my chores. There was something really pathetic about her doglike devotion, and I wished with all my heart that she would make some friends of her own.

Another Sunday came at last, after a week of grinding study. I woke up feeling sick and hot, but forced myself to get up as normal. As I sat through the long church service, I barely noticed what was being said. It seemed to me that the church was full of shadows, peopled by a long-dead congregation mouthing gloomy prayers and hymns: *I go whence I shall not return, even to the land of darkness and the shadow of death. . . .* Their ghostly shapes were more real to me than the bored Wyldcliffe students sitting in their neat rows. *The past, you can never get away from the past at Wyldcliffe. . . .*

I tried to shake myself out of my daze, telling myself I was just tired, but I couldn't relax as we walked back to school, buffeted by the wind that raced over the hills. There seemed to be some kind of tension in the air, as though something were about to happen, as though someone were watching me.

"Evie, are you ready?"

I blinked and looked up in surprise. I was sitting on the end of my bed and Sarah was waiting by the door.

"Ready for what?"

"To go riding, of course."

I looked down at my boots and jodhpurs with a puzzled frown. I couldn't even remember getting changed after returning from church, I had been so lost in my thoughts.

"Riding?" I said vaguely. "Are we going riding today?"

"You've got your lesson, Evie," she said anxiously. "You know—your riding lesson with Josh."

Josh. Of course, the nice boy who was trying to teach me. I liked him, and yet I wished I didn't have to spend an hour in his company. I wished I didn't have to carry on with the riding lessons. *You can get hurt. . . . It's danger-ous. . . . You might fall. . . .* A nameless feeling of dread was creeping over me, almost paralyzing me. I remembered what they had said about Agnes. *It was a riding accident . . . an accident . . . she died . . . that cursed place . . .*

"Are you all right, Evie?" Sarah asked. "You've been so quiet all day, and you look so pale."

"It's nothing, honestly." I made a huge effort to be posi-tive. Nothing would happen. Josh was perfectly capable of seeing that I didn't come to harm trotting around a prac-tice field. And there was Sarah, dear Sarah, looking so concerned and trying to help. I didn't want her to be wor-ried. "Sorry, Sarah, I'm just so tired, that's all. I'd better go and find Josh. See you after my lesson."

A few minutes later, I led Bonny out to the paddock.

"Evie!" Someone was calling me. It was Harriet, wrapped in a heavy coat and scarf, her long, thin nose showing red in the wind. "Can I watch, Evie? Can I watch your lesson?"

My head had started to ache again. I didn't want her there, watching me. Even the windows of the gray school building seemed to glare down like hostile eyes. "No, Harriet, not today. You don't want to stand around in this wind. Go inside."

"I'm not cold, honestly. Please let me stay, Evie."

It was too much of an effort to argue. Let her watch if she wanted; what did it matter? Perhaps if I ignored her she would lose interest and go away. I mounted and began to walk Bonny slowly around the ring that was marked out on the ground.

"That's better," said a cheerful, warm voice behind me. "You're improving already."

Josh. I made myself smile at him and he smiled back. There was a light in his eyes like a tiny flame. . . .

He made me work hard, and by the time the class was over I was exhausted. All the new muscles I was discovering were screaming at me to stop. As I slithered from Bonny's back, my knees seemed to give way. I staggered slightly, and in an instant Josh was by my side to support me, his arm around my waist.

"Evie, what's the matter?"

"My legs felt kind of funny," I said. He still held on to me, and I was aware of his body close to mine and the eager look in his eyes. Embarrassed, I wriggled out of his arms and tried to laugh. "I'm obviously not in good enough shape for this riding business."

"What's really wrong, Evie?" Josh asked, with a look of puzzled concern. "I can't help feeling that you're . . . well, worried about something."

I felt Harriet watching me from the other side of the field. She was still there, like a little old woman wrapped up in a bundle of ill-fitting clothes. Rooks were settling in the ancient trees of the grounds, their cries shrill and urgent in the dusk. The short winter day was already dying. For a fleeting second I wished I could talk to Josh. He seemed so . . . well, *ordinary*, so far away from the world I now inhabited. But there was no sense in that. I couldn't go around unburdening myself on him just because he was warm and kind. I didn't need a crutch to lean on. I could cope.

"It's such a gloomy afternoon, that's all," I said. "And listen to the wind howling! It's been giving me the creeps all day."

Josh looked at me searchingly. "I'll take care of Bonny for you," he said, taking her bridle from me. "Go and get some rest. And Evie . . ." He began to say something, then seemed to change his mind, busying himself with the pony. "I hope you feel better. Same time next week?"

"Yeah."

I walked slowly back to the stables. The wind was tearing around the shadowy buildings of the Abbey. It seemed to push me here and there as though I were no heavier than a dead leaf, with no will left of my own. I drifted away from the stable yard and over to the terrace. I hovered there for a moment, looking across the wintry lawns that led down to the lake.

The lake. Deep, deep water. Black depths of water. So cool, so heavy, so still and inviting. It was calling me. . . . I had to get closer. I began to stumble across the lawns, but something was wrong. Everything was slowing down, fading into black. . . . I was ice-cold. . . .

Evie . . . Evie . . . where are you?

It was Sebastian, I was sure of it, calling me from the ruins.

He was there.

He was looking for me.

He had come back at last.

Nothing else mattered. Nothing else existed. Energy blazed through me and I ran heedlessly, slipping on the icy paths, calling under my breath, "I'm here; I'm coming; wait for me, Sebastian. . . ." I dashed under the black arches of the ruined chapel, then came skidding to a halt. Six women, cloaked and hooded, were grouped by the mound where the altar had once stood. The next moment I was surrounded and their hands stretched out graspingly. One of them spoke in a muffled, eerie voice: "Ah, so good of you to answer our call—"

"No!" A great cry tore the air and a wall of light sprang up between me and the women like a shield. As I fell to the ground, everything whirled around me and I saw them turn and retreat, their black cloaks flapping in the wind. Then the light seemed to change and the heavy scent of candles filled my mind like drowsy incense. Soft voices were chanting, as sad and profound as the song of the sea. I was still in the chapel, but the roof was no longer the inky sky. Carved and gilded beams soared over me, and the stained-glass window behind the altar glowed with a hundred jeweled colors. Rows of women in white habits, holy sisters, were singing in the candlelight, their faces lifted in solemn ecstasy. One of them turned her face to me, and I knew her eyes. . . .

The candles blew out. The music stopped abruptly. The chapel was a ruined, meaningless shell once more, with the stars gleaming in the sky above my head. The menacing women in their dark cloaks had gone, and so had the ranks of chanting nuns. I had the sense that a long time had passed.

"Evie . . . Evie . . ."

The voice came again, but it wasn't Sebastian. A moment later Sarah ran up to me, out of breath and looking worried. "Evie, are you all right?" she said. "Josh said you finished your lesson hours ago. I've been looking for you everywhere."

I quickly told her everything that I had seen.

"So the Dark Sisters were here?" she said, horrified.

"And some other women, from long ago, but I thought I knew one of them. And, oh, Sarah, I'm sure Sebastian was here too! Do you . . . Can you sense anything?"

"I don't know—the atmosphere is confused. There's the scent of danger . . . and fear . . . and hope."

"He was here, I swear. I heard his voice!"

"That could have been a trap by the coven, some kind of setup to lure you down here on your own," Sarah said doubtfully. "Evie, I really don't think you should go out by yourself after sunset, not even on the grounds like this. And I think we should get back inside. You've been out here for hours; you missed dinner. You look so pale."

I glanced around one last time at the broken pillars and tumbled walls of the ancient church, reluctant to leave somehow. Had I really been here for so long? It had seemed like only a few moments, and yet perhaps I had wandered into some other time and lingered there without knowing it. I couldn't shake the faces of the women singing in the chapel from my mind. Had they really been the holy nuns from the ancient days? Where had the other hooded women vanished to? And was it Sebastian's voice I had heard calling me, or had it all been some cruel trick?

"Evie, come on. It's freezing out here. You're shaking." Sarah tugged at my arm and I followed her back to the school, my mind racing. We went in through a side door and made our way to the marble staircase in the entrance hall. A few students were lingering there by the fire that was burning as usual in the stone hearth. My teeth were chattering and I felt sick.

"Stand here for a while and get warm," Sarah said anxiously, leading me to a place in front of the fire. The flames danced and fought, red and purple and gold. As I stretched out my hands to them, a scream shattered the evening gloom. The heavy front door swung open and a plump twelve-year-old with a rosy face dashed into the hall. She was crying uncontrollably.

"I saw him, I saw him," she moaned, weeping and clinging to the girls nearest to her. Miss Scratton glided out of the shadows.

"What's going on? Constance, whom did you see?"

But the girl could only cry and hide her face in her hands.

Miss Scratton made her look up and said, "Now tell me what happened. It's all right. I am here. There's nothing to worry about."

"It was h-horrible," the red-faced girl stammered, hiccupping and gasping for breath. "I was up by the gates with my camera, because Emma Duncan told me that she'd seen a b-barn owl flying in the lane a few nights ago—you know, the ones with the white faces that come out at sunset—and I wanted to try to get a photo and . . . and—" She broke off, crying again.

"Go on," said Miss Scratton. "What happened next?"

"I heard this noise, like a groan, like someone in pain. It was coming from the other side of the gates, so I looked and I saw . . . I saw something white and I thought perhaps it was the owl, but it wasn't. It was this man in a long black coat and his face was all white and scary and I think he was dying." She burst into incoherent sobs.

"It was very silly to wander about at the far side of the grounds in the dark, Constance; no wonder you gave yourself a fright. It was probably one of the farm workers walking home. You must have scared him to death too. Now come with me," Miss Scratton said briskly. "We'll get you some hot cocoa and forget all about it." She swept Constance and the other girls out of the hall, but as she did so she glanced over to where I was standing, and her sharp black eyes seemed to hold a message for me.

Sebastian. It must have been Sebastian. My heart surged. He had been out there, looking for me. If only I had known, if only he had waited by the lake—then the girl's words hit me. *I think he was dying.* In a flash I saw Sebastian's chalk-white face, his bloodshot eyes; I heard his labored breath. But he wasn't dying; he couldn't die. . . .

I knew what it meant, though. Sebastian must be reaching the last stages of fading. There was only a fine veil hanging between him and his dreadful fate. He would soon leave this earth for his everlasting imprisonment in the Shadows. Time was running out. Sebastian was getting weaker and weaker; he could hardly breathe. I could hardly breathe. . . . I was so weak . . . everything was fading away.

The checkerboard tiles swam in front of my eyes, my legs trembled, and I fell into utter blackness, as dark and close as a tomb.

Twenty-one

FROM THE PRIVATE PAPERS OF
Sebastian James Fairfax
I am back here, in my living tomb.

My strength fades—but I have to tell you—

*I did try to find you; believe me, my darling love—
you must believe me.*

I tried to see you, Evie—I tried so hard.

*My vision of you had made me stronger. I thought I
would be able to reach you. I believed that if I could only
reach you, I would be healed. And so I strained my will
to make my journey.*

*For one brief hour I felt the wind upon my face again;
I watched the sun sink into the winter sky, and the first
stars flicker overhead. I breathed the damp, cool air of*

the lake where once we swam together, our bodies reaching out for each other. Under the arches of the old ruins, I waited for you as the day died and the night deepened. I closed my eyes and sank to the ground, exhausted by my journey, seeing nothing, hearing nothing, thinking only of you.

Evie, I called to you and you came! But everything turned to ashes and I saw that I had led you into a trap. Some of my former servants were waiting for you, ready to gloat over their innocent prey. I called to warn you and used the dregs of my powers to shield you, and they scattered like ants stirred by a stick.

I saw you. I was there, I tried—I tried—

Then something happened that I had not expected: a swell of holy song, glowing colors and lights, and a vision of high, rare power. It all seemed to come from you, I could have sworn, and yet you were somehow apart, and beyond any help I could give you. I could not stay in that bright company—I had to flee.

Someone saw me, a young girl. She shrank from me, as though I were a monster. And so, like a monster, I have retreated into my darkness.

Forgive me, Evie. I tried to find you and I failed. Oh, God, will I never stop failing?

It is because of me that Agnes died. It is because of me that the first women of the coven left their simple homes to pursue my corrupt ambitions. It is because of me that they are Dark Sisters. It is because of me that you are in danger. And now, when there is only a fine veil hanging between me and my fate, is it too late for me to redeem myself? Is there not one single act of good that I could be remembered by when I am gone? Will I never be healed?

Perhaps it is too late.

Perhaps that is my truth now.

I am so sorry, Evie. Forgive me. I am sorry for everything—except for loving you.

Twenty-two

I'm sorry," I murmured. "I'm so sorry." I lifted my head groggily and opened my eyes. The face of the school nurse swam into focus. Sarah was hovering next to her anxiously.

"Are you okay, Evie?" Sarah asked. "What happened?"

"My head . . . I must have fainted. Stupid of me."

"You're prone to this, aren't you?" the nurse asked briskly. "This is what comes of riding in the freezing cold and getting exhausted and then baking yourself next to the fire." She sounded severe, but she fussed over me kindly. Brushing aside her suggestion that I should spend the night in the infirmary, I pleaded with her to ignore what had happened. "I'm not ill," I swore. "It was like you said: The fire was so hot, and it was really stuffy after being outside. It's nothing serious."

Eventually she took me up to my dorm, making me promise to let her know if I got dizzy again. Sarah reluctantly left me at the door of the dormitory and went to look for Helen to tell her what had happened, while the nurse made sure I was tucked up in bed. As soon as she had gone, Celeste, who was lounging on the window seat painting her toenails, sneered, "Quite the little heroine with these fainting fits, aren't you, Johnson?"

"It's just a sad attempt to make herself interesting," added India.

"Absolutely pathetic."

It wasn't worth rising to the bait and arguing with them. I drew the drapes around my bed, though I was sure I wouldn't be able to rest. But the nurse had been right when she had said I was exhausted, as a few moments later I felt my eyes droop and I fell into an uneasy sleep.

I didn't dream.

The next thing I knew was that I could hear someone pacing softly across the floor of the dorm. I sat upright and listened. Perhaps it was Helen. Cautiously, I pushed aside the drape and peered into the dimly lit room.

I had to force myself not to cry out. It had happened

again. I was seeing into a different Wyldcliffe, not the distant time of the old nunnery, but the rich, splendid heyday of the nineteenth century, when the Abbey had been Agnes's beloved home. I was in the same room with the arched windows and the cushioned seat below them. But the walls were no longer bare and white, and I could no longer see the beds of my dorm mates. Through a kind of mist, I could see richly colored wallpaper and carpets, velvet curtains and hangings, a heaped silken bed, carved furniture, and glowing candlelight. It was Agnes's bedroom, and she was there in front of me, pacing up and down.

Agnes seemed to turn and see me, though I couldn't be sure. Then she threw a shawl across her shoulders, opened the door, and went out of the room. Without stopping to think I got out of bed. My feet felt the usual scuffed linoleum on the floor, though my eyes saw the richly woven carpet. I was somehow hovering between two worlds. I followed Agnes into the corridor and she led me to the top of the marble stairs. The landing was decorated with a profusion of pictures and mirrors and exotic ferns in ornate pots, but the white marble stairs were exactly the same as I had known them.

Slowly, as though hypnotized, I followed Agnes down

the stairs, unable to speak. But with each step I took, her outline became fainter, and soon I could no longer see her.

"Wait, Agnes, wait!" My voice came back to me, but the hangings and pictures vanished, and I was left with only the bare white steps, leading me down and down and down. . . .

Lying across the bottom step, like a broken doll, was a young girl. It wasn't Agnes. I was firmly back in my own time, and the girl lying unconscious at the bottom of the stairs was Harriet Templeton.

I was allowed to go and see her in the infirmary a couple of days later.

"She's very lucky to have gotten nothing worse than a broken wrist and a concussion after that dreadful fall," the nurse scolded. "Why didn't you tell us you were prone to sleepwalking, Harriet?"

"I . . . um . . . I didn't think it was important," she muttered.

"With all these stairs and twists and turns in this old building? You need to be much more careful. Anyway," she went on, softening slightly, "here's your friend to keep you company for a bit, so don't look so miserable. It's a good thing that Evie heard you in the night and came to fetch me. And there was Evie dropping down in a dead faint herself the other day. What a pair you are!"

"I'm absolutely fine now, I promise," I said.

"But you can only stay ten minutes at the most. We don't want Harriet to get too tired." The nurse bustled out, leaving us alone.

"So how is your wrist, Harriet?"

"It's nothing. It's my head that hurts."

We looked at each other rather awkwardly. I couldn't help feeling guilty that I hadn't made Harriet go to the nurse when I first found out about her sleepwalking, and yet somehow I was angry with her. In a weird way I felt we were now tied together by this secret. But I didn't want to get closer to Harriet. I didn't want the school staff thinking that we were special friends.

"Thanks so much for finding me and getting the nurse when I . . . um . . . fell down," Harriet said, blushing with embarrassment.

"Yeah, well, you should have told them before about the sleepwalking—gotten a dorm on the ground floor or something," I grumbled. "You could have been killed!"

"I know." She played restlessly with the fringes on the edge of the blankets, frowning to herself. Then she suddenly leaned over and grabbed my arm, her eyes wide and afraid. "Evie, did you see her?"

"What do you mean?"

"That woman, you know, that night on the stairs?"

I stared at her in disbelief, not knowing what to say. Was she talking about Agnes? Could she possibly have seen her too?

"Um . . . what kind of woman?"

Harriet frowned again. "I don't know; I can't really remember. All I can remember is her voice, leading me on somehow . . . and now I can't get rid of it."

"Get rid of what?"

"Her voice in my head." She began to cry quietly, like an overtired child. "Sometimes I think I'd like to fall asleep in the snow and never wake up."

"I think I'd better go, Harriet," I said, feeling alarmed by her fragile state of mind. "You need to get some rest." I went to fetch the nurse and then slipped away, trying to work things out. Perhaps Harriet had somehow tuned in to Agnes's presence on the stairs and it had given her a kind of psychic shock, which had made her slip and fall. Or perhaps she really was related to Agnes and now Agnes was trying to reach her, just as she had reached out to me? For some reason I didn't like the idea of that. My relationship with Agnes was special; I didn't want anyone else butting into it. But that was so petty—how could I be jealous of poor Harriet?

I walked slowly back to my dorm. Not everything that happened at Wyldcliffe had some mysterious meaning, I reminded myself. It was probably all very simple. Harriet had been sleepwalking, she had fallen and banged her head, and now she was confused and upset. But Harriet's problems were not my problems. Her world was not my world. And in my world I had to concentrate on the job I had to do, not get sidetracked by every drama that boarding school threw up. I began to run down the corridor. I had to find Helen and Sarah and get back to work.

Twenty-three

"Look!" I waved my hand and filled the attic with a thick covering of snow. The dusty shelves glittered with sparkling icicles. Sarah replaced the snow with a carpet of primroses. Then Helen made a breeze rustle through the icicles and made them chime like silver bells. We laughed and returned the room to its original state, then looked at one another, suddenly sobering up.

"I wish it could all be for fun like that." Sarah sighed.

"I know, but we're ready now for more than fun. Don't you feel that?" I said. "Aren't we ready to try the Talisman again, before it's too late?"

"I think we are," replied Helen slowly. "What about you, Sarah?"

Sarah hesitated for a moment, then nodded. "Yes, we're ready."

Sunday, our only day of freedom, arrived again at last. I sent a message to Josh that I had a cold and didn't feel up to my riding lesson, then met Sarah at the school gates with the ponies so that we could set off to Uppercliffe.

"Won't Josh wonder how you're well enough to ride out, but not well enough for his class?"

"He probably won't notice that we've gone out," I said. "I'm sure he couldn't care less what I do." But it wasn't true. I knew that his brown eyes followed me whenever I happened to be down in the stables, and I knew that I was avoiding him for that very reason. "Anyway, Sarah, I can't afford to spend time messing around having a riding lesson when we've got so much to do today. Helen will be at Uppercliffe by now. That's the only thing that matters."

Sarah looked kind of troubled, but I turned away and urged Bonny on as fast as I dared. Perhaps my love for Sebastian was making me selfish, brushing Josh and Harriet and everything else to one side as unimportant. I didn't want that to happen; I didn't want to hurt anyone, but I couldn't let down Sebastian. He had to come first. I would sort everything else out later, I promised myself, if only I could find Sebastian.

Helen was already waiting for us when we reached Uppercliffe. She had dug up the Talisman and was examining it closely. I couldn't help wondering whether, if the Talisman had been left to Helen, she would have already discovered how to use it. Again I had a faint, troubling feeling of jealousy as I took it from her.

"Is everything okay?" she asked. "Shall we start?"

There's no need to dwell on the failure of our efforts. The frustration, the rising anger, the terrible powerlessness. It is enough to say that nothing worked. The Talisman hung proud and cold and useless on its silver chain.

"What are we going to do?" I stormed, tempted to fling it from me in rage. I was furiously angry, but not with the Talisman or Agnes or the others. I was angry with myself. Why couldn't I awaken Agnes's powers? What was wrong with me? Everything I had tried and learned seemed feeble and less than nothing. But I had worked so hard. *Follow my path. . . .* I had tried, hadn't I? And then it dawned on me. The answer was stunningly, glaringly obvious. I didn't know whether to laugh or scream.

"We've been doing it all wrong," I said blankly.

"What do you mean, Evie?" asked Sarah.

"We're calling to the Talisman through our own

powers. But Agnes's element was fire, not water or earth or air. If we want to unlock Agnes's power in the Talisman, we have to do it through her element, not our own." I looked up at the others, convinced that I was right. "We need to channel the power of fire. She said I had to follow her path—I thought she just meant the Mystic Way, but she must have been talking about her own special powers. The fire is the only way to the Talisman."

"But can you do anything with fire?" asked Sarah quickly.

"I don't know; I've never tried."

"Then try now," said Helen.

Sarah found some scraps of rotten wood and made a campfire in the ruins of the old house. The wood spat and smoked, but a thin orange flame began to flicker and glow. I felt keyed up with excitement. This time I really would do it; everything would make sense at last. Agnes would help me this time; I was sure of it.

"See if you can control the flame with the power of your thought," Helen said. "That's one of the things Agnes learned to do first."

"All right. I'll try."

We formed a circle and held hands and the chanting began. As I let my mind drift with the lulling incantations, the voices of the distant sea and the underground streams and the rain clouds high over the hills began to call to me, but I had to try to block them out.

Fire. That was what I needed now. I had to think of warmth and color and life. I clasped the Talisman in my hands and focused on the dancing flames that licked around the little shards of wood. Fire. Heat. Life. *The fire of our desires . . .* I closed my eyes and tried to concentrate.

In my mind I saw the flames flare up like blazing rockets. There was a flash of heat and I seemed to see a girl with auburn hair standing in a shabby room. It was Agnes. She was surrounded by dancing, fiery lights. She flicked her wrist to control them and they made brilliant shapes that swooped around her, stars and dragonflies and birds of paradise. She gazed into my eyes and held her hands out to me. *You can do it, Evie.* My face and hands grew hot; I was panting for breath; I opened my eyes and reached toward the fire that glowed on the earthen floor of the cottage. With all the force of my mind I willed the flames to change, commanding them to obey me.

Nothing happened.

"I—I can't do it." I stepped back, feeling weak and shaky. "I can't. Sorry."

Sarah and Helen glanced at each other. There was an awkward silence.

"Perhaps you could learn to do it, eventually," Helen said slowly. "But how long would that take? And it's not just about controlling a simple flame. Agnes's powers were much deeper than that."

"I know," I groaned. "I know, I know, I know." I stumbled outside, desperate for some fresh air. Leaning against the rough walls of the cottage, I let the wind blow through my hair, as though it could also blow away the weight of my despair. I looked across the valley to where the village lay tucked in the folds of land. I could see the towers of the Abbey behind a screen of leafless trees. Down there, girls were enjoying the Sunday relaxation that even Wyldcliffe allowed. They were writing letters home, or reading, or chatting, or having music lessons, or learning to ride. . . . For one second I saw myself walking away from the Talisman and everything it represented. I could hide it again up here and no one would ever know it had existed. Wouldn't Helen and Sarah say I had tried hard enough to help Sebastian? Wouldn't they understand if I gave up now? For those fleeting moments, I saw another Evie, walking hand in hand with a boy with straw-colored hair and quiet brown eyes, laughing in the sunshine. . . .

No.

I wrenched my thoughts away. Sebastian had chosen to dwell in the shadows, but I would follow him there and bring him back to the light, however impossible it seemed. I would not give up. I would not grow weary.

I would not betray him.

Twenty-four

FROM THE PRIVATE PAPERS OF
SEBASTIAN JAMES FAIRFAX

Do you grow weary of your poor friend? I saw you, Evie. You were laughing—smiling—looking so beautiful. It was so good to see you like that, but you were not smiling at me.

Your smiles were for a tall boy with hair like corn, and you looked so happy. As though you had never known me.

Have you forgotten me already? Or was this one more cruelty sent to me by my tormentors, as they wait hour by hour for me to fall into their grasp?

The end is getting closer, closer—

Perhaps I was crazy to think that you could stay

true to me, when all I bring to those I love is danger and despair.

My parents, my friends—I spurned them all.

The women who served me I corrupted and then abandoned.

Dear Agnes, whom I valued above all others, my dearest Agnes whom I loved as a sister—I killed her as surely as though I had strangled her with my bare hands.

How, then, can I expect you to remain faithful to me?

Everything is leaving me.

Everything fades into mist.

Listen. This is important. You must listen to me, my darling, while I can still form these labored words—listen—

Our story may end well. Even now, there is still a flicker of hope, like a candle in a storm. One day, I may be saved. One day, I may see you face-to-face. Then I will tell you—I will tell you the whole of my heart. But there is another possible ending. Perhaps I have already glimpsed it.

In this story, you become discouraged. The road is too hard. You turn aside. There is someone else at your side. He walks in the living air, a young man with brown eyes and sunshine in his smile. Do you recognize this story? Is this the path you have chosen?

If so, don't blame yourself.

Dark—so dark—so tired—

I ache for you. I scratch out words for you: "My darling, my dearest, love, longing . . ." But these words are worn and tattered, used in a thousand trite Valentine's cards. How can I tell our story? What can I say? "For a little while, we walked the earth together, and it was enough." What words can truly speak of that bliss?

I am so very weary; my strength fades—

I have no words to tell you how I crave your touch and the scent of your hair, and the trusting look in your eyes. But I must tell you this:

If you choose to bestow those graces upon another, I would understand. I will never blame you, Evie. All I want now is for you to walk in the sun. And if in your new life, you ever remember Sebastian James Fairfax, remember him with a smile, not with tears. Too many people have wept over me.

Everything fades.

My story must end soon. But yours must continue, and your path must be paved with every joy.

Twenty-five

It was the start of another joyless week without Sebastian. There was no sign of the sun that morning. Another heavy load of snow had fallen in the night, and the world outside was as cold as a frozen, miserly heart.

I dragged myself out of bed and lingered in the chilly bathroom, trying to find some energy to face the day. My reflection stared back at me, tired and strained. I had lain awake most of the night going over and over in my head how I could learn how to control the fire element, but I hadn't stumbled across any great revelation. I sighed and wrapped my robe around me and went back to the dorm. When I got there, the others had already left for breakfast.

The warning bell rang. I had to hurry. I quickly found my skirt and blouse and started to dress. As I fastened my school tie, I realized that I was no longer wearing the little gold locket that contained the scrap of Effie's hair.

"Oh no!" I quickly searched through the rumpled sheets on my bed. How could I have lost it? Had I dropped it in the bathroom, or lost it out riding? *Think, Evie, think. . . .* I didn't dare to ask if anyone had found it, in case Miss Raglan heard about it. She would no doubt make me hand it over to her, and I hated the idea of her pawing anything that was connected to Agnes. I made my way downstairs, angry with myself for so carelessly losing this link with my past.

I slipped into my place next to Helen and Sarah in the dining hall. "Did you hear about what happened in the village last night?" asked Sarah.

"No—what do you mean?"

"It's kind of weird, horrible really. I went down to the stables early this morning and saw Josh, and he told me that someone in the village had found a dead fox nailed to their front door, and blood daubed everywhere."

"But that's totally—"

"Sick. I know; it's disgusting. And I heard the women who work in the kitchens talking about it as well." Sarah lowered her voice. "Do you think it could have anything to do with . . . the coven?"

It did sound like some kind of horrible voodoo. "But why would they do that? What would it mean? What do you think, Helen?"

Helen shrugged. "I don't know. But they're capable of anything. They wouldn't cry over a dead fox."

"It could be something completely different," said Sarah. "A local quarrel, mindless vandalism, anything. Josh thought that maybe it had something to do with the travelers' camp."

Josh hadn't struck me as the kind of person who would listen to prejudiced gossip about the traveling Gypsies.

"Why would he assume that they would be behind this?" I said indignantly.

"No! He didn't mean that. The person who lives in that cottage apparently supported letting the Gypsies camp on that bit of land in the village. Josh thinks maybe some of the people who don't want them in Wyldcliffe did this to him as a protest."

"Or to try to pin the blame on the Gypsies," added Helen.

"Exactly. There are plenty of people who don't recognize the Romany people or their way of life, who think they are thieves and scroungers going from place to place and causing trouble. It makes me so angry." Sarah sighed.

"I wish the travelers could know that we don't all think like that."

It seemed that there might be another battle going on in Wyldcliffe, not just our own, but our conversation was cut short as Miss Raglan marched into the room. She stood on the raised platform and two hundred girls rose to their feet in silence. Miss Raglan didn't look up and said grace in a subdued voice.

"Amen . . . Amen . . ." The dutiful response echoed around the room. We sat down, and I helped myself to eggs and toast from the serving dish, but Sarah pushed her food around listlessly.

"Listen, Sarah," I said. "Why don't we try to visit the camp and see what's going on, if you'd like to?"

Her face lit up. "Would you really?"

"Sure," I said. "As soon as we get a chance. I promise."

After breakfast, we walked back through the entrance hall on our way to our first class. Harriet was hanging about by the table, looking at the students' mail that was left there every morning. I hadn't seen her since she had been lying in bed in the infirmary, and she looked up and smiled self-consciously, as though she were half pleased and half anxious to see me. A feeling of exasperation welled up in me, and for the hundredth time I wished she hadn't sat next to me on the train that first day. Then I pulled myself together and made myself speak to her kindly.

"Are you feeling better, Harriet? How's the wrist?"

"Much better, not too sore," she said, waving her bandaged wrist to show me. In her other hand she held a large square envelope. "This is for you."

I took the envelope from her, and as my fingers brushed hers I had a feeling of revulsion, as though I had touched something dead.

"Is it something important?" she asked.

"What? Oh . . . um . . . no, it's nothing." I shoved the letter in my pocket. "I'm glad you're feeling better, Harriet. See you later."

My heart was jumping. I had already seen the printed names on the front of the envelope: *Carter, Coleman, and Tallen.* I knew those names. And I was pretty sure that I knew what this was all about.

Miss Raglan strode up behind us. "You should be in my classroom by now, going over your math assignment, not fussing over the mail," she said sharply. "We have a lot to get through this morning and exams coming up soon. Please hurry."

"Yes, Miss Raglan, sorry, Miss Raglan."

The letter would have to wait.

* * *

As soon as the bell rang for break I grabbed Sarah and headed for the stables. Helen was in trouble over a piece of unsatisfactory work and had to stay behind with Miss Raglan.

"What's going on, Evie?" asked Sarah as we hurried across the cobbled yard to Bonny's stall. "Who is the letter from?"

"Frankie's lawyers. It can only be something to do with her will. I don't want any of her money, or anything like that. Why they have written to me and not Dad?" As soon as were we safely hidden in the stable, I tore open the envelope, but I couldn't get past the first few lines of the letter:

Dear Evelyn, We are writing in relation to your late grandmother. . . .

I didn't want to have anything to do with all this. I didn't want to be reminded that Frankie wasn't there anymore. I passed the letter to Sarah with a lump in my throat. "You read it," I said. "Please."

"'Dear Evelyn,'" she began. "Umm . . . then there's a whole lot of introductory stuff. Who they are and everything . . . you know all that. . . . Oh, wait . . . it says, 'You may be aware that your grandmother left certain personal items in a safe-deposit box at her bank. One of them was addressed to you. Your father, as official executor of the will, has given us permission to send this item to you directly. It is a document, which we now have pleasure in enclosing.' Then it says would you please acknowledge safe receipt, best regards and condolences, blah, blah. . . ."

"So what's this document?" I felt sick with nerves. The term before I had received a letter showing my family's connection with Agnes's daughter, Effie: a letter that had changed my life. What would this new document bring?

Sarah pulled a sealed, folded paper from the envelope. "This looks really old," she said, handing it to me. My fingers trembled as I touched the yellowish paper and recognized the small sloping script, written in faded black ink. It said:

I ask my daughter to hand this on unread to her daughter, and so on, until the girl with red hair and gray eyes—the girl from the sea—may receive it. I pray that that this will be done as I request. A. T. H.

"Look at the initials," Sarah exclaimed. "A for Agnes!"

The first two letters had to be for Agnes Templeton. I searched my memory for the details of the story Agnes had told in her journal. What was her husband's name? Francis . . . Francis Howard, that was it. A. T. H. Everything fit.

At the bottom of the paper someone had added a few lines in pencil.

To be given to Evie on her eighteenth birthday, or on my death, whichever is earlier. Dearest Evie, I have kept this curious family relic for you. Take care of it, my lamb, and yourself. With endless love, Frankie.

I kissed the place where she had written her name, then turned to Sarah.

"Shall I open it?"

She nodded. "Yes. Open it now."

I carefully removed the red discs of sealing wax, and unfolded the paper. Inside was another scrap of Agnes's handwriting. *A memory of the gift I once received and which now lies hidden at Fairfax Hall.* This message was pinned to an even older sheet of parchment. It was thin and worn, with a ragged edge as though it had been torn from a book. The words on it were printed in cramped black letters, and around the edge of the paper there were drawings in colored inks—stars and flowers and exotic symbols.

"What does it say? What is it?"

"'For the healing of Blindnesse and to give good Sight for those who are in need of it . . .'" I stopped, bewildered for a moment, then began to laugh. "Blind! Of course, I have been so blind! But now I know what to do!"

"What is it?" said Sarah. "What do you mean?"

"Don't you see, Sarah?" I replied excitedly. "This is a page torn from the book that Sebastian found and gave to Agnes. The Book of the Mystic Way! She described it in her journal and said she learned most of what she knew from it. She's telling me that if I want to learn to control the fire, I must find the Book and study what she studied. Oh, why didn't I think of that before?"

"Of course! The Book was a gift to her, and then it was taken back by Sebastian. Presumably he took it to his home at the Hall. It all makes sense. But if Agnes really wanted to help you, why couldn't she have somehow left you the whole Book, not just this scrap of paper?"

"I don't know. Maybe she didn't have it with her anymore when she realized I was going to be involved one day. Anyway, I don't think it's as simple as that. I mean, why doesn't Agnes appear to me in a vision and give me all the answers?"

"Well, it would help," Sarah replied with a wry smile.

"Yes, but I don't think it's meant to be that easy. We have to do this ourselves. The Mystic Way is only another tool we can use to help us through life; it's not a magic wand to take all our problems away. That's what Sebastian didn't understand."

As I mentioned his name my excitement died down. There were still so many obstacles to overcome. Even if we could get to Fairfax Hall, how could we be sure that the Book would still be there so many years after Agnes had left me this clue? What if it had been taken—or destroyed?

Twenty-six

"Miss Scratton, you remember that we couldn't go inside Fairfax Hall last term because of the break-in over there?" said Sarah. We were standing next to Miss Scratton's desk after her history class, trying to appear innocently enthusiastic. "Well, we were wondering whether we could go again and see the house properly this time."

"Why?" Miss Scratton's brow creased in a faint frown.

"We're . . . um . . . really interested in history," said Helen.

"Local history," I added.

"Indeed. I hadn't noticed that you were particularly interested in any of your school subjects, Helen."

Helen looked embarrassed. She was constantly getting into trouble for daydreaming in class and forgetting to hand in assignments. Miss Scratton gave us a piercing stare, then seemed to relent.

"I admire your curiosity. However, I'm afraid we won't be able to go on any visits at the moment. The weather is too bad for that." Miss Scratton glanced out of the window, where the snow had started to fall again. "It's almost as though we are shut off from the outside world," she added quietly, "cloistered here within the walls of the Abbey, like in the old days."

She turned her gaze back to us, and as she did so, my heart jumped with a strange sense of recognition. *I've seen her before somewhere,* I thought. *Where? Where could it have been?* My mind flashed back to that night down in the crypt. Was it there that I had seen her, among the baying women of the coven? I couldn't believe that. I didn't want to believe that. Yet there was something familiar about her, so strict, so disciplined, so self-contained. . . .

"Now I really must get ready for my next class," she said. "Good afternoon, girls."

Miss Scratton swept out, her black academic gown billowing around her.

"Well, it was worth trying," said Sarah. "She wasn't

going along with the idea, though."

"It doesn't matter," I said. "We don't want to traipse around with a whole lot of sightseers anyway. We need to sneak in when the hall is shut and nobody's there."

"I could go," Helen suggested. "I thought myself over there once before. I'll go and see if I can find the Book."

"You can't go on your own," said Sarah. "What if you got into some kind of trouble and couldn't get back? We've got to stick together."

"Tonight then," I whispered. "We'll go tonight."

The Abbey might be shut off by the snow, but that wouldn't stop us. We had other ways of getting there.

It was freezing cold. The sky over our heads was brilliant black, studded with stars. Sarah and Helen stood in the hushed stable yard, wearing their thickest sweaters and looking at me apprehensively.

"Ready?" asked Helen.

"Yes, let's go for it," I said, trying not to show that I was nervous.

"Well, if you're sure," she replied. "I've never done this before, but I think it will work. Okay, let's try."

She stood between us, winding an arm around each of our waists, then closed her eyes and muttered to herself.

I braced myself for what was to come. For a split second I seemed to see Helen standing on the top of a bleak hill, raising her arms up to the sky, her gossamer hair blowing in the wind. Then the wind seemed to be inside me, a shrieking, turbulent force that would tear me to pieces. I heard Helen's thought echoing in my mind: *Hold on, hold on.* . . .

I seemed to be blown off my feet, and the stable yard slipped away from underneath me. The gables and turrets of the Abbey began to spin, and the stars flashed crimson and purple and gold. I was in a tunnel of light and sound, traveling faster than thought itself as we hurtled down the wind. The breath was being squeezed out of my lungs. I heard Helen calling, *Don't let go.* . . . I clung to her until I felt I could hold on no longer; then the three of us suddenly landed with a crash on a polished wooden floor.

"That was . . . amazing," Sarah said, gasping for breath.

"That was insane," I groaned.

"But we made it," said Helen. "We're in Fairfax Hall."

She stood up and pulled a flashlight out of her pocket, then helped us to our feet. I was still breathless and stunned as I looked around in wonder. We were in an elegant pillared room furnished with silk-covered sofas and little tables with spindly gold legs. Fairfax Hall. I could hardly take it in. One minute I had been in the stable yard, and now I was actually inside the hall, inside Sebastian's home.

Helen beckoned us to follow her, and we left the elegant sitting room and found ourselves in a shadowy corridor.

"If anyone finds us we'll be in spectacular trouble," Sarah said. "I've never actually broken into a museum before."

"There's no point in turning back now," Helen replied. "Follow me."

"Where are we going, Helen?" I asked, trying to sound calm.

"Miss Scratton told me that the house is arranged exactly as it was in the old days, when Sebastian's family lived here. And there's a library full of old books. It seems kind of obvious, but we might as well start there. Do you know what this Book looks like, Evie?"

"All I know is that it was given to Agnes by Sebastian after he had found it in a bazaar in Morocco. In her journal she described it as old and shabby, with a green leather cover."

"Come on then," Helen said. "Let's find the library."

We followed Helen farther into the shrouded house.

The flashlight picked out glimpses of ghostly white statues and gilt-framed paintings. I felt as though the darkness were alive, as though the walls could see us passing by. Sebastian lived here, I kept saying to myself; *he* knew these pictures; *he* walked in these corridors; *he* ran in and out of these rooms when he was a child. This expensive, antique furniture was as familiar to him as my simple cottage home was to me. As I crept along like a thief, I actually felt happy. I was in Sebastian's home. For that one moment it was enough. Then I seemed to hear a voice echoing in the silent house. *You grow weary, Evie ... the road is too hard ... there is someone else....*

I turned around, startled, but Sarah hurried me forward as Helen pushed open some carved double doors.

"Wow," breathed Sarah. "Look at this."

We peered into a vast, cavernous room, heavy with darkness. I glimpsed tall bookcases and leather sofas and two huge writing desks. It was incredibly still, as though the whole room drowsed in an enchanted slumber, waiting for someone to open the books and breathe life back into their dusty pages. We stepped into the room and Helen swept her flashlight over the bookshelves. There were novels and books of poetry and French plays; there were books about law and history; books about fishing and gardening; books about everything that had ever interested the Fairfax family. My heart sank. How would we have enough time to search through all of them? It was an impossible task.

"We'll never find it here," I said, then stood transfixed as Helen shone the light onto a pair of portraits hanging above the fireplace. *Sir Edward Fairfax, Lady Rosalind Fairfax*, the printed labels said. They stared out at us, caught in time, comfortable and serene, not yet knowing that they would lose their darling son in scandalous circumstances—a rumored suicide, the body never found. Sir Edward was florid and dull-looking, the typical country squire with his dogs and horses, but Lady Rosalind was beautiful. Her eyes, blue as cornflowers, brimming with restless life, were Sebastian's eyes looking down and calling to me—calling me to help him before it was too late.

He walks in the living air . . . a young man with brown eyes . . . he is there by your side. . . .

"Stop!"

I would understand . . . I will never blame you. . . .

"What is it, Evie?" said Helen.

"Voices—in my head . . . no, Sebastian, no, it's not like that! There's no one else. You've got to believe me!"

I snatched the flashlight from Helen's hand and

stumbled out of the library and ran toward the softly carpeted staircase. The others ran after me. Forcing my legs to work I climbed higher and higher, not knowing where I was going, driven on by the voice in my head. *I ache for you . . . long for your touch . . . you choose another. . . .*

"No, I only want you, Sebastian," I sobbed under my breath. "I only ever wanted you."

Sebastian was near; I was sure of it. This had been his home, and now perhaps it was his hiding place. I kicked myself for not coming here earlier to look for him and ran crazily from room to room, throwing open doors that revealed glimpses of empty, elegant bedrooms. "Where are you? Where are you?" I cried in anguish. But the house refused to reveal its secrets. It was all old-fashioned and lifeless and dead, a museum, not a home. There was no sign of any inhabitants, past or present.

"It's no good," I said, dropping wearily onto a low chair. "He's not here."

Then we heard it: a faint stirring sound, coming from over our heads.

"What's that?" asked Helen, looking up in alarm.

We froze. Silence. Then another low, muffled noise.

"It's coming from up there," Sarah murmured.

"I'm going to look."

"No, Evie, wait—"

But I didn't listen. I wasn't afraid anymore. At the end of the broad landing there was another set of stairs that turned and twisted higher. I ran up them, and a strange pulse of inexplicable joy seemed to tug under my ribs. When I got to the top of the steps, I saw that I had reached the servants' floor. A plain corridor ran the length of the house, with low doors stretching out in a uniform row.

The first door I opened led into a bare room with sloping ceilings, furnished with an iron bedstead and a plain white jug on a stand. The beam of the flashlight lit up a printed museum notice on the wall: *An Example of a Maid's Bedroom, circa 1875*. Another dead end.

I marched to the next door and flung it open. There was a display of old photographs of the hall and its many servants. *Annie May, Laundry Maid, 1895–1914, John Hall, Butler, 1906–1925* . . . The next few doors were locked. I ran impatiently to the last door in the row. As I turned the handle a tingling sensation shot up my arm, like a hit of electricity. I could hear the sound of my own heart beating, and then it came again, that other sound, the echo of a muffled groan. I pushed the door open and shone the flashlight into the room.

It was completely empty, except for one thing.

Twenty-seven

I stooped to pick up the round, silvery object from where it lay gleaming on the dusty floor. It was smooth and cool in my hand, and I recognized it at once: an old-fashioned pocket watch on a tarnished chain. I pressed the side of the case and it sprang open. The initials S.J.F. were engraved on the inside of the case, and a date, 1883. It had been a gift for Sebastian's eighteenth birthday. I was actually touching something he had touched. I wanted to shout and sing.

Then the voice in my head started up again. *Remember Sebastian James Fairfax . . . remember him. . . .*

"What is it? What have you found?" Sarah and Helen crowded into the little room behind me, and I showed them the old watch and its markings.

"We're so close," I said. "He's here somewhere."

Sarah began to examine the empty room, tracing signs in the dust on the floor. Then she laid her hands on the walls and felt her way around the edge of the room. Her fingers found a twisted knot in the wood of the wainscoting. She pushed it sharply, and a door swung open to reveal crooked steps leading up to the very eaves of the building.

Without thinking, I ran up the steps to where a velvet drape hung in tatters across an archway. I flung the drape to one side and saw a low chamber littered with a muddle of jars and parchments and curious brass instruments and piles of musty books. It was like Agnes's secret study, but there was no air of promise here, only the sharp breath of decay and disappointment. Everything was moldering away, like an abandoned castle in a half-forgotten dream.

A dream. A faint moan. The echo of a sigh. Someone was hunched over a desk in the darkest corner, poring over some papers.

"Sebastian! Oh, Sebastian!"

I threw myself across the room and the next second I was at his side and in his arms.

"Evie . . . I called you. . . ."

The rest of the world wheeled about us unheeded as we held on to each other. Nothing else mattered. But when I finally let him go, I saw that Sebastian was as haggard and beautiful as a dying star. He was pale and gaunt, his ink-stained fingers shook, and his eyes were wide with pain. I kissed his forehead and eyes, my heart choking with pity. "What are they doing to you; how can I bear it?"

"I know I am changed," he groaned, slowly pushing back his long hair from his face. "I am ashamed to be like this."

"Don't say that—"

"I wanted to be strong. I wanted us to walk and ride and journey, and live free young lives together. But it's too late. It's all too late. Everything is destroyed and finished."

"It's not, Sebastian. We can still do those things, and more." I kissed his hands and tried not to cry. "I've come to help you. I promise."

"No one can help me now. All I could hope for was to see you again. I've been thinking of you, writing to you . . . trying to reach you." He began to cough weakly. I beckoned to Sarah and Helen, who were hesitating by the entrance to the room. They helped me to move Sebastian to a shabby sofa, but he grimaced as we touched him, as though every bone in his body were on fire. His eyes rested on the others and a tremor passed over his face.

"Do you remember my friends?" I asked gently. "Helen

and Sarah are like sisters to me. They understand about the Mystic Way, about everything. They've seen you before; they were in the crypt that night at the end of last term. They helped us to escape. Do you remember?"

"Not really. Everything is going; everything is leaving me . . . everything except you." He clutched my hand. "You found me, Evie. I didn't think you would."

"That's all I've wanted ever since I got back to Wyld-cliffe," I said. "And now I'm here. Everything will be all right, I promise."

"No . . . no . . . it's too late. I went down to the Abbey. I saw that girl. She recognized me for what I am—a monster. And I saw the boy too. He loves you, Evie. I know he does. And you . . . you must forget me. . . . Walk with him in the sun. . . ."

"Don't say that! He's just a friend—he's nothing. And I love only you, Sebastian; you must know that. I don't want anyone else. I'll never love anyone but you."

"But you must," Sebastian said urgently. "You must live and love and have children—" He coughed again and gasped for breath. "You must travel and work and see the world, and do all the things I can never do."

"I only want to do those things with you."

"It's over for me. It's too late." Sebastian touched my

face and tried to wipe away my tears. "Don't cry, my darling." He shut his eyes and fell back onto the mildewed cushions, exhausted by the effort of speaking. "I want you to be free of me."

"I don't want that kind of freedom. I can't let you go, Sebastian," I said through my tears. "It's not over yet."

"You can't stop this. The fading process is nearly complete. I am hanging on by a thread." He paused for breath. "Soon I will no longer be myself. When the next new moon rises, I fear I will no longer be human."

"Sebastian, it's not going to happen; it can't. I'm going to reverse the fading; I'm going to use the powers that Agnes left me to stop it. We just need a little more time."

"There is no more time left." The shadows in the room seemed to quiver blacker and deeper, like demons dancing and gibbering in the lost lands of the shadow world. I saw their hideous faces; I smelled the foul stench of their breath and sensed their vile desires for torment and unhappiness. Sebastian couldn't become like them, no, no, no, never, never, never. . . .

"I'll make time," I said fiercely. "Sebastian, don't you remember what the coven did for you? The Dark Sisters each gave you a year of their lives to give you back your strength. I can do that too."

"No!" His voice was harsh, but clear. "There will be no more soul stealing. I want you to live for me, not die for me. That girl . . . Laura, I killed her doing that. . . . I deserve what is happening to me now."

"You didn't kill her; it was Celia Hartle," said Helen in a low voice. "It was my mother who murdered Laura. You shouldn't blame yourself for that."

"I blame myself for everything," he groaned. "I took the beauty of the Mystic Way and twisted it. It was wrong. I broke Agnes's heart."

"Yes, you did wrong," Helen replied. She was as stern as a judge, wrapped in her remote beauty, but there was pity in her eyes. "Agnes forgives you, Sebastian. She wants us to help."

"Agnes. . . ." He sighed. "I see her, surrounded by light, and Evie next to her—"

"Sebastian, you must listen," I said. "Agnes told us to find the Book. She wants us to learn its secrets so that we can save you. I'll become a healer, like Agnes. Do you have it?"

"The Book. Of course. I had forgotten about such things." Sebastian looked up at Helen, his eyes bleary with pain. "Your mother—she claimed it from me when I was weak. She wanted to know everything, as I once did."

He laughed bitterly, then bent over and coughed long and low, before dragging himself upright again. "The Book is at the Abbey, with the High Mistress."

"She's not there," I said. "She has gone."

"I don't believe that. I feel her searching for me, like a fire in the dark, trying to find a way to betray me. I no longer have the strength to fight her. I am wounded, Evie, right to my soul. Not even Agnes could heal me." Sebastian closed his eyes and started to mutter to himself. "I was afraid of dying—wanted to live forever. And now dying isn't the worst thing. I have lost myself. . . . Soon I will be a slave . . . a demon lost to humankind. . . ." He suddenly called out, "Evie, Evie, where are you?"

"I'm here," I murmured, frightened and horrified, yet glad to be at his side. "I'm here, Sebastian, I'll take care of you—"

"Oh, Evie," he said, quiet again, "how I wish I could die and go where Agnes has gone before me. All I want now is to pass into the next world, our true home, where even the poorest beggar is welcomed by death across God's threshold. I do not want to be exiled in the shadows as an outcast. But the way is barred. I cannot follow Agnes. I cannot even put an end to my wretched life. And now I am falling into eternal darkness."

"You mustn't torment yourself like this," I pleaded. "You must rest until I come back."

"Yes, rest . . . rest." He sighed. "To rest . . . and sleep . . . and die. . . . I'm burning . . . burning. . . ."

I glanced around to see if there was any water in all the confusion of that crowded room, however dusty and stale. *The water of life* . . . I noticed a small glass beaker half-hidden by the paraphernalia on the writing desk and asked Sarah to pass it to me. The beaker was empty. I circled my hands around it and, closing my eyes, I reached out in my mind to the silent, mysterious lake by the ruins. For an instant I was there again, swimming in the cool water with Sebastian, my body entwined with his, tasting his wet skin against my lips.

The water of our veins . . . the rivers of our blood . . . the water of life . . .

When I opened my eyes the glass was full of water, as cool and pure as melted ice.

I wet Sebastian's lips; then I bathed his face as gently as I could. For a moment his eyes shone clear and blue, straight into my heart. We clung to each other and kissed, as though our life together were just beginning, not coming to an end.

"Evie, it's time," I heard Helen say. "We have to go."

I tore myself from Sebastian's embrace. "I'll be back."

"You mustn't come back!" he cried. "Not unless you can truly heal me. I don't want you to see me at the very end. Promise me, Evie; do this for me. Don't come back." He grew wilder. "You must promise, you must!"

"Yes, yes, all right," I stammered. "I promise."

He seemed soothed and, making a great effort, raised my hands to his lips. "Let this be good-bye, girl from the sea," he said haltingly. "Let this be my last memory of you, before I lose everything."

But I wasn't going to let that happen. As Helen gently tugged me away from Sebastian's side, I knew that I wasn't ready to say good-bye.

Twenty-eight

Time was running out. The silver watch that Sebastian had dropped outside his hiding place ticked quietly in my pocket. I had found him, but that wasn't enough. That moment had passed, and now time was my enemy just as much as the Dark Sisters and their absent leader. *When the next new moon rises, I fear I will no longer be human. . . .*

Every day, every hour was precious in the search for the Book, and I was impatient with anything that got in the way of our search. We had surreptitiously examined nearly every volume in the library, but we had found nothing. Time . . . time . . . time . . . The days slipped by relentlessly and another week was swallowed up into the past.

When Sunday afternoon came again with its few precious free hours I set off reluctantly to the stables. I'd had a letter from Dad asking how I was getting on with my riding lessons. For his sake I felt obliged to continue with them, but they seemed a total waste of time. *I could be searching for the Book; I could be doing something useful*, I thought resentfully, as I dragged Bonny's saddle from its stand.

"I think this belongs to you."

Josh strolled into the tack room and handed me a small parcel. My heart sank. I didn't want anything from Josh. I couldn't accept what he had to offer. But it was becoming difficult to ignore the glow in his eyes when he talked to me, or the hurt in Sarah's face when she saw us together. *He's nothing*, I had said to Sebastian, and although I had meant it, I was ashamed of my heartlessness. I wasn't the only one who had feelings. I tried to forget my own concerns for a moment.

"Oh . . . um, thanks, Josh. Great."

"I don't think we'll be able to have a lesson today," he said. "The ground is so frozen that the ponies might slip." A heavy frost had turned the snow to hard, packed ice, and the school into an enchanted palace of white gables and sparkling towers.

"Okay, don't worry about it," I replied, secretly relieved.

"Aren't you going to open your parcel?"

I fumbled open the twist of brown paper, and something bright and hard fell into my hand. For a moment, I didn't recognize it, and then I remembered. It was the little locket from Uppercliffe Farm, lovingly polished until it glinted like a magpie's treasure.

"Oh, thank you so much! I had thought I had lost this! Where did you find it?"

"On the floor of the stables. The ribbon had frayed. The locket must have fallen off without your noticing. I've had it put on a chain for you."

"That's so sweet. You needn't have done that."

"I know," he replied softly. "But I wanted to."

Josh picked the locket out of my hand, gently turned me to face the other way, and fastened the chain around my neck. It felt quietly intimate, and I was conscious of him standing tall and protective behind me. *He loves you, Evie. I know he does. . . .* I swept the thought away.

"Thanks so much," I gabbled. "I really must go now if we aren't having a class—"

"Wait a bit, Evie. There's something else." He stepped closer to me and his smile was warm and golden. "Let's go for a walk."

"Oh, but I can't—"

"Why not?" he asked. "I thought Sunday afternoon was free time."

"But—"

"You can't have your riding lesson, so I will lecture you about the noble art of equestrianism as we walk around the lake," he said with a laugh. Then he became serious. "Please, Evie, I need to talk to you. Just a couple of minutes."

I couldn't say no. As we crossed the frozen courtyard together, I dreaded what he might say. The winter sun was hanging low in the clear, cold sky. Some of the youngest girls were throwing snowballs at one another, laughing and red cheeked. They looked so normal, shrieking and sliding in the frosty air. No doubt one of the mistresses would pounce on them at any moment for being so rowdy, but for a moment I envied them. I wished I could be eleven years old again, playing in the snow, carefree.

We walked past them and down to the lake. Beyond its glassy waters, the ruins were shrouded in pale, icy beauty.

"So what did you want to talk about?"

Josh pulled a piece of card from his pocket and gave it to me. I glanced down and saw that it was an old photograph, a portrait of a stout woman in a long skirt and a lace cap. She was no longer young, and her homely face looked into the camera with an honest, open expression.

A small girl clung to the woman's skirt, hiding her face but not her thick, shiny curls. *You be good now, my chick . . . my lamb,* a voice echoed in my head. I pored over the black-and-white image and saw that the woman was wearing a little locket around her neck. It was the same one that Josh had returned to me a moment ago. I had seen the woman before. I knew who she was.

"Martha!" I couldn't stop myself from exclaiming her name. It was Martha—Agnes's old nurse who had taken care of Effie at Uppercliffe when Agnes died. And the little girl next to her in the photograph was Effie herself. "Where did you get this?"

"How do you know Martha's name?" Josh asked quickly. "And why do you have the same necklace?"

"I . . . um . . ." My mind was whirling. How could I possibly explain? "I don't know. I found the necklace when we rode over to Uppercliffe." That much was true, but I knew I didn't sound sincere. I felt guilty, as though I had been caught with stolen goods.

"So it is the same one," he said. "Martha lived at Uppercliffe. She was a distant relation on my mum's side, going way back. We've got all these old photos at home of the old farm and the people who lived there." He looked at me curiously. "I can understand how you might have found the locket up there, but how do you know Martha's name?"

"I got kind of interested in . . . um . . . the history of Wyldcliffe, when I first came here. I looked up all this stuff about the Templetons, you know, Lady Agnes and her family. There's a book in the school library." I rattled the words out, making up more and more as I went along. "It had this photo of the old servants at Wyldcliffe, and she was in it—Martha, I mean. It said she was Lady Agnes's old nurse. And I remembered her face and name when you showed me your photo just now."

I paused for breath.

Josh stared at me, frowning slightly. "You're a terrible liar, you know, Evie. What really happened?"

"Nothing," I protested. Avoiding Josh's glance, I stared up at the distant, unfriendly hills, where the sky was beginning to grow dark. I suddenly longed to be free of secrets, and to be somewhere light and warm and safe. I shivered. "Nothing I can tell you, anyway."

"Evie, I've lived in the village all my life, and I know this place. People have always said crazy things about Wyld-cliffe, about ghosts and tragedy and revenge and all that nonsense. It does have a strange past, though, and there are other rumors too, about the school. Things have been seen and heard, odd things going on at night. And a girl died here last year. She drowned in the lake."

"Yes, I know," I said, my voice barely audible.

"People are beginning to gossip about the way the school is run, especially now that the High Mistress has gone off like that. Some of the old folks in the village swear they have heard her ghost moaning and sobbing in the churchyard. And now these animals being killed. People are hinting about some kind of weird black-magic blood rituals."

I tried to laugh it off. "They're taking it all a bit too seriously, aren't they? It's probably just some nutcase killing those foxes."

"Perhaps. But you haven't answered my question."

"I told you, I happened to find an old necklace. There's no big mystery in that, is there?"

Josh took the photo and slipped it back into his pocket, looking unconvinced.

"Strange things happen at Wyldcliffe, Evie. Be careful."

"I can take care of myself, honestly. But the locket—I should give it back to you. It belongs to your family."

I began to unfasten it, but Josh stopped me.

"Keep it," he said. "I'd like you to have it. It suits you."

"Thank you," I said. "Thank you so much." He was being so kind, and I was repaying his kindness with lies and deceit. I felt terrible.

"Here, have you noticed something?" Josh took the locket in his fingers, pressed the catch, and lifted out the little curl that Martha had kept all those years ago. He held it against my untidy hair. "It's exactly the same color as yours," he said softly. "What about that, Evie? Is there any mystery in that?"

There was nothing I could say. I hid the twist of hair back inside the locket, then pushed everything out of sight under my shirt.

"I'd better go." I began to walk away, crunching across the snow. This was all getting too difficult. It was no good. I would have to write to Dad and ask him to cancel the riding lessons. I would say that I was nervous of horses, that I couldn't cope with it. . . . He wouldn't know that what I really couldn't cope with was telling lies to a boy I liked, and who deserved more than I could give.

"Wait!" Josh caught up with me. "Look, I'm sorry if I've been prying, or making a fuss over nothing. It's just that . . . well, I like you, Evie, and I don't want you to be unhappy about anything."

"I'm not unhappy." It wasn't exactly a lie, but not exactly the truth either.

"All right, I believe you, but if you ever need to talk,

I'm always around. Okay?"

"Okay."

"Good. Then that's the end of the lecture. Let's forget it." He smiled at me encouragingly, and I couldn't help smiling back. We began to walk slowly toward the school. Long purple shadows were creeping across the ground. Josh didn't mention the locket again but chatted about his family and his riding and his plans to study. He asked me about my family too. Somehow it was easy to tell him about Mom and Dad and Frankie, and how much I missed them. We stood under the snow-laden fir trees, talking quietly, and by the time we got back to the stables it was nearly dark. The girls who had been playing in the snow had gone.

"Where have you been, Evie?" It was Sarah, waiting anxiously for me. "We were supposed to go to the library after your riding lesson. Did you forget?"

"Sorry, it was my fault," Josh replied.

"No, it's mine," I said. "I should have remembered." For the second time that day I had an uncomfortable feeling of guilt. How could I have forgotten that Sarah and I had arranged to check through yet another corner of the library in our quest for the Book? "Let's go straight there. We've time before dinner."

"Sure," said Sarah serenely. "'Night, Josh."

As she turned away, I saw the pain in her eyes. And I knew, with the clear instinct that Sarah herself possessed, that she was beginning to lose hope that she would ever be the one lingering with Josh in the twilight.

Twenty-nine

How many more days and night can I linger here, before I am taken?

I hated this place before as a prison, but since you were here, your spirit seems to haunt these walls. There is nowhere I would rather be now.

How puzzling love is! Greater than storms and wealth and science and wars—

When I lived in this house, I never gave a thought to love. I was above such weak fancies. I did not love Agnes. I only desired her beauty and her power—but you know all my shameful secrets. You forgive everything.

My parents loved me, but I was impatient with their

rules and conventions. I never stopped to find out what kind of people they really were. My father was busy with his lands, his horses and dogs. My mother was beautiful, but I never saw beyond her beauty. I never asked myself whether they truly loved each other, or if they needed each other, or how they spoke to each other when they were alone.

Did they ever feel like I feel about you? Would my father have laid down his life for my mother as I will lay down my life for you?

I will do this. I will fade and wither, so that you can live. Yet temptation crawls out of every corner into my mind—and I know that there is a way to avoid what is to come. There is a way. But that way would destroy you. It would kill you.

I told you to hide the treasure you guard, so that I could not be tempted by it. I swore I would not touch the Talisman, not even if it lay at my feet, if that meant hurting one hair of your head—one single strand of your beautiful hair.

Don't come back—you mustn't come back—

But I am not tempted. I am not. I do not desire the Talisman.

You say you will use it to heal me: You will find the

Book; you will do everything; you will save me. Oh, Evie, sweet Evie, I no longer believe that. It is too late, and everything is fading, everyone is leaving me—even you.

When I have gone, you will be the only one who mourns me. Those other souls who were kind enough to feel affection for Sebastian Fairfax have passed from these valleys already. Only the wild brotherhood I once rode with might remember me—yes, they might remember. Yet why should they? I have not made myself their companion for many a year. Let them forget.

Let the darkness cover me.

Let them all forget.

And let me forget that the Talisman ever existed.

No one can help me now.

Thirty

Over the next few days we searched for the Book in the library and in every classroom and on every shelf, as well as the hidden attic, but we discovered nothing. There was only one person left who could help me now.

Agnes. I still had her diary. Perhaps there would be some clue there, something to guide me. . . .

One evening after supper, we had a late study period. The class trooped into Miss Scratton's classroom, all slightly tired and bored, but dutiful as usual, getting on with their work without complaint. I glanced around. Sarah was writing notes methodically. Helen's face was half-hidden by her hair, but I could tell that her mind was far away from the intricacies of English history.

"Helen Black, I will be handing out a detention to

anyone who does not complete this assignment satisfactorily," Miss Scratton said crisply.

Helen sighed and tried to concentrate. I wrote quickly and neatly, churning out a whole lot of stuff about King Henry VIII and the dissolution of the monasteries, when he had smashed up the old religious orders and taken their lands for himself and his cronies. It was odd to think that Wyldcliffe itself had once been a great house of religion, where aristocratic young girls had been sent into the care of the holy sisters until they were of marriageable age. Perhaps nothing much had changed, really. I looked around the classroom. Celeste was poised confidently over her work. India, Sophie, Rachel Talbot-Spencer—whose mother was actually Lady Something-or-other—Lucy Lambton, Caroline and Katie and Charlotte—the whole crowd of them were there to be turned into perfect English young ladies, polished, polite, and slightly dead. We lived side by side and yet I hardly knew them.

I thought about what Josh had said about the rumors swirling around Wyldcliffe and wondered if any of the girls' parents would take them away. Probably not. They would see only what they wanted to see: nicely brought-up girls with the right accent and dress code and social skills. A Wyldcliffe education was more important than worrying about gossip in the local village.

I scribbled a few more sentences, racing through my assignment. As soon as I had finished, I raised my hand.

"Please, can I go to the library?"

"Finished so soon, Evie?" said Miss Scratton dryly. "Very well."

I walked down the corridor, my footsteps echoing on the polished floor, then crossed the tiled entrance hall and slipped into the library. There were only a couple of other students there, leafing through some old magazines and yawning to themselves.

Grabbing the first book from the nearest pile, I found a seat at a table in the corner. I glanced around to make sure no one was looking, then pulled a small black book from my pocket. It was Agnes's journal. I wanted to read it again and search for any clue that could help, however small or insignificant it might seem. I hid the diary inside the covers of the dull-looking textbook I had picked up and began to read, my eyes skimming quickly across the familiar pages.

SEPTEMBER 13, 1882

My news is that dearest S. is back from his travels at last, after months of wandering abroad . . . so good to see my

childhood friend . . . remarkably tall and handsome . . .
the same eager air, the same desire to share everything
with me, the same intense blue gaze . . . truly the brother
I never had . . . suffered a fever in Morocco . . . dreadfully
ill . . . he is troubled . . . This year of 1882 has been so
very tedious, so long and dreary without him . . . I must
remember that I am Lady Agnes Templeton . . . driven to
distraction . . . Mama . . . a decorated doll . . . I have felt
myself changing . . . tingling with some unseen, unknown
power . . . flames dance like bright leaves in the wind . . .
I am afraid, though exhilarated. . . . childhood behind
me . . . my destiny ahead . . .

"Oh!" I jumped. Someone had crept up silently and was reading over my shoulder. I slammed the book shut to hide the journal and twisted around.

It was Harriet.

"I didn't see you," I said, trying to speak casually. "You gave me a shock."

"What are you reading?" Harriet seemed as tense as a cornered animal, but I was the one who felt trapped.

"Um . . ." I showed her the cover of the book. "*Intermediate Biology . . .*"

Harriet leaned toward me. "What are you really

reading?" She put her hand on the book and tried to wrench it out of my grip.

"No!" I shouted, and one of the girls reading the magazines looked up and frowned. "It's private," I whispered desperately. "Please don't look, Harriet. It's my diary."

"I don't believe you," she snarled. I stared at her in amazement. All her awkward timidity had vanished, and she reminded me of a drunk I had once seen outside the local pub, his eyes full of fire and self-pity. "I need it. I want it. Give it to me."

She suddenly let go of the science book, raised her hand, and slapped me across the face. I cried out in astonishment, and the girls on the sofa turned to stare at us.

"What's going on?" one of them said. Harriet had collapsed on a chair and was weeping noisily.

"I'm so sorry, Evie, I'm so sorry."

"It's okay," I said quickly to the others. "She's upset—homesick, that's all." I didn't understand why I was protecting Harriet, but I didn't want anyone to know what had happened. "Can you go and get Miss Barnard? Harriet's in her class."

They nodded and went out. Harriet clutched my hand. "I'm so sorry, Evie," she repeated. "I like you; I want you to be my friend. You've been nice to me, and nobody else is.

And now you'll h-hate me. . . ." Her voice trailed off into incoherent sobs.

"I don't hate you, Harriet, I just don't understand—"

"I've got such a headache," she wailed.

"Don't cry; it will only make it worse." But there was nothing I could do or say to comfort her.

The door opened and Miss Barnard appeared. She was younger than most of the teachers, and she looked concerned.

"What happened? Jenny said there was some kind of incident."

"No, not really." I hesitated, not sure how much to say. "It's just that Harriet isn't feeling very well."

"I'm afraid this is the time of year for flu and fever," Miss Barnard replied, and she reached out to feel Harriet's forehead. The girl jumped away like a ferocious animal. "Don't touch me!" she spat, the wild look burning in her eyes again, but the next minute she slumped limply in her chair again, looking exhausted. "It's so dark in here," she murmured. "So dark."

I looked at Miss Barnard, feeling really alarmed. "What's wrong with her? Is it because of the accident she had?"

"She should have gotten over that by now. But boarding

school isn't for everyone. Harriet seems to be finding it hard to settle here. I think we may have to get in touch with her family."

"No! Please don't tell my mom! You mustn't!" Harriet stopped crying and blew her nose. "I'm sorry. I just got upset and silly because I've got such a bad headache. But I'll be better tomorrow, I promise. Please tell her, Evie."

I hesitated. Part of me felt that if I told her how Harriet had exploded and slapped me, Miss Bernard would arrange for her to be sent home. I was so tempted. It would be such a relief not to have Harriet around the place with her awkward, needy presence. But her frightened eyes pleaded with mine.

"It must be awful to have migraines like that," I said with an effort. "Poor Harriet. She's just really worn out. I'll keep an eye on her, if you like." As if I didn't have enough to worry about.

Harriet looked at me, embarrassed but grateful. "Thank you, Evie. You're my friend. You're my only friend."

I smiled back uneasily. If Harriet liked me so much, why had she been glaring at me a few minutes ago with such hatred? Why on earth had she slapped me? And why was she so desperate to read Agnes's diary?

* * *

The church clock in the sleeping village struck midnight. Another restless night. I had tried to put Harriet out of my mind, but I couldn't relax. Agnes's words in her journal haunted me as I lay in the still, white dormitory.

He still has the same eager air, the same desire to share everything with me, the same intense blue gaze . . . dreadfully ill . . . he is troubled . . . making new discoveries each day . . . hours studying the pages of the Book . . . I would do anything for him. . . .

I had read the whole journal again, hiding in the bathroom, but I didn't feel any closer to finding what I needed to know. Turning over in bed, I tried to think for the hundredth time of where the Book could be. Helen was able to pass through locked doors, and she had already told us that it was not in the High Mistress's study, which Miss Raglan now occupied. I mentally checked off all the places we had looked, and my mind was drawn back to the library, and Harriet's outburst. Her face seemed to float behind my eyelids, and I experienced again the moment of panic when she had crept up behind me and I slammed the book shut. *Slam the book shut . . . hide the book . . . lock it away like a secret. . . .*

I sat up suddenly. That had happened before, here at Wyldcliffe. A book had been shut up in panic and hidden away. I had seen it happen . . . I had seen the faces with their looks of alarm, and the quick movements to conceal the precious object.

I remembered. I remembered everything. My heart was hammering with excitement. In my first term, when I had been so new that I didn't even know my way around the building, I had blundered by mistake into the teachers' private common room. There had been six or seven mistresses huddled around a table, reading from an old book that looked like an ancient Bible. Miss Raglan had been there, and Miss Dalrymple, I remembered. And the book—they had covered it with a rich cloth when they had seen me, and Miss Raglan had been furious. Now I knew why. I had unknowingly caught sight of *the* Book, the ancient relic of the Mystic Way. It was here at Wyldcliffe, only a few yards away from me, hidden away on the floor below.

I didn't stop to think. Reaching in the dark for my robe, I crept out of the dorm and down the corridor, then peered over the banister of the marble staircase and listened carefully. The whole house lay still and silent. A small lamp gleamed faintly. I thought I could risk using the main stairs down to the second floor. If anyone saw me, I would say that I was feeling ill and on my way to the nurse's room. Oh, I didn't care what I would have to say, or what story I might have to invent. All I cared about was getting hold of the Book. Once I had it in my possession, nothing would stop me from devouring its secrets. Knowledge was power. Soon, very soon, I promised myself, I would know enough to awaken the Talisman and end this nightmare forever.

Thirty-one

As silently as a ghost, I entered the staff common room and shut the door behind me. Two tall windows overlooked the front drive. Their shutters were open and a cold shaft of moonlight spilled into the room. There was a large wooden table in the middle, and a group of easy chairs by the fireplace. A pile of essays and academic journals had been left on the table, next to a bag of knitting. It was orderly and calm, just as you would expect from a bunch of old-fashioned schoolteachers.

Between the windows, there was a low bookcase with a glass front. I hurried over and rifled through its contents: dictionaries and reference books, and the odd volume of crosswords. Then I heard voices outside in the corridor, coming nearer, creeping closer like a black mist.

I sprang up and looked around in panic. On the wall that faced the fireplace there was a large cupboard, like a wardrobe. I wrenched open the door and climbed in. It was full of the dark academic robes that the mistresses wore. I pulled the door to, leaving just a crack, and held my breath.

I could make out the movement of five or six women gathering around the table, their backs toward me in the gloom. One of them placed a heavy candlestick in the middle of the table and lit its four black candles, intoning, "Fire of the south, air of the east, earth of the north, water of the west, protect our gathering. May the light be no light, may the darkness be our guide, may our hearts speak, yet our tongues guard our secrets."

The woman who had lit the candles moved over to the fireplace and seemed to tug at a carved block of marble in the center of the elaborate chimneypiece. There was the sound of stone scraping against stone, and the block moved, revealing a black space. She reached in and lifted out an object that was wrapped in tasseled cloths. I peered through the crack in the door, desperate to see what was going on. The woman removed the cloths and I stifled a gasp. It was the Book, ancient and mystical, just as I had thought. She placed it on the table and chanted: "By the word we learn, by the word we curse, by the word we shall conquer."

Then all the women bowed to the Book, and one of them stepped forward into the light.

"Thank you, Sister," she said. It was Miss Raglan. So we had been right about her all along. She was part of Wyldcliffe's secret coven. Miss Raglan was standing with her back to the fireplace, her hands resting on the table. From my hiding place I could see her face in the dull glare of the candles. "Thank you all for answering my summons tonight," she said. "You have served our coven long and faithfully. It is you who must help to decide our next step."

"What is there to decide?" said a cloying, unpleasant voice. My heart squeezed inside my chest. Miss Dalrymple. Fussy, smiling, and utterly treacherous. "Our way is clear," she was saying. "Lord Sebastian, wherever he is hiding, cannot survive much longer in human form. He is on the brink of failure and destruction. If we do not act now, it will be too late for him to achieve immortality and take us with him into that eternal glory. Our High Mistress, too, has failed us. She has left us empty-handed."

"Yet the girl is still here, among us!" hissed the woman who had set out the candles. I couldn't see her face and didn't recognize her voice, but she sounded furiously angry. "She must still have the Talisman. But what are we doing about it? I sent her those warning messages, but nothing seems to dismay her. She even evaded us when I had her surrounded in the ruins."

"You should not have approached her without me!" replied Miss Raglan. "It was foolhardy."

"We need the Talisman, and I was prepared to take a chance to get it."

"But you failed!"

"All the more reason now that we should tear the school—and the girl—to pieces in order to find it," the other woman urged.

"We have already searched the whole school for the Talisman, when we staged those thefts as an excuse to go through the girls' possessions," Miss Raglan replied testily. "We cannot do more than that at this moment. Not all of the mistresses are part of our deep sisterhood. They know nothing of our true aim, and some of them are already complaining about my appointment and my ways. Wyldcliffe may be strict, but it is not a prison, and any more heavy-handed dealings with the students will meet with resistance."

"Then do not involve the other students!" said the

angry woman. "What do we care about them? Get this girl alone and seize her! We should force her to reveal the Talisman's hiding place and make her lead us to our so-called lord before it is too late."

Miss Raglan paused. "You may be right, Sister. The time has come for decisive action."

"But what can we do against the girl without the High Mistress?" Another voice. This time plaintive and fearful.

My stomach twisted again. I was sure this was the voice of the tired-looking woman in the school kitchen. I had talked to her and worked with her and never suspected for a moment that she was mixed up in this. "She attacked us last term in the crypt when we expected to overcome her easily," she was saying. "Why risk that again?"

"Because without risk there is no gain!" Miss Raglan replied. "I see now that the time has come for a new approach. If we sit and wait for our precious High Mistress to return we will be waiting until old age and infirmity overtake us all. I say that Celia Hartle is dead, and a new High Mistress must take her place. We must act now!" She suddenly banged her fist on the table and glared at the others. Her gaze swept over the door of the cupboard and I shrank back, terrified that they would find me.

"Who knows that she is dead?" said a quiet, dry voice. I had to stop myself from crying out. It was Miss Scratton, here in this room, in this deadly gathering. I didn't want to believe it; I would not believe it; this couldn't be happening—yet I would have recognized her voice anywhere. I froze and listened, straining every nerve.

"You are very keen to name a new High Mistress," Miss Scratton said. "I suppose you wish to fill that role yourself?"

"And who would you suggest?" Miss Raglan sneered. "We all know your ambitions. You barely concealed your rivalry with Celia Hartle when she was with us, so don't pretend to be devoted to her now that she has gone."

"One of the first rules of any sisterhood is loyalty," Miss Scratton flashed back. "I have never betrayed my sisters or my appointed superior. I would not want to be in your place when the High Mistress returns and finds you installed in her robes." She paused and lowered her voice. "And believe me, she will return."

"Then why does she send no sign?" asked Miss Dalrymple impatiently. "Does she no longer need us?"

"If she does return, perhaps she will find that we no longer need her," replied Miss Raglan. "The Book has been in our possession for some time. We have studied its mysteries. We are not without powers—why use them simply to serve the High Mistress when she has abandoned us? Why not seize the moment and force Sebastian to do our bidding? The Book will aid us to seek him out, and the precious Talisman, if we let it."

"The Book was not meant for those who seek to serve themselves, however deserving the cause. You twist its words at your own peril," said Miss Scratton.

"So what do you suggest?" asked Miss Dalrymple, her voice as silky and smooth as a poisoned drink. "You are so wise, Sister, so patient, so full of cunning. What do you suggest, now that Sebastian is on the brink of the demon world and everything we have worked for is about to be snatched away?"

There was a long pause; then Miss Scratton began, "I am not a leader. I would wait for the true High Mistress to show herself—"

"Wait? Wait?" Miss Raglan snarled furiously. "I cannot wait. I am getting old. We cannot simply wait and wait, then die as our mothers and grandmothers did. I have no daughter to take my place. I want the reward for our labors that Sebastian Fairfax promised, here and now, without further delay. Nothing will stop me—not you, not Celia Hartle, and certainly not that stupid redheaded girl. She holds the key to all this."

"We cannot approach her openly," said Miss Scratton, "She has no idea of our identity. We should keep it that way."

"And she has remarkable powers," protested the woman from the kitchen.

"That was nothing more than beginner's luck. She will not withstand us again." Miss Raglan smiled coldly. "We must shake off our timidity, separate her from her little friends, and seize her. Then she can be used to revive Sebastian enough to enable our plans to come to fruition. We will steal her soul and then discard her, presenting the Talisman to Sebastian as a final gift. He will not be able to refuse us then. We will achieve what the High Mistress could not."

My leg was cramped awkwardly, but I was too scared to move, too frightened to breathe. I was sure they would hear my heart beating, betraying me to them.

"But if she dies . . . how would we hide her death?" said the fearful woman.

"An accident. A novice rider thrown from her horse. Any story will do. She is nothing."

"And was Laura nothing?" asked Miss Scratton. "People are beginning to talk."

"Then you must silence them! I claim stewardship of this coven," Miss Raglan declared. "I am the High Mistress now. We will use our energies to seek out Sebastian from his hiding place. And at the next new moon we will gather our whole Sisterhood together and call upon them to confirm my claim. Then I will be strong enough to move openly against the girl."

"So be it," said Miss Dalrymple eagerly. One by one, the others agreed.

"So be it."

"So be it."

Miss Scratton hesitated. "So be it," she said.

"In the meantime, the girl must be watched," Miss Raglan continued. "We need to know if she is trying to communicate with Sebastian, and where she is hiding the Talisman." She turned to Miss Scratton. "You will do this. It will keep you from meddling in other matters."

"I shall be glad to undertake this task, Sister," replied Miss Scratton. "I believe she trusts me a little. I will watch her. Evelyn Johnson will not sleep or breathe or move without my being aware of it."

"Then this gathering is ended, until we meet at the new moon, two weeks from now," Miss Raglan said with a self-satisfied sigh. "May the shadows of night be our

Thirty-two

Silence.

They had gone.

Slowly, I pushed the door open and climbed out of my hiding place. My legs were shaking and my mouth was dry. Now I knew the truth at last. I had long suspected that Miss Raglan and Miss Dalrymple were my enemies, but Miss Scratton—upright, grave, and just—how could she be part of their twisted world? I felt sick with disgust, but I had to face it. Miss Scratton was a Dark Sister who had vowed to spy on me. The last shred of any faith I had in the school that was supposed to be my home had been utterly annihilated.

There was a fire burning in me, and it was fueled by hatred. Yes, I hated those women who were supposed to

225

teach us and care for us but who regarded us as no more than pawns in their insane game. I wanted to lash out and destroy everything that was around me, to smash their bookcases and their pictures and their school. I would go to the police, I thought; I would tell them everything I had seen and heard, how Mrs. Hartle had killed Laura by draining her life force from her to prolong Sebastian's existence, and how they were planning to do the same to me.

Even as the thoughts formed themselves in my mind I knew it was hopeless. Nobody would listen. Nobody would believe it.

That wasn't the way, I told myself. I had to stay calm. I had to make my plans before the new moon hung in the sky like a branch of white fire. Everything was leading to that moment. *Think, Evie, think. . . .*

I crept over to the fancy fireplace and felt carefully amid its marble leaves and carved fruit, found the secret place, and pressed hard. The narrow chamber swung open. I reached inside for the Book. But first my hand touched something else: something cold and steely. The silver dagger. Mrs. Hartle had dropped it as we battled in the crypt and her sisters must have brought it back here for safekeeping. After a moment's hesitation I stuffed it in my pocket. Then I picked up the Book, and as I touched it a voice seemed to sound in my mind, chanting an old rhyme:

> Reader, if you bee not pure,
> Stay your hande and reade no more;
> The Mysteries Ancient here proclaimed
> Must not bee by Evil stained.

I knew I should get out of there and go back to the dorm as soon as I could, but I was desperate to open the Book and devour its secrets. I placed it carefully on the table. The green leather cover was exactly as Agnes had described, with the words *The Mysticke Way* gleaming faint and silver in the moonlight. How many people had held this ancient object in their hands? How many of them had been led into despair by its words? *The Mysticke Way is a path of Healing*, I repeated to myself. *I seek Healing for Sebastian . . . for Wyldcliffe . . . for all of us. . . .*

I began to flick through the pages at random. They were dry and musty and the lettering was difficult to read. Some of the pages were decorated with red and green inks, just like the page that Agnes had left me, and some were written in Latin and Greek and other languages that

I didn't recognize. I was in too much of a hurry to take in what I was looking at, and the Book seemed to have a mind of its own. Some of the pages were stuck together and wouldn't open, and sometimes they flipped open as though blown by an invisible wind. I caught glimpses of many obscure spells and charms: *For Finding a True Friend; To Foretell the Weather; To Charm Poison from a Toad; For Making Rain; To Cure Rheumatics; The Gift of Sight; The Gift of Death . . .*

The Gift of Death. The bold black letters seemed to stare up at me and pierce my mind. The rest of the page was decorated with some kind of woodcut, showing a grim figure of Death and a bright angel, side by side. *The Gift of Death.* For some reason I wanted to know more. I tried to turn the page to read the details of the spell, but the pages wouldn't open. This part of the Book had been sealed against me.

The church bell sounded in the distance, its thin peal clear and sharp in the winter night. Midnight. In a few seconds it would be a new day. A wind stirred through the room, and the pages of the Book flapped in the breeze, then fell still, opening at a new place. I looked down. The letters on the page were shaped like tongues of red flame.

To Summon the Secret Fire.

The church bell struck one last time. The secret fire, the sacred flame, the source of light and power—Agnes had served it faithfully. And when she wanted to seal her powers inside the Talisman she had summoned the flame and thrust the silver trinket into its fiery heart. I remembered the words from her journal. *My life force seemed to be dragged out of me and into the silver jewel. . . . My powers are sealed in its silvery heart. . . .*

It was all so clear, so simple now. I knew what I had to do. If I could summon that fire myself, I would be able to put the Talisman back into the mystical flames and unseal it once again. And then Agnes's powers would be mine and I would be armed with her strength as I fought to free Sebastian from his doom.

Hugging the Book to my heart, I whispered, "Thank you. Thank you, Agnes."

I had found what I was looking for.

Thirty-three

The next morning Helen had to shake me from sleep.

"Evie, the bell rang. Why aren't you getting up?"

"What . . ? Uhh . . . so tired . . ." I sat up and yawned; then everything from the night before came flooding back to me. I grabbed hold of Helen's wrist in excitement. "I've got so much to tell you."

"Me too," she replied. "I just heard two of the cleaning women talking in the corridor. Apparently it's happened again."

"What?"

"An attack in the village. Another creature nailed to a door. This time it was a chicken, with its head cut off and feathers everywhere. It's awful. The locals are getting pretty angry about it, talking about chucking the Gypsies off the land. Sarah's going to be upset."

I looked around. Sophie was slowly getting dressed, and Celeste was still lying in bed.

"That's not all Sarah's going to be upset about," I said in a low voice, not wanting to be overheard. "We need to talk." I threw my clothes on and we hurried downstairs to find Sarah in the stables before the bell rang for breakfast. It was a bright, clear morning, and the frost sparkled on the ground with a hundred tiny points of light. Sarah was mucking out Starlight, her cheeks pink with exertion, but the color drained from her face when I told her and Helen what I had found and seen.

"I can't believe it," Sarah said. "Any of the others, but not Miss Scratton."

"I saw her. I heard what she said. She's as bad as the rest of them."

"But it doesn't make sense," replied Sarah stubbornly. "It doesn't feel right."

"Anyone is capable of doing wrong, Sarah." Helen sighed. "And immortality is a powerful temptation. People have stolen and killed for much less."

"Miss Scratton would never do anything like that."

"I wish it weren't true, but it is," I said. "It doesn't make any difference, though. We always knew we were on our own in this. She couldn't have helped us anyway, and it's better to know who our enemies are."

"Enemies?" said a thin, nasal voice. "Who's got enemies?" We spun around and saw Harriet standing in the doorway of the stable.

"We were talking about . . . the . . . the next lacrosse match," I gabbled. "Planning tactics."

"Oh. I thought you hated lacrosse."

"Yeah, well, I can't duck out of it, so I might as well try. . . . Um . . . are you okay, Harriet? Any more headaches?"

"No . . . no." She suddenly looked around nervously, then scurried off.

"What was all that about?" Helen asked when she had gone. "How much do you think she heard?"

"I don't know," said Sarah. "We'll have to be more careful. Although I don't suppose there's anything in it except Harriet being weird as usual."

I wasn't so sure. As Harriet had walked away, I had noticed something. There were some streaks of reddish brown dirt on the side of her skirt, like mud or rust. Or even, perhaps, like blood.

* * *

Dinner was over. It was our official letter-writing time. A duty once a week. Some of the girls grumbled about not being allowed to call home. "I mean, haven't they heard of cell phones?" they moaned. But Wyldcliffe had its own way of doing things. Wyldcliffe students were expected to be able to write expressive, elegant, polite letters just as the students of fifty years ago had done. So there we were, heads bent, scribbling away, clinging to another fading custom, pretending that the modern world could be blotted out as easily as the snow blotted out the grass.

Miss Scratton walked slowly up and down the room, handing out pieces of writing paper, ticking off untidy handwriting, watching everything with her sharp black eyes. I felt her gaze sweep over me, and my stomach heaved with revulsion. Did she really think I would be so stupid as to mention Sebastian in my letters to Dad? Did she really think she would catch me so easily? I bent my head and tried to write my letter. I hated Miss Scratton now; I would never stop hating her, and the hatred burned in my head like an obsession. But I had to pretend that I was perfectly happy, that I was a carefree student, writing home, chatting about nothing.

Dear Dad,

I am fine, and working hard. I think I am even beginning to understand what the chemistry teacher is trying to tell me. I have been thinking—perhaps I will study medicine at college. It seems a good thing to be a healer.

In history we have been learning about the old monasteries and the great religious houses before they were all destroyed by Henry VIII. I don't like the idea of the Wyldcliffe nuns being thrown out of their home all those hundreds of years ago, poor things. Sometimes I think I can imagine them singing in the ruins of the chapel, and sometimes I feel we are still like them in a weird way, shut away up here, cut off from the rest of the world.

The weather is still cold—we didn't get snow like this at home by the sea!

My riding is making progress, though I'm afraid I will never be really good. My teacher is nice, very encouraging. Thanks so much for paying for all that. I really appreciate it.

Dearest Dad, I miss you so much. I'm doing my best, I promise.

Loads of love,

Evie xxx

I stuffed the letter into an envelope. I couldn't say what I really wanted to say:

> Dear Dad,
> Tonight we are going to cast our Circle and attempt to summon the fire element. I don't know what will happen. It might be dangerous. It might be a complete failure. But one soul depends on me, so I have to try it. One lost, despairing soul. Funny, people don't talk about souls much anymore, do they? And yet, this was once a place where the nuns thought and prayed about nothing else. A teacher I trusted has turned out to be my enemy, and I feel sick to my guts, but I'm not going to let them win this. I can't.
>
> There's another thing bothering me, Dad. The guy who teaches me to ride is so nice, but I'm frightened of hurting him. He has a look in his eyes when he sees me, a kind of tenderness. Perhaps if I had known him before all this began, it might have meant something to me, but now it's too late; I belong to Sebastian, and nothing can ever change that. Oh, Dad, I'm so scared. I never meant for any of this to happen. I never meant to fall in love. . . .

There were some things that were impossible to say. I didn't sleep that night. One by one, Helen, Sarah, and

I slipped out of our dorms and made our way to the secret attic. I was the last to arrive, hiding a small bundle under my robe. Helen and Sarah gathered around me eagerly as I brought out the book and turned the pages to the right place.

To Summon the Sacred Fire

There are those rare Souls who are called to minister to the Sacred Flame, which is a spark of the great furnace of Creation. These women, for such they are, have no need of Instructions or Ritual. They will contact their Element as a bird makes contact with the air, or a child with its mother, that is, through Nature alone. Yet it is still possible to reach the Fire through study and perseverance, if the Heart be pure.

"Look! There in the margin," I said. Someone had added notes in pencil at the edge of the page. "Sebastian . . . That's his writing, I'm sure."

Helen held the candle closer to decipher the faint words. "'I have attempted this many times,'" she read slowly. "'Each time I have failed and been rejected by the Powers. Yet I will master this, if it takes every drop of my blood.'"

"He never did," I said. "Only Agnes could reach the sacred fire, and she didn't need the Book to do it."

"Are you ready to try, Evie?"

"I'm ready."

Helen set the candles out in a circle around us. "Let all our deeds be pleasing to the Light of Lights; let them be as clear and pure as the mountain air."

Then Sarah laid bunches of fresh evergreen leaves between the wavering candles. "Let our thoughts be as strong as the trees that grow in the earth; let them bear fruit that is good and wholesome."

I scooped water into my hands from one of the stone jars and let the shining droplets fall on the greenery. "Let our lives be cleansed; let our minds be without stain."

We held hands and chanted together: "Let this be our circle of protection and knowledge. Let the Mystic Rites begin."

I cannot betray the secrets of all that we did. But when all was prepared, we burned the oils and the herbs prescribed in the Book and watched the smoke curl up to the roof. Then I closed my eyes as Sarah pressed the silver dagger against my bare arm and let a single drop of my blood fall into the smoking mixture.

The blood of our veins . . . the fire of our desires . . . show us the fire . . . the fire of life. . . .

I was falling. The air rushed past me like the beating of angels' wings. I was spinning into darkness, and the voices of Sarah and Helen were lost to me. I was entirely alone in the whole universe. Then there was a light ahead, and everything slowed down. I had arrived at the heart of a deep cavern, and the light in front of my eyes was so dazzling that I could hardly bear to look at it. But I had no choice. Somehow, I approached and saw that the light was coming from a column of leaping fire, great flames twisting silver and red and blue, orange and purple and white, like living diamonds. The heat was terrible and I was afraid that I would burn away like a dry leaf, but at the same time I knew that I must reach out to the flame. As I tried to do so, I was blasted back by the force of the fire, and a voice seemed to say, "You cannot approach the sacred fire; it is not for you. . . . The living water calls to you, sister. Go back; you do not belong here."

"No," I called out in desperation, "you must let me approach. I was sent here; Agnes sent me. . . ."

Then the voice, or the thoughts in my head—I couldn't be sure—seemed to speak again. "There is light in your soul and courage in your heart. But these are deep mysteries and only a few may be welcomed. You cannot pass through the flames without a token of belonging. A token of fire. Bring that next time and the powers may be more gracious."

Then it seemed that the light and the heat would destroy me utterly, burning away every particle of my being, and I screamed as the flames surrounded me.

"Evie! Evie, it's all right! Come back!" Someone splashed water on my face and I woke up in the attic, sprawled on the faded carpet. The leaves and herbs had been scattered and the circle was broken. Sarah and Helen were bending over me, looking anxious. I shook my head wearily.

"I couldn't do it. I don't belong in the realm of fire."

I felt so flat and dull, aching with emptiness. I had been so sure that it would work. Why hadn't Agnes appeared to me? Where had she gone? I missed her, and I seemed to be losing her as well as Sebastian. I had failed; I couldn't do it. . . .

"So what happened? Can you try again?" asked Helen.

"I'm not sure. They said—or someone seemed to say—that I could, but I would have to take something with me, something from Agnes, I think."

"What?"

"I don't know—a token of fire, whatever that is."

"Do they mean the Talisman?"

"No—not that. I don't know how they told me, but I have to find something else. The token." I slammed my hand on the floor in frustration. "I was so close! All I had to do was reach out . . . and now I've no idea what to do."

"We'll find the way, Evie, I promise," said Sarah soothingly.

"But when? How? If Miss Raglan is confirmed as the High Mistress at the next new moon, I think she'll be strong enough to act openly against us. And Sebastian can't hold on forever."

"Let's give it one more try, at least," Helen said, her green-yellow eyes shining in the candlelight. "A token of fire. We've got to find that before we do anything else."

"I'll find it," I said grimly. "I'll find it, whatever it takes."

I will master this, if it takes every drop of my blood. . . .

I would give my blood, my tears, my hope. Oh, I would go on and on until the bitter end, until I had nothing else left to give.

Thirty-four

I had never seen Miss Raglan so angry.

"This cannot be tolerated!" Her face was mottled and red, and she scanned the faces of the uneasy Wyldcliffe students with something close to loathing. "Someone has taken an antique letter opener and a very valuable book. They are both the property of the school, and I will have them returned!"

Part of me wanted to laugh at her impotent rage as she spluttered like a dictator who had suddenly lost control of an army. It wasn't really funny, though. Now that Miss Raglan and the coven had discovered the loss of the Book and the dagger, I knew that I would be top on the list of their suspects.

"Never, in our long history, have we had thieves at

Wyldcliffe," she blustered. "I will not put up with this while I am responsible for the school. This is the second time this term that there has been an incident like this. The book in question was an extremely rare volume of great interest. If the culprit does not come forward, I will be forced to call in the police."

Yeah, right, I thought. It wasn't very likely that Miss Raglan would run to the police with everything that she had to hide. She was bluffing, and I knew we were still safe. The Book was hidden in Agnes's secret attic, and so was the silver dagger. Let her storm, I thought. As long as she was angry, I knew that she was empty-handed.

Miss Raglan stumped out of the dining hall and the girls split up into little groups, slightly shocked over the scene we had just witnessed. I felt kind of sorry for them. Those blond, pretty Lucys and Camillas and Carolines would never dream of taking something that didn't belong to them, and yet they had been harangued like common street kids. First the High Mistress had disappeared; now there was a thief at Wyldcliffe. Their little world was beginning to show cracks. Celeste and India were holding court, giving out their opinions in silky voices that were full of spite.

"Well, I wouldn't put it past Helen Black," Celeste was

saying. "She's completely nuts, and everyone knows she hasn't got any money at all. If this dumb book really is worth a fortune, she'd be only too happy to get her hands on it. Personally I wouldn't have these scholarship girls at Wyldcliffe." She glared in my direction. "It really lowers the tone, don't you think, Sophie?"

Sophie blushed scarlet and mumbled, "I can't believe anyone from Wyldcliffe would steal stuff from the school. . . . I really can't."

"I think you're right, Sophie," said India smoothly. "Helen Black and her crowd are too stupid to pull off a stunt like that. I blame outsiders. I'm sure the missing book is down at that horrible Gypsy camp at this very moment. Everyone knows they are thieves, and worse— look at what they've been doing with those dead animals on people's doorsteps; it's completely sick."

Sarah had been listening in disgust, and she couldn't contain herself any longer. "How dare you say that? There's no proof that any of this is connected to the travelers. Just because people are different from you—and thank God some people are—you automatically despise them."

India laughed. "Oh, listen to Saint Sarah, always defending the weak. But I happen to think that the weak have only themselves to blame."

"Come on, Sarah," said Helen. "It isn't worth arguing with her." She dragged us both away and we headed for our next class. It was history with Miss Scratton. I took my seat in the familiar classroom in the old wing, with the narrow lattice windows and the whitewashed walls. The poster of the witches from *Macbeth* was still displayed behind Miss Scratton's desk. *Ironic,* I thought bitterly. She was worse than any witch. I couldn't even take an interest in her lessons anymore, though they had previously been my favorites. I wanted to get out there and out of her sight as quickly as possible.

"When Henry the Eighth dissolved the monasteries and the great religious houses in the sixteenth century, there was a period of great upheaval and uncertainty, even rebellion. . . ." Her monotonous voice droned on as we took notes. "For the ordinary people, places like our own Abbey had for many years been sources of education, charity, and medicine—the sisters would have cared for anyone who needed healing."

A wave of exhaustion swept over me. I could hardly concentrate.

"Of course, even in pagan times the people would have valued their healers. Long before the Abbey was built, the ancient settlers who worshiped on their hilltop temple would have had their wise women. . . ."

The light in the room dimmed. I sat up and gripped the edge of my desk, willing it not to happen. But everything was changing again, just as it had once before, when I had first glimpsed Agnes in her long-ago schoolroom. The colors and sounds swirled into a confused blur. . . . It was happening again. . . .

The low lattice windows and the whitewashed walls dissolved and faded. I was in simple wooden building, hardly more than a shelter. A young child wrapped in a rough woolen cloak lay on the straw-covered floor, and his face was gray with pain. His mother held his hand and tried not to weep. Another woman, who wore a silver amulet around her neck and a veil over her hair, was tending the child. She wiped the boy's face and gave him sips of a bitter-looking mixture, while repeating some secret prayers. The boy's pain seemed eased, and he fell into a deep sleep. The woman with the amulet turned to me, and though her face was half-hidden by the veil, I saw her eyes burning with fierce intelligence and pity . . . a healer . . . a wise woman . . . a holy sister. . . .

Miss Scratton's harsh voice jolted me back to the present. "Like the Wyldcliffe nuns, the wise women would be highly respected as teachers and holy sisters—"

"No!" I couldn't help crying out. How dared she talk about sisterhood when she had betrayed every ideal of learning and love and loyalty?

"What's wrong, Evie?" Miss Scratton said, looking up at me. "Do you disagree with my views?"

"I . . . I'm sorry," I stammered, trying to cover my confusion and find something to say. "It's just that, um . . . at my old school, um . . . the teacher said that in the old days women weren't important. . . . They just had babies and did the cooking and stuff. . . ."

"And isn't having babies and caring for a family important? But in any case, I think you'll find that if you look deeper, women have always done much, much more. Oh, yes, women have always wielded great power," she added softly, "even if it largely went unseen."

Unseen power . . . the great sisterhood . . . the Mystic Way . . . I felt dizzy as her eyes stared unrelentingly into mine.

"But that would be an interesting topic of discussion for another time." She seemed to lose interest in me and turned away abruptly. "Right now I want you to read the source material on page thirty-two of the textbook and then plan your written report."

My head was bursting. What had I just seen? Was there some clue in the vision? Perhaps I needed to connect with the women of the deep, unknown past—perhaps they had some ancient knowledge that would help Sebastian. Perhaps he needed to drink the herbal mixture, like the boy. But how would that be connected with the fire token? If only I knew what it all meant!

I bent over my books and pretended to do my work, but I was really scribbling down anything that could trigger the answer I needed: *Fire—heat—flame. Red—red rose? Ruby? A ruby ring. Red—sign of blood. Healing potions—look in Book. To cleanse blood? Poppies. Crimson. Scarlet. Fire. A token. A love token. FIRE.*

Think, Evie, think, I told myself, but my mind was blank, as empty as the mournful hills and the gray, gray sky.

Thirty-five

FROM THE PRIVATE PAPERS OF
SEBASTIAN JAMES FAIRFAX

A memory stirs in the darkness—

We were riding under the gray sky, not far from here. Galloping like thunder, laughing as we flew across the valley, riding to escape, riding to forget.

My brothers were with me.

The Fairfaxes are dead and gone, and I was the only child of my parents. But they asked me to call them brother—

My memories fade except this. Pain—the pain is consuming me. I am drowning in pain and fire—

Must hold to the memory. Must not let go. Must fight. Fight for Evie—

I am so alone.

Long ago, I had my brothers.

We journeyed together—Niko and Stefan and Tamas and all the rest. Their sturdy horses. Their beautiful women.

Why do they come back to me now? They ride in my mind like bright flames.

I must tell you—I feel the wind on my face as we ride from place to place. I hear laughter and singing. I see the glitter of their black eyes and the flash of their sharp daggers. I smell wood smoke. I taste hot, savory broth; the sun goes down. We eat and sing and tell stories.

I must tell you—the end of the story—

When was this? Twenty, thirty, sixty summers ago? Why does this come to my mind?

My mind . . . The Talisman hovers in my mind—calling me, tempting me—

No.

No.

If I could choose—if I could find you again, Evie, I would ride with you across the moors as I once rode with my brothers, wild and free and sure.

I see you riding like fire—a red rose—a crimson slash of silk—the fire—

I am falling—falling—pain and darkness.

All is hidden and lost. I write these words—My voice fails—I must reach you. I write my name in the dust—I am consumed by fire—

My brothers will help you.

Help me, Evie.

My story is nearly over.

Help me.

Thirty-six

In my dream it is snowing and I am outside in the sparkling air, as comfortable as a fox or a deer in the deep woods. I am wearing a long, heavy skirt, with a bright shawl wrapped around my shoulders. A cooking fire glows in a ring of stones dug into the cold earth. The flames heat a pot of broth that hangs from a metal trivet over the fire. Behind me is a huddle of tents and wooden carts, and a couple of ragged boys playing in the snow. I am watching and waiting, and the smell of the fire mingles with the smell of the tall pine trees. I am waiting for someone, waiting for him to return to me.

And then Sebastian is there, running over the snow, his face full of young, strong joy. He takes me into his arms and we kiss, and our mouths are warm and sweet as honey.

The white world fades and the red sun burns low on the horizon. But there's something I need, something I'm looking for; I try to remember. *Sebastian*, I say urgently, *you've got to help me find the fire token. What is it? Where is it?* He looks at me so tenderly and strokes my hair; then a rough voice calls out, "Prala! Av akai!" Brother . . . *my brother* . . . Three dark-haired riders, wary-looking men with strong, proud faces, are waiting for him under the trees, holding the reins of Sebastian's black horse. One of them comes nearer, leading the horse and speaking urgently to Sebastian. Then Sebastian lets go of me and leaps into the saddle. *I can't stay*, he says. *My brothers will help, I have to move on, move on, move on*. . . . He gallops away with the men, and I am left alone as the sun sets and the world blazes into fire.

When I woke up, the dream was still bright and alive, like a picture in my mind. I looked at the little alarm clock by my bedside and groaned. Three o'clock in the morning. I just wanted to go back to sleep, to my dream world where Sebastian's kisses were real.

The dream. I suddenly sat up, bolt upright, my heart racing. *My brothers will help.* But Sebastian didn't have any brothers; he had been an only child. His brothers, the riders in the snow . . . those men on the wild-looking horses, what did they remind me of? My thoughts were jumbling over one another, struggling to make sense, as scraps of forgotten conversation rose from the layers of my mind. *I hope she haunts you,* Celeste had said. *But I don't believe in ghosts, do you, Sarah? Yes . . . I think I do . . . the old beliefs . . . The dead can come back; the dead can come back to haunt the living; that's what the Romany people say. . . .*

That was it; that was the connection—those men in the dream, they reminded me of the traveler boy, the Gypsy we had seen on his shaggy pony out on the moors. And Sebastian's brothers—what had Sebastian told me of his long and restless existence since Agnes's death? *I lived for a while with some Romany wanderers. They were good to me, like brothers.*

Was there a connection? *My brothers will help,* the dream Sebastian had said. But perhaps I was just grasping at any wild idea. Yesterday my mind had been full of images of the woman with the amulet, and now I was buzzing with dreams of Sebastian. Was it all just crazy nonsense, brought on by worry and lack of sleep? Or had my dream really contained a message of some kind?

There was only one way to find out.

The following Sunday Harriet ran after us down the drive just as we got near to the school gates. I guessed she had been hanging around, waiting for us to appear.

"Hey, Evie," she said, panting. "Where are you going?"

"Out," I said shortly.

"Can I come with you?"

"You younger ones aren't allowed out without a mistress," Helen replied.

"But that's not fair. Anyway, they'd never know. I could walk behind you." Her face screwed up, as though she were trying not to cry. "I just want to get out of here for a while."

"Don't be silly, Harriet. It's impossible," I said. "Come on, let's go."

"Look, perhaps we could ask Miss Scratton if you could come another time," Sarah said kindly. "But we can't do it today. Why don't you run back to school and curl up with a book or something? We'll see you later."

Harriet's black eyes were mutinous with disappointment. "Oh, all right," she replied sulkily, as we hurried through the gates and set off along the rough lane that led to the village. I seemed to feel her eyes boring into my back as we left her behind.

"Poor Harriet," murmured Sarah. My conscience twinged. I would be extra nice to Harriet when we got back, I promised myself. I would play Scrabble with her after supper, whatever she wanted. I would let her think I was her best friend; I would do anything—but right now I had to get to the travelers' camp.

We walked briskly, and had soon passed the churchyard and reached the far side of the village. The field by the road had a sad, untidy look. Four or five trailer vans and a couple of beaten-up cars were parked, seemingly haphazardly, around the edge of the field, and here and there piles of scrap metal, a broken chair, and a stripped-down motorbike added to the sense of transience and confusion. Someone had strung some washing to dry on a line, and the clothes flapped stiff and frozen in the chill wind. There were no gaily-colored wooden carts, no exotic women in bright skirts, nothing of the storybook image of the ancient Gypsy folk. A low hum of pop music was coming from one of the trailers, and the smell of cooking. Three horses were tethered by coarse ropes to the fence, and they stood patiently, nuzzling against one another, waiting.

"Do you really think we'll be welcome?" Helen wondered, as we hesitated by the gate. I was glad we weren't wearing our conspicuous school uniform, but instead were dressed for a Sunday-afternoon walk to the village in our jeans and jackets.

"We'll soon find out," I replied, pushing the gate open and walking into the field. A dog barked; then a girl opened the door of one of the vans and ran down the steps. When she saw us she stopped and stared wordlessly. It was the young girl we had seen out riding.

"Hello," I ventured. "Is your . . . um . . . brother around?"

The girl continued to stare at us, then turned and fled back into the trailer. We heard voices and then the door opened again. The boy we had seen before stepped out, eyeing us warily. I guessed he was about seventeen. He had untidy brown hair and broad shoulders and a closed, defensive expression. I nudged Sarah in the ribs.

"*Sastipe*," she said haltingly. Sarah had made the effort to learn a few Romany words before our visit, and had persuaded us to do the same. "*Devlesa avilan.*"

Greetings, my friend. It is God who brought you. . . .

The boy looked up in surprise, then growled, "I can speak English, you know." He stared at us for another moment, then broke into a reluctant grin. "Your pronunciation is terrible. But at least you tried. *Devlesa araklam tume*—It is with God that I found you."

"Thank you," Sarah replied delightedly. "So . . . can we talk to you?"

"Sure. I won't bite." He smiled at her again. "I've seen you out riding. You're not bad. Quite good, in fact. What do you want to talk about?"

Sarah hesitated for a second. "It might sound stupid. . . ."

"Wait a second." He turned and stepped back into the trailer and spoke briefly to the people inside, then zipped up his jacket and walked over to us. "Let's go somewhere else. My mother's resting. I don't want to disturb her. She doesn't really like . . . I mean, it would just be easier."

We walked down the lane, away from the village, and found ourselves taking the path that led to the little river, hardly more than a stream, that ran down to Wyldcliffe from the hills above. The boy said his name was Cal, and we told him our names. "So what brought you to the camp? Most of the locals avoid us like the plague, especially since all that trouble about those dead animals being found in the village. We'd never do that," he added quietly. "We have too much respect for our fellow creatures."

"We don't think it was you," Sarah said in a rush. "I'm sorry if you've been given a hard time."

Cal's face clouded over, and he stopped to lean against the old stone bridge that spanned the river's shallow bed. "Yeah, well, I don't care what people say about me, but some of those stuck-up girls from that big school at the Abbey have been giving my kid sister grief. They've been hassling Rosie when she's riding her pony, calling her names, making fun of her. That's out of line." He looked up suspiciously. "You're not from that place, are you?"

"We are, but not all of us think like that, I promise you," said Helen. "We don't like those kinds of girls much either."

Cal didn't look entirely convinced. The news that we were from the Abbey seemed to have put him on his guard again. "That's easy to say. Perhaps I'd better go." He began to walk away, but Sarah ran after him.

"Please, Cal, please look at this. Look," she said, pulling something out of her pocket. "This is a photo of my great-grandmother, Maria. She was one of the Roma— like you. And these were her parents." She showed him another photo of a handsome dark-skinned young couple sitting outside a *vardo*, or traditional wagon, a little wooden house on wheels with a campfire nearby. The mists of my dream moved and swirled in my head again. . . . "Maria was adopted into a rich *gaje* family," Sarah went on. "The girls at the Abbey gave her a really hard time when she was there. She knew what it felt like. And I haven't forgotten her. I'll never forget. That's why we're not like those girls who were mean to your sister."

The boy took the faded sepia photograph in his hands and examined it. He gazed at Sarah for a second. "I'm sorry," he said quietly, giving back the photo. "I should have known. I should have seen it in your eyes. You're beautiful enough to be Roma anyway. *T'ave baxtalo.* You are welcome here."

Sarah blushed scarlet. "Thank you."

"Okay," he said. "Let's talk. What do you want to know?"

I pushed forward eagerly. "Has your family been coming this way for a long time?"

"As long as I can remember this has been one of the winter stopping grounds. Doesn't makes sense, really, as it's miles from anywhere. We usually stay nearer to towns in the winter. But there's a kind of tradition in our family not to let too many years go by before we come back to Wyldcliffe. Something to do with an old promise."

"Do you know anyone called Sebastian?" I said, my heart in my mouth.

Cal thought for a while, then shook his head. "Can't think of anyone called that."

"Oh." Disappointment washed over me. I had been clutching at straws, perhaps, but I had been so convinced that my dream had meant something. "Are you sure? Sebastian Fairfax?"

A flash of amazement passed over Cal's face. "Fairfax?" he said. "Do you mean Fairfax James?"

"I—I don't know . . . maybe. Who was he?"

Cal looked around cautiously. "My dad told me about him before he died. Said he had to hand on the tradition. Fairfax James was, well, a sort of legend for us. He was a conjurer, a kind of wandering magician."

"Oh my God . . ."

"Fairfax traveled with our family for a while, in the old days, way before I was born, performing at fairs and shows. Then there was some kind of trouble—I don't know what—and he disappeared, but not before he helped our family. A deed worthy of a brother, my dad said."

"A brother—that's exactly what Sebastian said! So when did he know your family?" I asked anxiously.

"That's the uncanny thing. Dad remembered seeing Fairfax when he was only a kid, and Fairfax was about twenty years old. But Dad said that my grandfather had known him too, years and years ago, and yet Fairfax was exactly the same age even then. He doesn't change, just turns up for a while, then vanishes. They say that every generation of our family is destined to meet him at some point in their lives. That's why we keep coming back here. In case he needs us." Cal looked defiant. "In case he comes back from the dead."

"It is him—Fairfax James is Sebastian; it has to be!"

"But what has he got to do with you?" asked Cal in astonishment.

"I know this sounds crazy, but we know him," said Sarah.

"And he sent me a kind of message," I added hurriedly. "He said his brothers would help, and I think that must have something to do with your family. I need to find a fire sign, something to do with fire—a token or symbol or object. Do you know what it might be?"

Cal frowned, then shook his head. "Sorry. I can't think of anything." He looked at us warily. "Are you sure this is for real? You're not winding me up?"

"I promise you, Cal, it's nothing like that," pleaded Sarah. "I swear on everything that's precious, on Maria's memory—"

His expression softened. "Okay, Gypsy girl. How about you come and meet my kid sister? You can show her your picture and tell me more about all this. If Fairfax really has come back to our family, I want to be ready for him."

He held out his hand to Sarah. She hesitated, then

took it in hers. "Thanks. I'd love that."

Cal turned to us. "Don't worry. I'll bring her back to the school before it gets dark." They walked away in the direction of the travelers' camp, and Helen and I set off back to the school. I was thinking furiously. It was good that we had made contact with Cal, and good to see the light in Sarah's eyes when she talked to him, but I was still no nearer to what I needed. I kicked a pebble on the path in frustration. Sebastian had once known the Gypsy travelers—that much was clear—but how could they help? And what was the fire token?

My stomach was tight with fear. I tried not to think about what might be happening to Sebastian: how the light in his eyes might be fading, how the threads that bound him to this life might be getting ready to break. I had to make progress—and quickly. There was a little over a week until the new moon. It would rise on the fulfillment of my hopes, or their utter annihilation.

Thirty-seven

I tried everything. Every night I tried a different charm from the Book. *To Cure Sicknesse, To bring Rain in time of Droughte, To improve Memorie* . . . But I knew I was fooling myself. These things might have filled me with wonder a year ago, but now they were like empty toys. Without the fire token my powers were meaningless and the Book offered me nothing but ways of killing time. *Time . . . time . . . time . . .* Every day that went by was another failure. I couldn't find the fire token, and I couldn't find a way of stopping the hours racing past.

Monday . . . Tuesday . . . Wednesday . . . Thursday . . . the last week before the new moon rose was almost over.

On Friday morning there was a rush of girls around the long table in the entrance hall. They were looking excitedly at the piles of mail, chattering and giggling like eager magpies. A huge bunch of red roses was displayed in a crystal vase in the middle of the table, and red ribbons had been fixed up all around the hall.

"What's all this about?" I asked Sarah as we pushed our way past the crowd of girls.

She grimaced in reply. "St. Valentine's Day, of course. They always make a big fuss about it."

"I wouldn't have thought Wyldcliffe would have encouraged such frivolities."

"Mrs. Hartle would have stamped it out if she could, but you know how the school clings to its traditions. In the old days, the girls would make little posies and poems for their favorite teachers, and the handing out of the flowers was an elaborate ritual. We don't do that anymore, thank goodness, but it's still a big deal for students to get valentine cards from well-connected boys from London or Eton College. Celeste will be in her element."

Celeste was indeed at the center of the crowd, gleefully waving a bunch of colored envelopes and exclaiming over their contents. She had a gang of girls hanging around her shrieking and giggling, but I couldn't help noticing that Sophie wasn't there and that India looked rather sour. Perhaps the preppy boys she knew had let her down. As

I watched the crowd of laughing girls, a desperate, crazy, ridiculous hope that Sebastian had sent me a valentine message shot through me like an arrow. I marched up to the table, scanning the letters.

"I don't know why you're bothering to look, Johnson," Celeste crowed, pushing past me with her triumphant haul. She was right, of course; it was hopeless. . . .

"Hey—aren't these for you?" A girl called Fiona Hamilton excitedly waved a small package and a plain white envelope under my nose. "Lucky you."

Lucky me. I grabbed them from her; then my heart sank. That wasn't Sebastian's writing—how could it be? How stupid of me even to imagine for a second that they would be from him. Sarah was at my shoulder, looking with curiosity at the package and letter.

"Why don't you open them?"

"Not here. Let's go outside."

I had a feeling that whatever they were, I didn't want Celeste or anyone else to see them. Sarah and I made our way to the terrace. It was cold but bright, and our breath hung like little clouds in the clear air. I opened the envelope and a strip of paper fell out.

THIEVES WILL BE PUNISHED

"Looks like the mystery letter writer has decided to contact me again. Just the thing for Valentine's Day," I said lightly, crumpling it up and throwing it away.

"Evie, you've got to take care," Sarah said in a low voice.

I tried to laugh it off and show a confidence I didn't quite feel. "Well, the thief has to be caught first before she can be punished, and they haven't managed that yet."

"But still—"

"So what's in this other one?" I said jokingly. "Rat poison? A letter bomb?" I ripped the packaging open and a small, heavy object made of polished wood fell into my hand. It was a carving of a horse, wild and free and exquisite.

"But that's beautiful!" exclaimed Sarah. "And there's a card."

The card had a simple flower on the front. Inside, someone had written, *For Evie. Happy Valentine's Day. J.P.*

"J.P.—so it's from Josh," Sarah said quietly.

Sarah and I stared at each other for a fraction of a second. "Sarah—listen, I'm so sorry. I never wanted—"

"It doesn't matter; I'm not stupid. I can see how much he likes you." She sighed. "I guess I've always known that Josh thinks of me as a kid. I've had plenty of time to accept that nothing will ever happen between us. Just because we both liked horses, and he was the only boy around for miles, and we were friends and chatted sometimes . . . Well, it wasn't enough. Like I said, I'm just not the kind of girl guys notice."

"I'm not so sure about that. Cal seemed to notice you all right."

Sarah looked down with a secret, self-conscious expression. "Perhaps he did. Don't worry, Evie; my heart isn't broken, only bruised."

"Oh, Sarah—"

She gave me a warm hug and forced herself to smile. "Don't they say that what doesn't kill you makes you stronger? It's all right, honestly."

"Are you sure?"

"I'm sure." Then she looked serious again. "But what about Josh? Won't he be upset?"

I didn't want to bruise anyone's heart, let alone break it. "It probably doesn't mean that much," I said. "I guess he likes me, and I do like him; he's a really nice guy. But this valentine thing . . . he's probably just being—"

"Being what? Being polite? Don't kid yourself, Evie. I've seen the way he looks at you."

I glanced down at the carved horse in my hand. It must

have taken him hours to make, I thought. It wasn't a gift to be given lightly. I remembered the way he had found Martha's locket and put it on a chain for me, they way he found any excuse to chat whenever I went to the stables, the way he looked at me. . . . I couldn't pretend to myself any longer that Josh was just being friendly. But I couldn't accept his gift.

"Why is everything so complicated?" I groaned. "I'll have to go and talk to him and explain. If anyone asks for me, will you say I've gone to see the nurse with a headache?"

"Sure."

I walked slowly across to the stable yard, hoping that Josh wouldn't be there and yet cursing myself for my cowardice. I would tell him the truth, thank him for the gift, and explain calmly that I had a boyfriend, that was all. But it would be only a fraction of the truth, and I hated lying to him.

"You're deep in thought."

I looked up. Josh was there, right in front of me. He was leading a beautiful white mare across the yard and smiling his golden, welcoming smile.

"Oh . . . Josh . . . hi . . . I mean, that's a lovely horse," I said lamely.

"She's really special. I'm taking very good care of her."

"Who does she belong to?" I asked, glad to talk about anything that wasn't Valentine's Day.

"One of the staff. Miss Scratton."

"Oh." So Miss Scratton did ride after all. She probably got this horse sent to the school so she could follow and spy on us if we went out riding. I hoped she would break her neck.

Josh tethered the horse, giving it a drink from a bucket, then came over to me.

"Are you okay, Evie?"

"Yeah . . . of course."

"It's just that I have the feeling that you've been avoiding me lately, making excuses to cut your classes with me. Do you really dislike riding so much?" He stepped closer and added, "Or is it me that's the problem?"

"No! I don't want you to think that. I . . . I got your card, and the carving. It's beautiful."

"It's beautiful, *but*—isn't that what you're gong to say? So what's the 'but' in all this, Evie?"

"I've already got a boyfriend," I muttered.

Josh took a quick breath, then smiled. "It doesn't surprise me. Who's the lucky guy? Someone back at home?"

"No."

"So he's from around here?" Josh said with a look of astonishment. "Then I must know him."

"Um . . . no . . . you won't know him; he's . . . um . . . It's difficult to explain. . . ." I trailed off unconvincingly.

"Are you sure he really exists, Evie? You don't have to make up some imaginary boyfriend to put me off, you know. If you're not interested I can take a hint."

"It's not that! I do really like you, Josh, but—"

"But you love someone else," he said softly. "Is that it?"

I nodded miserably. "I'm sorry. And the carving was such a sweet gift. I really appreciate it."

"Well, keep it anyway. Maybe it will bring you luck. More luck than I've had."

"Josh, I—"

"I think we've both said enough. Look, it's no big deal. I won't embarrass you again, I promise. In any case, my mom will be back soon, so you won't have to put up with me as your teacher for much longer."

"I'll be sorry," I said. "You've been great."

"So have you." He made as if to go, then turned back. "I just feel worried about you, Evie. Whoever this guy is, it doesn't seem to me that he's making you particularly happy."

Tears sprang unexpectedly to my eyes. Sebastian had

given me a few precious moments of the greatest happiness I had ever known, but loving him had also taught me about pain and fear. How had this happened to me? How had one chance meeting with a boy with laughing blue eyes led me to this? Oh, it was feeble and selfish of me, but for one weak moment I longed to be sensible Evie Johnson again, who laughed at stories about ghosts and vampires and evil spirits, who knew that such things could never exist. I wished I could tell Josh everything. He was good and wise and calm, and I was so tempted to lean on his strength. But I couldn't betray Sebastian's secrets, or my own. I had to be strong without help from anyone else.

"I'm okay, honestly."

"Well, if you ever feel differently, you know where to find me. I want to be your friend, Evie, simple as that. No strings, no pressure. Just friends."

"Oh, Josh, you're so kind. I don't deserve it."

"Hey, don't cry, please, Evie." He put his hands on my shoulders and tried to calm me down. "Come on; it can't be as bad as that." He smudged my tears away and smiled at me. "Even when you're crying you look fantastic."

I tried to laugh everything off and pull myself together, but Josh kept hold of me, his face suddenly different, intense and eager. "Has anyone ever told you that your eyes are the color of the sea?" he whispered. "And your hair is like fire? You're beautiful, Evie."

"And late for class." I wiped my face and blew my nose. "I'm sorry for being stupid."

Josh dropped his arms and stepped away.

"I'm sorry too. I guess 'just friends' don't say that kind of stuff. Forget it. I won't go on like that again."

We both hesitated, awkward and unsure.

"Well, I'd better go," I said, trying to speak normally.

"Yeah. Sure. So . . . will you be there for your lesson next time?"

"Of course," I said. "You're a good teacher. And a good friend."

Josh smiled again, with only a hint of sadness in his eyes. "That's settled then. See you soon."

"See you." He walked off and I waited for a moment, watching him go, then jumped out of my skin. Someone had been watching us from the corner of the stable yard. It was Harriet, her strange old-lady eyes staring at me blankly. She had been there the whole time. Guilt swept over me. I still hadn't spent any time with her, as I had promised. I stepped toward her with a false, bright smile. "Hi, Harriet, what are you doing out here?" But she pretended not to see me and hurried away.

I felt so annoyed with myself. I had let Harriet down, as well as hurting Josh.

Josh. It suddenly hit me. What had he said? Eyes the color of the sea and hair the color of fire . . . red hair . . . the red hair that had been passed to Agnes's descendants . . . I felt under my blouse for the hidden locket that contained the lock of Effie's hair, as bright as a burning flame.

The fire token. That was it. Josh had helped me to solve the mystery, just in time. Hope came crashing over me like the roll of the sea on the shore.

This time I would do it. I would summon the sacred fire. The circle was prepared; the incantations were spoken. I held hands with Sarah and Helen as the candles in the attic room flickered like marsh lights. The powers were coming to me. I felt a crackle of electricity down my spine. I was freeing my mind, willing myself to go beyond the everyday dimensions into secret and unknown realms. . . . *Agnes, help me now.* . . . I was falling, falling into the center of all things.

Helen and Sarah seemed to vanish from sight. I crouched down on the floor, then looked up. I was in the sanctuary again, the cave of white crystal where the pillar of living fire burned without ever diminishing. I approached the flames and felt the heat reach out, ready to engulf me.

"Let me approach the fire!" I called, and the mysterious voice echoed again in the corners of my thoughts. *Go back . . . go back . . . you do not belong. . . .* I opened the locket and took out the burnished lock of hair.

"Here is my claim," I said steadily. "I stand here in the name of Lady Agnes, sister of the fire. This is her sign, her fire token—a lock of her daughter's hair. I am a daughter of that blood, and I reach out now to the sacred flame."

Shielding my eyes, I threw the bright curl into the pillar of fire. It blazed up, brilliant red and bronze and orange, like all the autumns the world has ever known, and then I saw an image of Agnes in the heart of the fire, her hair streaming out, her arms wide in welcome. At last she had shown herself to me; at last she was at my side once more. I had proved worthy of her gift. As I stepped forward joyfully, the flames no longer scorched me but filled me with dazzling light and power. I wanted to stay there forever, burning like a star in the sky, but I heard Agnes say, "Go, my sister; fulfill your task."

I fell to the ground and for a moment lay in a dazed dream. Then I heard voices: "Evie, are you all right? . . ." "Don't disturb her. . . . Let her be. . . ." I raised my head and looked around groggily. The attic under the eaves seemed so dark and small after the vast light and energy I had just witnessed. Helen was kneeling at my side, feeling my pulse. I gently pushed her away and got to my feet.

"I am reborn." I held out my hands in wonder. Tiny white flames danced on my outstretched palms. I threw my hands aloft and the flames shot away and became stars and birds and flowers, shining like jewels in the night.

"You can do it . . ." breathed Sarah.

I laughed recklessly. "I can do anything now. I've seen Agnes again. She's in me now, always. We have both touched the fire. And I'm ready to use her Talisman."

Thirty-eight

The birds were beginning to call to one another as Sarah and I rode to Uppercliffe Farm in the early morning light. We were going to collect the Talisman. There was a fresh, bracing wind, and tight new buds were just beginning to appear in the hedgerows. There was change in the air. Spring wasn't so far away.

My heart was lighter than it had been for so long. For once, I indulged myself as we jogged along, allowing myself to think of what the future might hold when Sebastian was free. I imagined that he was riding next to me on his black horse, the wind blowing his dark hair and ruffling his shirt. I saw his mocking smile as he challenged me to gallop over the hills. I saw us tumbling breathless from our horses and lying close together on the rough grass, sheltering each other from the wide world and all its harshness. . . .

"Hey!" A voice cut across my daydreams. "Wait!"

We halted and looked around. Two other riders were coming nearer, and I recognized Cal and his sister, Rosie. I glanced over at Sarah. "They're out early."

"Well, so are we. It's not a crime."

Cal trotted up, and I could see that he was delighted by the unexpected encounter.

"Hey, Sarah. I didn't think you would be up so early."

"We wanted to see the dawn before school starts. We're allowed to ride out and exercise the ponies as long as we're back in time for breakfast." Sarah smiled. "How are you, Cal? *Sar'shan?* You see, I've been practicing."

"You're doing well." He smiled back. Sarah dismounted and went over to talk to Rosie, who was hanging back shyly. Cal looked pleased, then glanced at me. "I have a message for you."

"What?" I asked, wondering if he could possibly have heard anything about Sebastian. My voice grew urgent. "What is it? Tell me!"

"My mother . . . she was watching you out of the window of the trailer. She said, 'Tell that *gaje* girl with the hair like autumn leaves that she's in danger.'"

"Tell your mother . . . tell her the *gaje* girl said thank you for the warning. But I have to go now. There's something I need to do." I turned to Sarah. "We can't wait around here any longer. Good-bye, Rosie. I hope we see you again."

The little girl looked at me, her gaze straight and direct and untamed. "Did you hear about last night?" she said abruptly. "They came again. They killed another fox."

"That is so sick," said Sarah. "Who on earth would do something like that? And why?"

"Everyone blames us," Rosie answered. "Mother says we might have to leave soon."

"But you can't!" I said to Cal. "You said you had to stay, in case, you know . . . what you told us—in case Fairfax James is looking for you."

"We have to take care of ourselves too," growled Cal. "You don't know what people do to Gypsies when they want them out. Burned trailers. Attacks in the night. We can't risk anything happening to Rosie."

"Let's hope nothing does happen," said Sarah calmly. "I'm sure the police won't let—"

"The police?" he snapped. "What can they do to stop an attack in the night? You need to open your eyes to what life is really like for us, Gypsy girl. Come on, Rosie, let's get out of here."

They began to canter away, churning up the soft ground, but then Cal wheeled back in a wide circle. He pulled up where Sarah was standing, flushed and upset.

"I'm sorry," he said. "I didn't mean that. It wasn't fair. It's just that I want to protect my family. I have to be the man now that my father has gone."

"I understand that," said Sarah.

Cal smiled at her, and the hunted look cleared from his face. "You understand a lot. Come and see Rosie again, if you can. You'll be welcome." Then he looked straight at me. "Didn't you say you had something to do? Don't wait any longer. Time isn't on your side."

He galloped off, and we didn't need any further urging. We rode as swiftly as we could, followed only by the sound of birds calling to greet the dawn. It was getting lighter and we had to hurry. Soon the tumbled remains of Uppercliffe Farm came into view. We scrambled off our ponies' backs and ran up to the door.

"Something feels different," said Sarah, halting by the entrance of the abandoned house.

"So let's get it as quickly as we can and get back to Helen." I pushed past her to the corner of the room where we had buried the Talisman. Kneeling down, I began to scrape at the earth. Soon my hands touched the side of the rusted tin box. I pulled it from the clinging soil and forced it open. A shower of dusty rose petals and a linen pouch fell out onto the earth. But there was nothing else. The box was empty. The Talisman was gone.

More than anything, I felt ashamed. I had made bad decisions; I had let everyone down. Why had I imagined that the Talisman would be safe at Uppercliffe? It could have been taken by anyone—Miss Raglan, Miss Scratton, or any of the other women who surrounded us and who were watching our every move. It could have been taken by hill walkers, poking about curiously in the ruins on the moors. It could have been found by kids, turning up a treasure like magpies, finders keepers.

I hated myself for being so stupid.

Helen and Sarah tried to soothe me and share the blame and dream up plans for getting the necklace back, but I felt curiously distant from them. Our sisterhood could not help me now. This was my failure, not theirs. I had betrayed the trust that Agnes had placed in me when she bequeathed the Talisman to me. I had betrayed Sebastian's hopes, and my own. There was no way we could save Sebastian without the Talisman. There was no time left for second chances. It was too late, and it was my fault.

When this was all over Sarah and Helen would be sorry and grieve, but the agony was mine alone to bear—now, every day, the rest of my life. Forever.

That day seemed to pass by like an old film, slow and unreal, a blur of sound and images. People talked and moved around me like puppets. The hours slipped past. I went to the library and prepared some French exercises for the following day. I saw Harriet, looking tired and anxious, and helped her with her math assignment. *Oh, thank you, Evie; what would I do without you?* The puppets flickered and moved and spoke and I heard and responded, but all the time I was thinking, *I lost the Talisman, I lost the Talisman, it's all my fault....*

"We could go to the attic tonight," Sarah said quietly after supper. "You know, look in the Book for any ideas. It might help."

I shook my head. The Book and its mysteries could no longer help me. It was all over, all finished. This was the end of the story.

There was only one thing left for me to do. I had to see Sebastian, tell him that I had failed, and beg his forgiveness. And I had to do it alone.

Thirty-nine

FROM THE PRIVATE PAPERS OF
SEBASTIAN JAMES FAIRFAX

I am alone.

On the brink of eternity.

This is my reward. My punishment.

Alone—alone in the everlasting night. Soon, the Unconquered will reach out to take me.

Leave me! Let me be! I beg—

No.

There is no one to hear.

There is no one to pity me.

I am nothing. Pain, fire, grief. They are nothing.

Demons in my head and heart.

Temptations.

My heart has died. Only the demons remain. My shadows. My brothers.

I am alone.

There was someone. A girl. I remember—

She is gone. I forget.

Her name, her face, her voice. All gone into the dark.

There are no choices left. No hope. No path ahead. I am broken.

When I am gone, my dearest, sing no sad songs for me. . . .

My dearest.

My darling.

A girl with bright hair. Lost now forever.

Words are all that is left. Hope. Life. Joy. Just words. Only pain and fear are real.

Pain forever. Eternal. Unending.

Everything has faded.

This is how it ends. Alone in the dark—the end—at last—

Forty

This was how it had all started, slipping down the servants' stairs at night to meet Sebastian in secret. It was right that it should end like this too. As I made my way slowly down the back steps, all the stolen hours with Sebastian rushed back to me: times of love and laughter and discovery. I heard his voice; I felt the spell of his blue eyes and the caress of his intense gaze. *You looked like a water nymph saying her prayers. . . . I want to know everything about you. . . . Please see me again. . . . I want this perfect moment together, just the two of us. . . . I never want to hurt you. . . . I love you, girl from the sea. . . .*

I sneaked along the musty passageway and out into the stable yard. I was not going to ride, as I couldn't risk being heard or take the chance of tumbling off. Instead, I would walk, and I was prepared with thick clothes and shoes, a map, and a flashlight. I had even hidden the silver dagger in my pocket, though I wasn't sure what I would do with it. But it had once belonged to Sebastian, and it seemed to offer some kind of protection against any other wanderers in the night. So practical. So sensible. *Sane, sensible Evie.* I thought I had left her behind forever.

Hurrying out of the grounds, I kept in the shadows, trying to stop myself from breaking into an eager run. The sky was veiled by a drift of sluggish clouds. *I can last until the new moon,* Sebastian had told me. Tomorrow night the new moon would rise and Miss Raglan would take control of the coven and swoop down to attack me. *Let them come,* I thought. I no longer had what they wanted. I couldn't give them the Talisman now.

But I didn't want to waste a moment thinking about the coven. I wouldn't let them be part of this night, when Sebastian and I said good-bye. As I strode across the rough tussocks of the sloping moor, the familiar paths glimmered in the starlight, wild and lonely and free. I should have been afraid, out on the moors, alone in the night, but I wasn't. I was part of this place now. I no longer feared or hated these bleak hills where Agnes and Effie and Martha had once walked. Now, in some deep way, Wyldcliffe was my home, and Sebastian was the end of my journey.

Suddenly, a high, inhuman scream tore across the air from the direction of the village, the desperate squeal of an animal in pain. I ducked down instinctively, my heart pounding. What had it been? A fox caught in a trap, or a baby rabbit snatched by an owl? Or something more sinister? A ritual killing: blood and fur and bone torn apart and scattered in the night?

Now I was afraid. I waited, crouching painfully for what seemed an eternity, but the only sound I could hear was the wind in the grass. The sky seemed endless above me, and as I waited the earth seemed to turn under my feet and the wind sang its song of endless yearning.

I couldn't wait forever.

I had to go on.

There were eyes watching me in the dark, someone behind me, tracking me across the moors. . . . I began to run, stumbling on and on until my breath turned to knives in my lungs and my legs were shaking. On and on I raced, until I saw the stately trees that surrounded the hall. I had made it; I was there at last. I passed by the granite monument to Sebastian, half-buried in the hillside above his home. I didn't stop to look. I didn't want to read those words again: *In memory of a beloved son . . . God rest his soul.*

I paused to take deep breaths of cold air and tried to calm down. I forced myself to look behind me. No, there was no one else there. I was alone, ready to face this final task. A low wall separated the grounds from the surrounding slopes. It was easy to scramble over it, then skirt around the lake to reach the back of the house, where the old kitchens and domestic offices had once been. Gritting my teeth, I picked up a stone and smashed a pane in one of the low windows, then forced the casement open and scrambled inside. I turned the flashlight on and groped forward, finding my way to the silent hallway. As I crept up the carpeted staircase, the dusty portraits stared down disapprovingly. I was a thief, an intruder, a stranger, but my heart belonged here. I stumbled farther in the dark and at last I reached the foot of the secret steps that led to Sebastian's hiding place.

"Sebastian?" I called softly. "Sebastian, it's me, Evie."

The silence was as deep and cold as a well. I began to climb, shining the light ahead of me, until I reached the top. The tiny attic room was full of the same confusion of drapes and furniture and broken equipment, but the low couch was empty and the air was stale. I swept the beam of light over to the corner. Sebastian wasn't there. A heap of papers lay on the desk. Snatching them up, I saw that there were pages and pages of them, all addressed to me: beautiful, broken love letters, the diary of his torment. I scanned them eagerly.

> *It's because I love you that I had to tell you the truth.*
> *You know everything now, Evie . . .*

I read them eagerly, greedily, then turned to the last page. The writing was badly formed and jagged, as though it had been painful for Sebastian even to hold the pen;

> *Words are all that is left. Hope. Life. Joy. Just*
> *words. Only pain and fear are real.*
> *Pain forever. Eternal. Unending.*
> *Everything has faded.*
> *This is how it ends.*
> *Alone in the dark—the end—at last—*

As my eyes devoured the words, my heart seemed to split in two.

I was too late, after all.

Forty-one

Now the house seemed full of menacing, unnamed threats. I was there alone, and Sebastian was gone. Where was he? Had he ... had he already come to the end of his tortured journey and faded from this world altogether? I couldn't believe it—I didn't want to believe it. I would have known; surely there would have been some sign, some message.

Perhaps, like an animal, Sebastian had crawled away into a lonely corner to face his end, his final moments before his masters snatched him into eternal bondage. Or perhaps the end had not yet come and he was lying ill in one of the other rooms, fading and helpless as the demon spirits hovered, getting ready for the final blow.

I drew the dagger from my pocket and held it tight, then crept down the stairs. "Sebastian? Sebastia-a-an!" My voice cracked and was swallowed up by the dark. I hurried back down to the ground floor and flitted through the grand public rooms: a drawing room of shrouded mirrors and dull gold brocade; a rich red dining room set out with a long mahogany table, where no one would ever dine again; a music room, where a piano waited for the touch of the long-dead hands; and the library, lined with a thousand books.

The library. I hesitated outside the door. It was standing ajar, and a flickering light glowed within. I slowly pushed the door open and stepped inside. A fire was burning in the grate. The books, the desks, the leather chairs, everything was the same as before. I walked over to the fire and looked up at the portraits of Sebastian's parents that hung over the carved mantelpiece. "If you can hear me, please help me," I begged.

"They cannot hear you."

I stifled a scream and whirled around. Sebastian was standing on the far side of the room, his eyes burning. There was blood on his face, and his breath rattled. He seemed to emit a shadow, a dark aura that sucked away life and light and hope. But he was still there; there was still time. . . .

"Sebastian," I sobbed, and stepped toward him, but he flung his arm up like a shield.

"Do not touch me! Do not come near me."

"Why not? What's happening?"

"My destiny. Soon, very soon I will be . . . a demon. I am almost there."

I felt I would go crazy with grief and fear and guilt, and sank onto one of the low chairs in front of the fire. "I'm so sorry, Sebastian, I'm so sorry. I came to tell you. I tried so hard, but I failed."

"You have failed." he repeated in a ghastly, dead voice. "You are sorry." Then he looked across the room and his eyes narrowed. "My memory . . . there was a girl . . . like you . . . a girl from the sea. She was going to save me. It is too late. By midnight tomorrow I will no longer be in this world." Then he staggered forward, shielding his eyes, gasping like a child. "I'm so afraid."

I couldn't bear to see him like that. I had been so convinced that I would rescue Sebastian that I hadn't allowed myself to think that I would fail. Even now, I couldn't let myself give up. "I will save you, Sebastian. I'll find a way somehow; we have one more day—we have tomorrow."

"It was you then?" His eyes flickered over me. "You are . . . that girl?"

"Yes, it's me, Evie. Oh, Sebastian, don't you remember?"

He clutched his head and gave a terrible cry. "Evie . . . Evie, it's you. . . ." The next moment he flew across the room and took me in his arms, holding me as though nothing would ever part us. "You're here; you've come back; oh God, don't ever leave me again."

"I won't, I promise," I replied joyfully, yet the sight of his gaunt face pulled me back to reality. "Sebastian, I have to tell you something. It's about the Talisman."

"Don't speak of it! If you knew how it has tormented my dreams—but I made a promise, didn't I, Evie?" he murmured. "I will fade, so that you can live. I swore it. Eternal slavery for me, in exchange for life for you." He kissed my forehead, then stepped back and let me go with a twisted smile. The red light of the hearth seemed to glow in his eyes, and a change came over his face. He stared at me strangely, and now there was no recognition in his eyes. "A fine bargain indeed."

"Sebastian—"

"Sebastian, Sebastian," he echoed mockingly. "Did you come to watch my final moments? Did you come to rejoice that I kept my promise?" He laughed. "But I do not choose to keep it. I do not choose to fade. Give me the Talisman!"

"I can't. I don't have it; that's what I had to tell you. The Talisman is lost—"

"Liar!" He pinned me against the wall as though possessed with a manic strength. "Give it to me! My last, my only hope. I will escape this torment, even now at this late hour. I will become the destroyer, not the destroyed. I will kill you in order to save myself."

"No, Sebastian," I pleaded. "No!"

"I did not understand then," he snarled. "I did not know this torment. Now that I can see into the abyss, I do not choose to become a slave. I do not condemn myself to wither and fade. I will become one of the mighty Unconquered and live as a king in the everlasting night. And you will help me, as you promised. Give me the heirloom that Agnes bequeathed to you."

"I can't...."

"You mean you won't? It should have been mine anyway; Agnes would have wanted me to have it...." Sebastian put his hands around my neck, searching for the Talisman, gripping me cruelly. "What's this?" he cried, as he found Martha's locket. "Where is the Talisman? You . . . you dare to cheat me—betray me?"

In desperation I groped for the dagger in my pocket to try to defend myself, but he was too quick for me. He twisted it out of my hand with an agonizing wrench and pressed the blade against my throat.

"You will give me the Talisman," he growled, "not this worthless trash." Tearing the locket from around my neck, Sebastian flung it in fury on the glowing embers in the fireplace. All at once a dazzling flame shot up from the hearth and a voice echoed, "I am with you, my sister. . . ."

I saw a circle of brilliant white fire in my mind, and I heard Agnes speak the word of power. Then I spoke it aloud, and a wall of flames sprang up around me like bright trees, and Sebastian was thrown to the other side of the room. He reached out for me again, screaming, "No, no, no! Come back!" But the fire swept me away from him like a shooting star, as I was taken far beyond the limits of the world and into a sea of never-ending light. . . .

When I opened my eyes, I was huddled against the wrought-iron gates that led to the school. "No, no, no . . ." I sobbed.

No, no, no . . . Come back, come back, come back. . . .

I hardly knew where I was, or what I said. I knew only

that Sebastian had finally betrayed me, and that our love was at an end.

There are many kinds of betrayals. There are the small ones: the unkind word, the laughter behind someone's back, the petty lies. And there are the betrayals that break hearts, destroy worlds, and turn the strong, sweet light of day into bitter dust.

Forty-two

The birds were awake and the sky was getting light. I forced myself to move. As I stood up I heard the soft clop of hooves in the lane. For one crazy moment I thought it was Sebastian coming to find me, but I saw the familiar figure of Josh, riding up to the school on his gray horse for the start of the new day. He saw me and quickly dismounted.

"Evie, what on earth are you doing out here? What's the matter?"

I threw myself into his arms and began to weep, as though I were drowning in sorrow.

"There, there, Evie, it's all right; I'm here. . . ." He rocked me gently, like a child, and eventually the storm passed. My tears were over.

"I'm . . . I'm so sorry, Josh," I stammered. "I'd better get back to school. I'll be in trouble if they find out I'm not there."

"Aren't you in bigger trouble than that already?" Josh asked. "What's going on, Evie? I guess you've been sneaking out to see this boyfriend of yours. If he's upsetting you—"

"No," I said quickly. "Nothing like that. It's . . . it's not his fault."

"So what is it?"

I sighed. "I wish I could tell you, but you'd think I was crazy."

"Just try me."

I looked up at his honest face and saw that there was real concern in his eyes. I longed to be able to open my heart to him.

"The thing is . . . I'm worried about my boyfriend. He's . . . well, he's sick. And I'm so worried. I don't know what's going to happen."

"I'm sorry to hear he's ill. But isn't he getting any help? Aren't his parents taking care of him?"

I didn't say anything. I didn't want to lie to Josh, but the truth was impossible. Cold and tired and miserable, I began to walk down the drive to the school. Josh followed me, leading his horse.

"I know that you don't want to tell me about it, Evie, but I wish you didn't have to keep everything a secret like this." He glanced up at the hills that encircled the school. "This place has always been full of secrets. I don't just mean all that stuff about Lady Agnes and her ghost. There's other talk too. Weird stuff. But the truth comes out eventually."

"Isn't that just silly gossip?" I said wearily.

"I'm not so sure. There are stories that there's some kind of mysterious cult based here—women worshippers who follow a pagan master, like a coven."

"A c-coven?" I stared at him, flushed and amazed.

"Evie, I'm right, aren't I?" Josh exclaimed. "Are you mixed up with all this? Are you in danger?"

"Y-you can't believe all that stuff," I stammered, trying to hide my feelings.

"I've lived on these hills all my life. They are full of mystery, like the stars and the rain and the sea. We know so little, really. I've learned that everything and anything is possible."

"Yes," I whispered.

"So who is this boy you're seeing? Does he have anything to do with these women?"

I felt so torn. I wanted to tell him, but I couldn't.

"Of course not," I blustered. "And look, I really must hurry back to school. If anyone sees me I'll say I got up early for a walk. Thank you so much, Josh, I'll see you later."

We had reached the stable yard.

I turned to go, but he caught my hand and gently drew me to him. "Look, Evie, I know your heart is somewhere else, but I want you to know that you can come to me if you need help." He looked at me as if trying to read my thoughts, and then he smiled. "I see you're still wearing the locket."

I lifted my hand automatically to my throat. "Oh . . . yes . . ."

But I had seen it being thrown into the fire, tarnished by the heat. The chain had been broken, and yet now it was whole again, and the battered little locket lay quietly against my skin. Another mystery.

"Evie . . . oh, Evie, thank God—where have you been?" Sarah and Helen came running up. "Are you okay?"

"She's tired and upset," Josh said lightly. "I'll let you look after her." He swung away, whistling under his breath, and Sarah dragged me into Bonny's warm stable.

"I woke up early and just knew that you weren't in the school," she said.

"We've been frantic about you," exclaimed Helen. "What happened?"

I told them everything, reliving each painful moment of the scene with Sebastian.

"He didn't want me in the end. It was the Talisman he wanted," I said, trying to keep my voice from shaking. "And now this is Sebastian's last day. I thought it was all going to be so different. But it was all for nothing. Everything that happened between us . . . he has forgotten it all. He's forgotten that he ever loved me. And now . . . now it will happen, just like he said. He'll become a . . ." I couldn't say it. I began to cry again.

Helen took my hand. "Remember there are other powers at work," she said. "We don't see the whole pattern. It's still not too late."

"Like Agnes said, even death isn't the end," murmured Sarah.

"But this isn't death, is it?" I said, almost crushed by misery. "Agnes died, and we know she has moved on in the journey; she lives in light in the next world, as the Creator planned. But Sebastian . . ." I fought for breath, then forced myself to speak the terrible words. "Sebastian will become a demon for all eternity, beyond the reach of prayers or hope. Endless night, endless suffering, lost to

God, lost to humanity. Lost to me. Don't talk to me about death! Death is a gift, a gateway and a release. This . . . this is evil beyond death!"

We fell silent; then I made the effort to speak again. "Look, I'm sorry. There's no point in talking about Sebastian. The new moon will rise and it will all be over. I thought he loved me. I thought I could save his immortal soul. I was wrong on both counts. But thank you for trying to help me. You've been amazing."

"We're still here for you, Evie," said Sarah, "if there is anything we can do."

"Sisters to the end," added Helen.

There was nothing else to say.

I walked across the stable yard and headed for my dorm to get changed. The rest of the girls had already gone to breakfast. I would be late for class, but I didn't care. What did anything matter anymore? I had to learn to live again without Sebastian, without hope and without love.

Forty-three

Everything on the third floor was quiet, apart from the swish of a broom as one of the cleaning women began to sweep the floor of the corridor. I walked past her and went straight to my dorm. I pushed the door open, then stopped in amazement. Someone was crouching over the small cupboard next to my bed, going through all my private stuff. It was Harriet.

"What the . . . ?"

Lying in a heap on the bed were my letters from Dad, my precious photographs from home, and several sheets of paper covered with small black script—Agnes's writing. Her journal had been ripped to pieces and scattered like leaves in the wind.

"Hey! Stop! What do you think you're doing?" I rushed

over to Harriet and dragged her away from my things.

"I wanted to find my necklace," she whined. "Someone told me it was you who took it for a joke that time it went missing."

I stared at Harriet in total disbelief. "Why on earth would I do that? Of course I don't have your necklace! Who told you that?"

"Celeste. She said she'd seen you hide it in your cupboard."

"Celeste? Celeste?" I stormed. "You chose to believe her after everything I've done for you?" All my fear and grief boiled up and poured out like poison. "How dare you touch my things without asking me? And look what you've done to this book—that was totally irreplaceable. I'll never forgive you for this!" I gathered the pieces of Agnes's diary together with shaking hands and tried to smooth out the torn pages. Harriet sat on the bed, her shoulders slumped and her head bowed.

"I'm sorry, Evie. I don't know what made me do it." She began to complain self-pityingly. "I really don't feel right: I hear things; I can't sleep. There's this voice in my head all the time—"

"Oh, be quiet!" I snapped. I had never, ever been so angry.

"But, Evie . . ."

I marched out of the dorm, still shaking with rage. I had never liked this girl; I had forced myself to be kind, to help her, and how had she repaid me? After all that stuff about wanting to connect with Agnes and wanting to be friends with me and being lonely and voices in her head—it was a pile of self-indulgent, attention-seeking garbage, and I had had enough. She ran after me.

"Please, Evie, I need to tell you. It's getting worse. I'm scared. . . ."

"Leave me alone!"

"But I need to talk to you, and you said I could—"

I whirled around and glared at her, hating her timid, sallow face and her scared-looking eyes. "I never want to talk to you again."

"What do you mean?" she said, looking shocked.

"Exactly what I said. Go and find someone else's stuff to trash, Harriet, because I don't ever want you coming anywhere near me again. Is that clear?"

Her mouth drooped and her dull skin became flushed with red blotches. She looked crumpled and useless and utterly pathetic. I felt my anger begin to cool, but she burst into tears and pushed past me, then ran clumsily down the marble stairs.

"Harriet, wait . . ."

It was too late. She was gone.

I felt sick with exhaustion, and secretly ashamed of myself. Then I remembered the torn journal that I was still clutching, and a wave of self-pity washed over me. I couldn't face going down to the classroom. I hurried over to the curtained alcove that led to the secret stairs and shut myself into the old servants' quarters, cut off from the rest of the school. Feeling my way in the dark, I crawled up the narrow steps to the attic and let myself into Agnes's secret study. Then I sat at her desk and laid my head on my arms, and allowed myself to leave this world as I fell into the embrace of a deep, dreamless sleep.

When I woke up, I didn't know where I was. For an instant I thought I was back at home in the cottage, but as I groped to light a candle that stood on the desk, I remembered everything. The burden of unhappiness settled onto me again like a great weight. I sat staring at the dancing candle flame, and realized there was nothing I could do about the way I felt. I had to live like this now, with this pain. My hands shook and my eyes were sore and my guts ached, but I had to go on living. I had to eat and sleep and study and be with people. There was no alternative. I had read books and magazines about girls who "couldn't live" without their perfect boyfriend, but I knew that it wasn't like that. Even when you're so unhappy that nothing is real, life doesn't stop.

I looked around the little room crammed with Agnes's possessions and wondered if I would ever come up here again. The jars of herbs and candles and secret ingredients hadn't given me what I had been looking for. The Mystic Way had failed me, or perhaps I had failed the Mystic Way. I found a piece of bright silk on one of the shelves and wrapped the torn fragments of Agnes's journal in it. I didn't need it anymore. As I opened the drawer of the desk to hide the little bundle away, I remembered that we had hidden the Book there too. I hesitated, then picked up the heavy, leather-bound volume. The silver letters on the cover seemed to glow like slivers of moonlight. A way of healing and power . . . I needed healing so badly. I flicked through the pages and the Book fell open of its own accord. I saw an image of an angel, side by side with a hooded skeleton. *The Gift of Death* . . .

For one terrible instant, the memory of Harriet lying crumpled at the bottom of the marble steps flashed into my mind. I could choose to leap down to those mesmerizing black-and-white tiles, throwing myself away like a sacrificed pawn in a great game of chess. Then the pain would be over. I would never hurt again. I shut the Book roughly and thrust it into the drawer with Agnes's journal.

No. I would never do that. That would not be the end of my story. I had to go on living, however much it hurt, just as Sebastian now had to face his fate. I glanced at my watch. I had slept through the day. It would be dark outside, the darkest night I had ever known. The new moon would rise like a silver promise. At midnight Sebastian would pass into the shadows forever, and there was nothing I could do about it. I stood up and slowly made my way downstairs, back to school. Back to reality.

Sarah and Helen were talking quietly by the fire in the entrance hall when I reached the bottom of the marble steps. They looked up anxiously and drew me over to the glowing hearth. "You're so cold!" Sarah said. "We told the staff you'd gone to the nurse with a headache this morning. Hopefully they won't check up on it. Oh, Evie, we're so sorry—"

The great front door suddenly blew open, and a blast of wind and rain spattered across the threshold. A storm was brewing outside, and the trees were swaying in the driving wind.

"Close that door, Evie!" said Miss Hetherington, who was passing through the hall. "It's going to be a wild night."

I shut the door as she told me, but not before I glimpsed the slender arc of the moon, riding high behind the scudding clouds.

We hung about aimlessly, then went to the library, hoping to find somewhere quiet to sit together before the bell rang for bedtime. I was thankful that the library was empty, and I remembered vaguely that there was a music recital being held in the school that evening. I guessed most of the students had gone there after dinner.

"You haven't eaten all day, Evie. You'd better have some of this."

Sarah passed me a bar of chocolate. I wasn't hungry, but I tried to eat some to please her while Helen stared abstractedly into space. There was nothing to say, nothing to do, nowhere to go. It was like waiting for bad news at a hospital, or sitting by the telephone and dreading that it would ring. As each minute passed, a tiny voice in my head started to drone. *Are you really just going to sit here? There's still some time left. Time enough for a miracle. Time to do something.*

There's nothing I can do, I answered myself wearily, but the voice started up again in a never-ending circle. *But are you really just going to sit here? There's still time . . . time . . . time. . . .*

The clock in the library chimed nine. I woke from my

reverie. I noticed that the sound of the wind outside had grown, until it was like an angry beast prowling around the school. There was a muffled crash. Sarah looked up. "Sounds like slates falling off the roof. It's a really bad storm."

The door of the library opened and a young girl came in, blinking and looking about her. I recognized her as a girl in Harriet's form. "Um . . . are you Evie Johnson?"

"Yeah."

"Then this is for you." She handed me a folded note, then scurried out again. An almighty crash of thunder rattled the building, and the lights flickered and went out. We could hear the sounds of startled screams and shouts in the corridors and distant rooms as the school was plunged into complete blackness.

"It's a power outage," said Helen. "Hang on." She rummaged in her bag and found her little flashlight and switched it on. "That's better. I guess the staff will organize candles and stuff until the power comes back on."

"Should we go and see if they need any help with the young kids?" asked Sarah. "Some of them might be scared."

"Wait, let me read this note first." I held it under Helen's flashlight and scanned the scribbled words.

Dear Evie,

After what you said this morning I can't go on. The voices in my head are getting worse. I don't know how to go on living. Do you remember I said I wanted to go out into the hills and fall asleep in the snow and never wake up? The snow has gone but it is still cold by Agnes's grave. I have a knife. They say you only have to make a tiny cut and it is enough; then you wait for the end to come. Good-bye. I will not bother you again. I'm sorry I let you down.

Harriet Templeton

"Oh, God . . ." I could hardly believe it. I felt faint as I read the note again, trying to make sense of it all. Harriet couldn't go on. . . . Now I bitterly regretted the harsh words I had spoken to her. But how could I have known she would get so desperate? "Oh, my God . . . we've got to do something. I've got to help her."

"Should we call the police?" asked Helen, her eyes round and anxious in the torchlight. "Or a doctor or someone?"

"The phone lines will be down with the power outage," said Sarah. "What about the staff, one of the mistresses—"

"No!" I said. "There's no one we can trust. They don't

care about the girls, anyway, and explaining it to them will only cause more delay. We'll have to go ourselves. If Harriet has only just left we might be able to stop her before she does anything stupid. We can get her back to school before anyone knows anything about it, what with all this confusion in the storm. Then we'll get in touch with her mother somehow. That's who she really needs."

Suddenly, I needed my mother too. *Please help me*, I prayed silently, as we hurried down the unlit corridors to one of the many side entrances. We passed a cloakroom and grabbed some coats at random from the pegs, then plunged outside. The rain lashed into my face, and the icy wind took my breath away. The storm was raging all around us as we raced toward the long drive that led to the wrought-iron gates and the village beyond, where the grave of Lady Agnes lay under the yew trees in the churchyard. All the brave messengers of spring that had been announcing themselves in the last few days—the tiny green shoots, the first trembling new leaves—would be torn to pieces that night. *Please let us be there in time*, I begged. I hadn't been able to save Sebastian, but perhaps I could at least reach Harriet, poor sad Harriet with her sick and fevered mind.

As soon as we were out of sight of the school, Helen

enfolded us in her powers, and a moment later we arrived at the lonely churchyard. The black trees swayed in the wild wind, and the little cottages in the village beyond were wrapped in darkness.

"Harriet? Harriet!"

The only answer was the sobbing of the wind and the groaning of the trees.

Passing the rows of slanting tombstones, we hurried to where a single grave was set slightly apart from the others. It was an old-fashioned tomb of stone, surmounted by a statue of an angel. The angel's face had worn away over the years, and now it looked down with a blank expression, holding a scroll carved with a simple inscription:

LADY AGNES TEMPLETON,

BELOVED OF THE LORD

Harriet was standing in the rain with her back to us, staring at the angel. And slumped at the foot of the statue like a dying man, looking up at her in horror, was Sebastian.

Forty-four

Sebastian?"

He raised his haggard white face to mine. I didn't know what to think or feel or do, and for a moment I stood paralyzed. Then Sebastian raised his hand and pointed to Harriet, gasping. "No . . . no . . . no . . ."

"Harriet, what's happening?" I cried. "What are you doing?" Harriet turned to me with a peculiar smile on her face. She was clutching Sebastian's silver dagger in her hand, and she passed it lightly over her wrist.

"No—wait!" Sarah shouted. But Harriet let the blade cut her skin. A single drop of blood fell from her wrist onto Agnes's grave. Harriet's face began to convulse, her eyes rolling in her head. A strangled noise came from deep inside her. "I . . . am . . . not . . . Harriet. . . ." Her breath curled and thickened in the wind like smoke. "I . . . am . . . Celia . . . Hartle."

The smoke grew into a billowing shape full of flickering fire. Harriet screamed and fell back unconscious, and Mrs. Hartle emerged from the thick fumes, dreadfully thin and scarred, but terrifyingly real. She clicked her fingers and the silver dagger flew from Harriet's hand to her own.

"So. Here we are again," she said silkily. "The High Mistress and her devoted students."

We stumbled backward, stunned and horrified. I feverishly called out in my mind to Agnes, trying to summon her fire to attack our enemy, but the High Mistress laughed as though she could read my thoughts. She flashed the dagger, making swift patterns in the air, and ropes flew from its point and bound our hands behind our backs. We fell to our knees before her, and a fog seemed to choke my mind and will. Both fire and water were beyond my reach, and I was helpless before Mrs. Hartle's hypnotic gaze.

"Dear Evie," she crooned. "So kind, so considerate, trying to save poor little Harriet—while all the time she was my creature, not your friend. Oh, you weakened me last term, I admit that. It was well done, most impressive."

She spoke lightly, but I sensed the anger inside her, like a snake, as she stroked the scar on her face. "But even though you had weakened me, I was able to linger in Wyldcliffe's secret places until you returned, bringing this pathetic girl with you. It was easy to enter her feeble mind and body and bend her will to do my bidding. She fed me, sacrificing animals that I used in ancient rituals, drinking their blood until I was fully restored. And dear Harriet was a most useful spy. She found out where you had hidden this."

Mrs. Hartle cut the air with her knife, and the next moment the Talisman hung from the blade, glinting in the fitful moonlight.

"Harriet would have killed you if I had told her to, while I inhabited her mind. But I wanted to keep your death for this moment." The High Mistress laughed exultantly. "Let me tell you how I have outwitted you at every turn, Miss Johnson. Last night I followed you to Fairfax Hall and you led me to Sebastian. I had searched long for him, but his only defense—his nauseating love for you—had repelled me. But once he turned his back on you, those defenses were destroyed and it was easy to take him. He is no longer my master. I rule over him now, not the other way around. Next, I worked through Harriet to destroy the papers Agnes left you—yes, I know all about them. I knew that this would anger you beyond any other thing and turn you against your poor, weak friend. Then I drove her to write that suicide note, knowing equally well that good, kind, noble Evie would not be able to resist its cry for help. Quite the little martyred heroine, aren't you? Always trying to save others. And now you need saving yourself."

She seemed to tower over me, and I shrank back, dreading her touch. But with a quick, deft movement she turned to Sebastian and slipped the Talisman over his head, laughing as he writhed with the pain of it. "Sebastian won't lift a finger to help you now, Evie. He will never return to your clinging embrace. He will destroy you, awaken the Talisman, and deliver me and my Sisters from death forever."

"No . . . no . . . no . . . ." Sebastian groaned. Mrs. Hartle ignored him and walked up to Helen.

"Ah, my daughter, so we meet again, here at the Traitor's grave," she taunted. "Why do you not greet your mother?"

Helen jerked her head away. "You're not my mother! You've never been a mother to me. My mother is the air and the wind and the stars. I despise you."

Mrs. Hartle's face grew thunderous. "By the end of this night you will acknowledge me as both your mother and your mistress, to be obeyed and feared. I have everything I need. The only thing missing is my circle of Dark Sisters—I wish them to see and share this moment. You will all come with me to where my Sisters are waiting." She looked around crazily and called out to the wind, "I come, my Sisters, I come!"

At that moment Sebastian raised his head and murmured, "My brothers . . . my brothers . . ."

He looked straight at me, and I saw that his eyes were clear and blue and brimming with an ocean of regret. And then he smiled, and his smile was no longer bitter or mocking, but clear and calm like a summer's day.

"Sebastian!" I tried to reach him, but the High Mistress screamed and flashed her knife in the air, and we were dragged away from the churchyard into a terrifying vortex of noise and speed and black, whirling stars.

Forty-five

We were thrown out of the whirlwind onto a barren hilltop. A hostile, storm-racked landscape stretched around us. Through the pain and shock I recognized the place. It had once been a fort, built hundreds of years ago by the people of the valley as a stronghold against their enemies. And before that it had been a pagan temple, as near to the heavens as the ancient worshipers could get. Here I had once sat with Sebastian under the deep midnight sky, and here, it seemed, the High Mistress would play out her moment of triumph.

The wind tore across the hills and parted the clouds and the high, pure arc of the new moon shone down. A crowd of cloaked and hooded figures stood around us, chanting in a circle like a gathering swarm. They didn't seem to be able to see us. We were hidden by Mrs. Hartle's paralyzing will, still unable to speak or move or think clearly. As she stood shrouded in mist, watching her Sisters, everything swam in front of my eyes like a haunted dream.

"This is the hour," one of the women intoned. It was Miss Raglan. She stepped forward from the ranks of the coven and raised her arms to the moon. "Our moment of destiny is upon us."

"Only the High Mistress can lead the coven to its destiny," replied a cool, dry voice, and I recognized Miss Scratton under the veil of her cloak.

"No doubt you want that honor for yourself!" snapped Miss Raglan angrily. "But our Sisters have seen through your plots. You will never lead this coven. Here and now, by the light of the moon, surrounded by the wild elements, I shall become the new High Mistress and achieve our long quest!"

The crowd behind her began to roar their approval, and a frenzied chanting began, but Miss Scratton shouted, "Fool! Do you not know that this coven still has a High Mistress? And that she is here among you?"

The chanting faltered, and there was another tremendous crack of lightning. It seemed to tear away the veil that had hidden us from the women's sight. They cried out as they saw Mrs. Hartle standing cold and proud and terrible in the night.

"It is I," said the High Mistress. "I have returned at last." There was a moment of confusion as exclamations ran through the crowd. "The High Mistress! She has returned!"

"Why do you not bow before me? Is there no loyalty among you? Did it take such a short time for you to forget your true mistress?"

"Welcome, welcome, we have longed for this moment," gushed one of the women, and I recognized the sycophantic voice of Miss Dalrymple, quick to abandon her former ally and throw herself at Mrs. Hartle's feet.

"I . . . We . . ." gabbled Miss Raglan, as the Dark Sisters made deep bows to her rival. "We thought you were dead!"

The High Mistress laughed wildly as lightning cracked across the sky and rain lashed the earth. "Celia Hartle will never taste death! After our defeat in the crypt, I confess that I was wounded. The elemental powers that were turned against me stripped me of my strength. So I hid, choosing not to show myself in my weakened state. But I have not studied the secret rites all these years for

nothing. And now here I am, back to claim my triumph."
Mrs. Hartle moved closer to Miss Raglan, and her voice
became a honeyed river of menace. "It will not be you who
brings our labors to fulfillment. Oh, I watched you. I saw
your lack of faith in me. For loyalty I bring rewards; for
betrayal—curses." She clicked her fingers and Miss Raglan staggered back and whimpered, as though reeling from
a savage blow.

Mrs. Hartle turned to Miss Scratton. "You have done
better. I am pleasantly surprised. Your reward will be of
another sort." Miss Scratton didn't move, except to bow
her head and lower her eyes.

"But all judgments can wait," Mrs. Hartle went on.
"The night draws deep. At midnight all will be fulfilled.
The foolish girls who dared to rise against me are prison-
ers at my feet. And I bring you another prize—our former
master. He is ready to do our bidding." She kicked Sebastian viciously, then forced him to his knees. The Talisman
swung heavily around his neck, like a great burden. "Pre-
pare the girl."

The cloaked women dragged Helen and Sarah away.
Miss Scratton stepped swiftly over to me and made me
kneel opposite Sebastian. Now we faced each other, as
though we were going to be betrothed in some mystical

ceremony. Evie and Sebastian, together again at last, but now only one of us could survive. The rain wept over us. The last minutes of the day were dying. Soon the bell would toll for midnight. Sebastian's head hung down and he swayed slightly. I couldn't see his face. It was better like that, I thought, better not to see the end.

My mind was slow and blurred, as though I had been stripped of my own self by the High Mistress's overpowering will. I was helpless against her. Celia Hartle had won, and I had lost, and there was nothing I could do about it. She pushed the silver dagger into Sebastian's grasp. Holding his weakened hands in her own, she raised the dagger over me. "When this strikes your heart, the Talisman will be his, and immortality will be ours!" Then she turned to Miss Scratton with her final order. "Sister, make her ready for the end."

Miss Scratton bent down and tore my shirt open, laying my neck bare for the bite of the knife. As she leaned over me, I thought I heard her whisper, "Your necklace, Evie, give her your necklace. . . ."

I looked up at her, suddenly jerked awake from my lethargy and despair. My necklace . . . the little locket . . . it still hung, small and insignificant, around my neck. I stared into Miss Scratton's eyes. *I can't believe it*, Sarah had said. *Any of the others, but not Miss Scratton . . .* And as I looked into those cool, pitying eyes, I recognized her at last. A wise woman, a holy sister, a healer . . .

"Come! Out of the way!" said Mrs. Hartle impatiently. "Let the blow be struck!"

"Your necklace, Evie, your necklace . . ." Miss Scratton whispered again.

Without stopping to think, I grabbed the little chain and twisted it until it snapped, then flung the locket at Mrs. Hartle.

It soared across the space between us in a wide arc and burst into flames with a dazzling light. Mrs. Hartle screamed, and her will and concentration wavered for a moment. The ropes around our wrists melted away, and Sebastian struggled to his feet.

"My brothers," he cried. "Ride, my brothers! Ride!"

All at once, the air was alive with the sound of hooves beating the ground. I looked behind me and saw Cal galloping wildly up the slope, leading a band of ghostly riders. Their horses flew over the turf like enchanted shadows, like a dream I'd once had . . . a long-ago dream. . . . The wild Gypsy riders were back from the dead to haunt the living, keeping their old vows to be true to their brother Fairfax James. The Dark Sisters began to howl in anger as

Sarah and Helen cheered the riders on.

"How dare you!" Mrs. Hartle screeched insanely. "Get back! Get back!"

Sebastian stood tall and unafraid. "Ride, my brothers! Ride to our aid!" His beauty shone through the mask of his pain, and his blue eyes flashed like stars.

This is the moment; you can do it, Evie; you can do anything. . . . Agnes was calling me, and my mother, and Frankie, telling me to believe in myself, telling me to fight for what I loved.

I flung open my arms and welcomed the rain. It drove down at my command like a flight of stinging arrows and blinded Mrs. Hartle for one precious moment. I lunged forward and knocked the dagger out of her hands, then pulled Sebastian toward me. Snatching the blade from the ground, I slashed the turf at our feet until we were standing in a protected circle, just the two of us. The noise and confusion of the hilltop fell away as though a curtain of water hung between us and the rest of the world.

Time seemed to stop. We were alone.

Sebastian fell to his knees in front of me, exhausted by his efforts. "Forgive me, Evie," he pleaded. "I can't explain the madness that overtook me last night. I only know that it has passed now, forever, whatever happens next. When you turned the power of fire against me last night it burned the fear from my soul. I was myself again. I called my brothers—to help you." He dragged the Talisman from around his neck and pressed it into my hand. "This . . . this is yours. Protect yourself with it. Forgive me."

I knelt down next to him.

"There's nothing to forgive, Sebastian. Nothing."

He held my hand to his lips for a moment. "All I can do . . . is say good-bye—before my master comes." His voice faded to a sigh. "I'm glad—so glad—that you are with me, my girl from the sea."

Sebastian sank to the ground and closed his eyes. I gently lifted his head and laid it in my lap. As his life in this world ebbed to its final flicker, I felt more alive than I ever had before. This was the moment that I would save Sebastian, and nothing would stop me now.

Forty-six

I held the Talisman up and called out, "Lord of all creation, hear me! I summon your sacred elements! Let their powers be my powers; let their justice be my justice; let their light shine on me!"

A crack of electricity leaped from the sparkling jewel.

"I serve the living waters and the eternal fire," I cried. "I claim my right to approach the sacred flame!" Everything began to spin and I seemed to fall a long way, falling endlessly. Then I was alone in the deep cavern of crystal that I had seen before. The pillar of fire twisted and turned in front of me, and a voice spoke from its depths.

"You are welcome, sister. You may approach."

I plunged the Talisman into the heart of the flame and cried, "I release you!"

And then . . . and then . . . I was light and air and fire. I was all my past and all my future. I was myself and yet I was Agnes too. She was standing by my side, and I had her memories, her thoughts, her knowledge. Scenes from her life flashed through my mind at top speed. As Agnes, I seemed to feel again the joy of Sebastian's return from his journey abroad; I saw him press the Book into my hands; I felt the touch of his kiss; I felt the pain that Agnes felt as he descended into the dark. I saw everything through her eyes. I understood everything. I forgave everything, as Agnes had done before me.

The fire burned inside me. Now I knew every one of its secrets; I understood its powers that would heal and cleanse, bringing life and strength. But I knew more than that. *The fire of our desires . . . the power of love . . . stronger than life . . . stronger than death . . .* Now I knew what Agnes had preserved in the Talisman. She had no anger for Sebastian's weaknesses and mistakes, only love and forgiveness. I turned to the girl at my side and said wonderingly, "Your real power . . . it's love, isn't it? All along, all this time, that was it. . . ."

"Yes," said Agnes. "Love is the greatest power of all, and it can never be corrupted. You cannot snatch Sebastian from the Unconquered by giving him immortal life, which would make him as evil as they are. I could not do this. You cannot do this. That is not the way. The Talisman bestows other gifts."

"But what can I do to save him?" I begged.

"Love him," she said simply. "It is enough. Let your love show you the way."

Love. A light in the darkness that can never be destroyed. The only reality.

My reality.

The next moment I was kneeling next to Sebastian on the cold ground, and I knew what I had to do.

"Sebastian, listen to me. I'm going to help you. I'm going to give you something."

His eyes fluttered opened, and he tried to focus on my face.

"I have a gift for you," I said. "Please take it." I saw that Sebastian understood what I meant, and was afraid. The Dark Sisters had done this willingly, hoping for a greater gift in return. Laura had been forced to do it, and had paid with her life. But I wanted to do this. No one was forcing me, and I didn't expect to get anything back. I was doing it freely, from my heart, for Sebastian. Now it was my turn to feed him with my life's blood, my very soul. "Let me do this for you, Sebastian. It's the only way."

"No," he groaned. "I won't accept this gift. I won't let you sacrifice your life for me."

"I'm not talking about my life. Just one day, that's all. It will be enough."

"Enough for what?"

I looked into the blue of his eyes and smiled. "Enough for me to give you my real gift. Please, Sebastian. If you love me, let me do this."

I grasped the Talisman tightly in my trembling fingers, and its light filled my mind. Unknown words sang in my head. I saw the two of us walking together by a river of endless light. The fire blazed inside me. I leaned forward and kissed Sebastian. At that moment, we knew every secret of each other's minds; we knew our pasts and our futures; we saw eternity stretching out around us. We knew the truth: *The greatest of all the powers is love. . . .* I felt a part of my life's breath leave me and flow into him. With that long, sweet kiss, I had given Sebastian a day of my life.

When I opened my eyes, the fatigue and pain had gone from Sebastian's face. He was young and strong again, just for one more day. We were ready to face whatever would come. Together we stepped out of the circle, back to the noise and confusion of the storm-lashed hilltop.

A battle was raging. Helen and Sarah, together with Cal and his riders, were fighting for their lives against the coven. Sarah had torn the earth open and uncovered ancient cairns of weathered stones, and Helen was sending them hurtling down the wind like a shower of hail onto our enemies. But the Dark Sisters were still fighting back, led by their High Mistress. Her hair had fallen around her face, and she was savage with fury and madness. As soon as she saw Sebastian she screamed, "Seize him!"

But even as the crazed words fell from her lips, the thin chimes of the church bell began to float across the valley from the little gray church.

Midnight had come at last.

A deathly chill spread over the hilltop, and a mist rose from the ground. The fighting stopped, and everyone fell silent as a black shape emerged from the gloom. It was the mighty figure of a king that glimmered in the night, as though we were seeing a dark angel reflected in a deep, black pool. His long robes swirled around him like smoke, and he was crowned with tongues of red fire. His face, once gloriously beautiful, was now wholly corrupt, twisted by scorn and hatred. It was the king of the Unconquered, ready to claim his prize.

"This is the hour. Sebastian has failed in his quest. I

have come to bind him to the Shadow world as our slave."

The High Mistress was the first to speak. "No—no, you cannot take him yet," she protested wildly. "He is mine . . . leave him to me. . . . I will make him reach out to grasp immortality, and then eternity shall also be mine . . . please, just a few more moments, I beg you . . ."

The Unconquered moved his head slightly toward her. "Silence! You will not deprive me of my prey."

"But I already have," I said quietly.

"You?" He turned his terrible glare on me. "What can you have done that would concern me?"

"Sebastian is no longer fading," I said, trying to speak without fear. "You cannot take him. I have given him one day of my life. He is healed."

"One day! One day! What will that achieve? In twenty-four short hours I will return and take him then."

"No, you will never touch him now. Being your equal or being your slave—they are as bad as each other. You are evil and Sebastian is not. He doesn't belong with you." I held the Talisman high, and its glittering light made the dark king stagger backward. "My gift for him is greater than you know, and I am stronger than you are. I always will be, because I haven't forgotten how to love."

Then the Unconquered blazed with anger and disgust.

Sparks fell from his shadowy garments, and his fury made the earth tremble. "Love! Love! You dare speak to me of love?"

"What will be the use of your feeble love when death comes to take you in the end?" said Mrs. Hartle bitterly. "Oh, you are young; you think life will go on forever, but it won't. Love dies. Hope dies. Everything dies in the end." She seemed to collapse in front of us, turning into nothing more than a sad, frustrated woman clinging to an impossible dream. "I have given all my life for this moment," she moaned. "I wanted to live forever, and you promised me, Sebastian Fairfax, that it would happen . . . you promised us . . ."

"Death is the gateway to immortal life, not these twisted spells," said Sebastian. "I was wrong—and you are wrong to cling to this mania that is poisoning the only life you have."

"What good is life if death will destroy everything I have ever worked for?"

"You have a daughter," said Sebastian. "After your death, her life will honor yours, and her children—"

"Oh, spare me your sentimental drivel," she sneered. "'You can die and rot, but your children will take your place, like little flowers springing up in the sunlight. . . .'

I do not wish anyone to take my place!" Mrs. Hartle suddenly bowed to the Unconquered lord. "If I cannot live forever in this world, take me into your world, I beg you. Take me into your kingdom as your servant. I will be faithful to your sublime powers. I will have immortal life through your greatness."

"No! Mother—no!" Helen darted forward and tried to drag Mrs. Hartle away.

But the High Mistress twisted from Helen's touch with a cold laugh. "I don't need your love, my daughter. You have chosen your path. I have chosen mine. I am the High Mistress—now and forever." She stepped into the shadows that were swirling around the dark king and threw herself down at his feet. The next moment she gave a terrible cry as his steel-clad hand gripped her throat.

"I will take you in place of the other." He laughed. "So be it! You will serve me well!"

She fell back, lifeless. A pale figure, like ash, rose from her body and hovered next to the Unconquered and was then sucked into his darkness. The next moment they had gone. Only Mrs. Hartle's body was left behind, as still as the heart of silence, and her blank eyes stared up into eternity.

Forty-seven

The storm was over. The women of the coven had gone, melted into the hills, and the spirits of the Gypsy riders had returned to their resting place. We hugged and wept and held one another through the darkest part of the night, trying to let it all sink in, trying to comfort Helen. Then I stood close to Sebastian, and Sarah leaned her head against Cal's shoulder, while Miss Scratton and Helen knelt by Mrs. Hartle's body and mourned. We didn't move or speak for a long time.

"And so . . . so, is she dead?" said Helen at last, as the first gleam of dawn crept over the hills.

Miss Scratton sighed. "Her mortal body is dead, but her soul is chained to the evil places her new master inhabits. I am sorry, Helen."

Helen's eyes were red with crying. "Is there any hope for her?"

"There is always hope." Miss Scratton stood lost in thought for a while; then she beckoned the three of us to follow her down the hill a little way, leaving Cal and Sebastian to embrace as brothers and talk quietly together. We stood and looked over the valley to where the Abbey lay beneath us in the morning mist. "The night is over," Miss Scratton said, "and although the way ahead is still unclear, a darkness has left us. My hope for you now, Helen, is that this will not make you bitter. You have already had a lot to bear."

"I just wanted . . . I just hoped . . . that she would love me," Helen said fiercely. "There's no one left now who ever will."

Miss Scratton took Helen's hands in her own. "Your sisters love you, Helen. And you have a father, and one day he will find you. After that, there will come another, neither mother nor father nor sister nor brother, and he will love you beyond the confines of this world. This I can promise you. It is your destiny."

"How do you know all this?" asked Helen. "Who are you?"

"I saw you," I interrupted. "I saw you long ago, Miss Scratton—singing and healing and praying—"

"Yes, you saw me, Evie. You have the gift of divining the past, through the river of time."

"So you were there, all those years ago. . . ."

"I was there. And I am here."

"But I still don't really understand," Helen said.

"Some things we can never truly understand," Miss Scratton replied. "Who can understand the miracle of creation? Who can understand the depths of the oceans and the life of the stars? And the human heart, which one of us really understands that?"

"But how can you have lived at different times?" I asked. "After all that has happened with Sebastian, we know it is wrong for humans to seek immortal life; it's not possible—"

"Not for humans, I agree." She smiled, and as I frowned up at her thin, plain face, I saw that she was no longer plain, but filled with radiant inner light, like a picture in a church, like an angel. . . .

"I am a Guardian, Evie, sent by the Great Power to wherever I am needed. This valley is both sacred and cursed. The story of Agnes and Sebastian and Evie is only one of many in its long history. You know that the hills beneath our feet are scored with tunnels and caverns. In one of them is a crack between this world and the shadows.

The valley has seen great marvels because of it, both good and bad. And I have been here to see some of them, to play what part I can. I have known failure and success, but the battle between the light and the darkness never ends. It is enough for you to know that much."

"But what are you going to do now?" asked Sarah. "Will you stay here?"

"For a while, at least. The coven is scattered, angry and afraid, and that may make them dangerous. I hope that they will not suspect me, but I cannot be sure. Celia Hartle never entirely trusted me, and she managed to send me on a wild errand the night that Laura died." She paused and looked away, then added softly, "That was indeed a failure. After that I had to pretend to be the High Mistress's most fervent supporter. It was useful to act as one of the Dark Sisters, both to help guard the other students, and for other purposes." Then she looked at the three of us and laughed warmly. It was the first time I had seen her laugh. "But you do not need a guard. If you stay true to one another, you will be strong enough for anything that life will send you."

"And what about poor Harriet?" I said anxiously. "Will she be all right?"

"Harriet will recover from this," replied Miss Scratton,

"if that's what you mean. She sleeps now by Agnes's grave, which, if Celia Hartle had but known it, gives her a kind of protection. I will ensure that she will wake with no knowledge of this night and nothing worse than a chill from being outside. But she has been possessed by a mind stronger than her own, and that takes longer to heal. We must tend to her." She looked down at Mrs. Hartle's body and covered it with her cloak, then gave a high, clear call. The next moment her magnificent white horse galloped out of the gloom and halted by her side, restlessly shaking its head and pawing the ground. Miss Scratton bent down and lifted up Mrs. Hartle's body with surprising strength, then gently laid it on the horse's back. "We must tend to this matter, too. But not you, Evie."

"Why not? I . . . I want to help."

"The new day is beginning. This is your day—for you and Sebastian. Go to him, Evie. Use your day well. And if you should chance to pass by the grounds of Fairfax Hall at sunset tonight, your sisters will be there to greet you."

I kissed Helen and Sarah, then walked up the hill to where a boy with dark hair and blue eyes was waiting for me.

Sebastian James Fairfax. My first, my only love.

Forty-eight

This is the day. This is now.

It is the perfect morning. The storm has passed and everything is beginning again. Although it is not yet March, the air is gentle, the sky is a soft, sweet blue, and the earth is warm in the sun. Under the trees, the rain-dashed buds of snow drops and crocuses are raising their heads again, determined to live.

Sebastian smiles at me and folds me in his arms.

"You gave me one day. So I want to give you this day in return. One perfect day that will last forever. And then . . . then I will receive your final gift."

It is a day when all things meet and make sense. A day to treasure, like a precious jewel. A day I can look back on: when Sebastian and I were together, and happy, and blessed. My heart goes out in gratitude to Agnes, to Sarah and Helen, who helped to make this happen.

I love . . . I am loved . . . just for one day.

We walk and walk over the high hills, as close to heaven as we can get. The sun shines, and the earth turns beneath our feet, and life flows on in an endless stream around us. All that we have is here and now, and it is enough. Each minute. Each second. A lifetime of love and laughter crammed into a few hours.

It is the only time that Sebastian and I have ever met in the sunlight, out in the open, away from the darkness and the shadows. We don't need to hide anymore. I see the clear blue sky reflected in Sebastian's eyes; I see the whole world in his smile. We walk far over the moors, talking of everything, asking questions, making confessions, searching for explanations.

"I couldn't leave this life with you thinking that I was your enemy. That was a greater torment than anything else I was facing. You don't know how much I love you, Evie."

"I loved you the first time I saw you," I reply.

"Liar!" He laughs. "You couldn't have. I was awful to you."

"Well, maybe the second time." I smile, taking his hand

and pulling him close. "I'll always love you, Sebastian; you know that."

"I know."

He leans down and kisses me, and our souls touch. Then we cling to each other and try to memorize each other's faces, trying to make it last forever, trying to hide from what is to come.

Memories.

Do you remember when we first walked up here on the moors . . . do you remember the moon . . . and the night we rowed across the lake . . . do you remember?

I remember everything. I'll always remember. I'll spend my whole life remembering.

A cloud covers the sun. "Let's not think about the past anymore," I say. "The past is done. I want to think about the future. Our future."

Oh, we plan it all. We talk about the places we will visit together: Paris, Italy, India . . . so many places. We'll see temples and museums and rivers and wide oceans. We'll lie in the sun, lazy from food and wine and happiness. We'll climb mountains and find new places, and study and write books and make discoveries, and give something back to the world. We'll do it all together, day after day, step by step, and all the time our love will be wrapped around us, like a blanket of stars. And our children—how lovely they will be, I tell him. I see them playing around the gray stones at Uppercliffe: a sweet, solemn girl and a little boy with bronze curls. They laugh and tumble and rush over to Sebastian and cling to him, as though they will never let him go. We see everything, rolling along on the river of time. . . .

Time.

We are running out of time.

The hours are slipping past. The sun begins to sink in the west and the air bites coldly. The bright day is fading into a dim haze of evening light. We pass the trees and gardens of Fairfax Hall and walk up the slope to the granite monument that Sebastian's parents left in memory of their son who could never die.

In memory of a beloved son . . . in memory of my beloved . . . beloved memories.

So many memories. Our golden day is nearly done.

Helen is there, and Sarah, waiting by the memorial stone, and I am glad they are with me, now that the end has come.

"Are you really going to do this for me, Evie?" Sebastian asks.

I nod slowly. It is all I can give him now, the meaning

of everything I saw in the Talisman. But it hurts. It hurts so much.

"Thank you." He clasps my hand tightly. "I wish I knew what to say. Do you remember that poem I tried to write for you? Words are useless, aren't they? 'I'm grateful.' 'I love you.' It's just not enough, is it?"

"It doesn't matter. You don't have to say anything. We've said it all."

I am crying now. I can't stop my tears. Sebastian reaches out and touches a strand of my hair, just like he did when we first met. "Don't cry, Evie. It won't always hurt. You have to trust me. I want you to do this. It's the only way."

I throw my arms around his neck as though I will never let him go. But I must, because I do trust him. I will always trust him. I will do this. I am strong enough.

"It's okay. I'll do it. Just for you." I manage to smile. I want him to remember me smiling.

"There's one more thing I want you to do for me," he says.

"Of course. Anything."

"Then live, Evie. Just live. Don't spend your life grieving. I don't want you to stop loving because I . . . because our story wasn't as we once hoped."

"I'll never love anyone else," I say passionately. Sebastian smiles, and there is only a trace of sadness in his bright eyes.

"Oh, yes, you will, Evie. You must. You must love and marry and have a daughter with hair like fire and eyes like the sea. And you will tell her that no life is wasted, however short, if it has been touched by love. Oh, Evie . . ."

One last embrace. The very last kiss.

"Good-bye, girl from the sea," he whispers. "Every ending is also a beginning. We'll meet again, I promise."

Sebastian lets go of my hand and walks over to the monument that catches the last few rays of the sun. He lies down on the bright turf with the great stone at his head, closes his eyes, and folds his hands over his chest.

"Are you ready, Evie?" asks Sarah softly.

My heart is on fire, but yes, I am ready.

I unfasten the Talisman and place it on Sebastian's breast, like a star, then hold out my hands. They fill with clear water, which I sprinkle in a circle around us on the grass. Sarah takes the silver dagger and scores the ground, following the circle I have made, cutting the damp, sweet earth. Then Helen summons a wind that races around us in an endless ring of power, hiding us from the world's eyes. Water, earth, and air. Three elements. Three sisters. We need one more.

The water of our veins . . . the earth of our bodies . . . the air of our breath . . . the fire of our desires . . . come to us now.

I reach out in my mind and see the sacred fire rising up like a wild, brilliant bird. I click my fingers and tiny flames dance along the edge of our circle. They look like flowers dancing in the grass. Now the fourth element, Agnes's power, is present through me. Water, air, earth and fire—we are ready to follow the Mystic Way, the path of healing.

Helen passes me the Book. It is heavy in my hands as I find the page I need.

The Gift of Death. That is the only thing I can give Sebastian now. Death, for so long feared and avoided, is now ready to save him, and only I can open the gateway. This is my final gift to Sebastian The pages that had refused before to reveal their secrets now fall open under my touch and I know their strange truths.

That death is not the end. That the Creator has given life everlasting to all who truly seek it, not in this life, but beyond the threshold of our final sleep . . .

We make the incantations. We scatter the offerings.

We do all that is required, secret and beautiful and sacred. And a fourth girl comes to join us, our sister Agnes, at the heart of the mystery. Her rich red hair hangs loose over her white dress; her arms are held out in gladness to me, her eyes full of love. "I have come for my brother," she says. "It is time."

I take the silver dagger and place it in Sebastian's hand. He puts his other hand on top of mine, intertwining our fingers so that we hold it together.

"Receive our brother into your eternal rest. . . . Receive him into the light. . . ." Helen and Sarah and Agnes speak the words of the mystery, but my heart is too full and I cannot speak. "Receive him into the light," I beg silently.

As the knife slides into his heart, Sebastian opens his eyes and looks up to the sky and his face is bathed in radiant light, so blinding that we cannot watch. And when the light passes, he has gone. The earth in front of the stone memorial is raw and soft, like a freshly dug grave. Only the Talisman remains, a bright jewel on the ground. I reach to pick it up. It is all I have left to tell me that this really happened. Our story.

And now it is over.

If the demons of the Unconquered realms ever come seeking Sebastian Fairfax again, they will not find him.

He is far beyond them now. He has taken my gift, and crossed the threshold of death into a new beginning.

I stand up and look across the hills. The sun is setting, and my heart is breaking, but Sebastian is at peace.

Forty-nine

Little by little, I was coming back to life. All around me, the school was recovering too, slowly getting used to the shocking news that Mrs. Hartle's body had been found out on the moors. We fell back into some kind of routine, the only difference being that Miss Raglan was no longer around. The students were told that she had suddenly had to leave due to urgent family reasons. She wasn't missed. Miss Dalrymple and the others kept quiet, ashamed or embarrassed. Or biding their time, perhaps.

The days crept past, and Wyldcliffe Abbey School for Young Ladies carried on in the only way it knew how— with rules and order and calm English self-discipline. For once I was glad of the rigid routine that had enabled the school to survive so long in a changing world. It helped me to get through each day with something like normality. The visits and inquiries from the police and press were hard to ignore, though, as plans were made for an inquest into Mrs. Hartle's death. The funeral would be held later, when all the investigations were over.

We managed to get hold of the newspapers and read everything we could about the case. The authorities were suggesting that the High Mistress had suffered some kind of breakdown. She must have been hiding out in the caves on the moors for weeks, they speculated, then had a fatal heart attack as she was wandering in the storm.

Sometimes reality is just too hard for people to accept. This story would do as well as any other. Something for the headlines, until the next sensation came along. Something for Celeste and India and the others to gossip over, then forget.

In those quiet, drifting days, Helen and Sarah and I stayed close together, united in grief and love. Whatever had happened, whatever we had lost, we had one another, and nothing would ever break that bond. With each passing day, the weather grew warmer and brighter, and the hills echoed with the sound of newborn lambs bleating to greet the bright and mysterious world.

The following weekend, Harriet's mother came to take

her home. I went to say good-bye in the black-and-white-tiled hall as they waited for the taxi to arrive. A fire was crackling in the grate and a bowl of roses glowed on the long polished table.

"Mum, this is Evie, the girl I told you about. She was my friend here."

Harriet looked different, thin and tired, but the strained, hysterical look had left her. She didn't know that she had been controlled by a warped mind and used as a pawn in an insane game. She didn't remember the dreadful paths that Mrs. Hartle had sent her down. She only knew that she had come to boarding school and had not fit in, that she had been nervous and anxious and overwhelmed by homesickness. Harriet's eyes shone as she introduced her mother to me. Mrs. Templeton was rather like Harriet, sallow and thin and eager to please.

"Thank you so much for being kind to Harriet," she said apologetically. "I had no idea she would be so homesick and upset, starting all that sleepwalking business again."

I felt like a fraud. I hadn't really been so kind. But Harriet's mother waved away my embarrassed denials.

"No, Miss Scratton says you've been wonderful. It's funny," she added, glancing at the marble steps and the trophy cabinets and the antique prints on the walls. "The school hasn't changed at all. But being back here . . . well . . . it makes me remember how lonely it could be."

"Yes," I said. "Wyldcliffe can seem very far from home sometimes."

"Guess what, Evie? Mum's going to start working part-time so she can be with me at home and send me to a local school in London. Isn't that great? Not that I won't miss you," Harriet hurried on. "And you will write to me, won't you?"

"Of course."

"Thanks! Tell me if you see Lady Agnes's ghost, won't you?" She laughed and pulled her mother by the sleeve. "Come on, the taxi's here. I can't wait to get home."

They bustled into the car and drove away. For a second I wished that I were still twelve years old and that my mother could arrive and make everything right. I remembered how close she had seemed to me that night out on the hilltop. I tried to send her a message. *I'm okay, Mom*, I told her. *I'll survive.* . . .

"What are you thinking about, Evie?"

I jumped and turned around. It was Helen.

"Mothers," I said softly. Our eyes met and I read the flash of pain in her face.

"Do you still miss not having her?" she asked.

"Of course. And I miss Frankie too. But I'm fine. I really am."

"I know. And you've got your dad too. That makes all the difference."

I looked at Helen curiously. She was holding a letter in her hand. "Miss Scratton gave me this. It was sent to her so that she could pass it on to me."

Dear Helen,

I can't quite believe I am writing this letter. Miss Scratton at the school tracked me down through the newspapers after the publicity about your mother's death. It seems that you and I are related. In fact, she seems to think that I might be your father. I don't know if that's good news for you or a terrible shock, Helen, but I am so happy to find out about you. I often wondered if this was the reason Celia suddenly disappeared like that when we were young kids together. I wish she had trusted me enough to tell me. But that's all in the past. I hope we can meet—soon. Please write.

Tony Black

I reached out and hugged Helen tightly.

"I'm so, so glad," I said.

She smiled, and her fragile beauty shone like a flower opening in the sun. "Me too. I'm going to write back. Where are you off to?"

"Oh . . . I've got a riding lesson. I'd better go."

I walked outside and made my way down to the stables. This would be my last lesson with Josh before his mother came back to work, and my stomach was twisted with nerves. A couple of days ago I had given him the torn fragments of Agnes's diary to read, and Sarah had promised to tell him the rest. He deserved to know the truth, but I didn't know whether he would think I was lying or crazy. Either way, I had to face him.

Josh was waiting for me in the yard, holding Bonny by the halter. I swung into the saddle and he grinned. "My mother will be impressed. I've turned you into a passable rider. Anyone would think you'd been at Wyldcliffe for years."

"Thanks." I smiled. "At least, I think that's a compliment."

"Where's Sarah?" he asked, as I rode into the paddock and he strode along next to me.

"She's riding up on the moors with Cal. Miss Scratton said it was okay."

"So is his family staying in Wyldcliffe?"

I shook my head. "I'm not sure. There's still so much rumor and gossip about them—all those horrible animal killings that Mrs. Hartle was behind." I halted and looked at him steadily. "That is, if you believe what Sarah told you."

Josh rested his hand lightly on mine. "I believe you, Evie. I know this valley. I know it hides many secrets. Besides, I knew you were in trouble all along. And so this guy, Sebastian . . . he's . . ."

"He's dead," I said briefly. "It's all over." There was a yawning hole where my heart had been, but I wouldn't cry. Sebastian wouldn't want that. *When I am dead, my dearest, sing no sad songs for me. . . .*

Josh tightened his hold on my hand. "Evie, I know you won't want to hear this yet, but you know that I . . . I can't help wondering if there'll ever be any hope for me."

I felt a wave of panic rise up in me. "I can't; it's too soon. I don't think I can ever . . . love . . . again. What you're saying . . . it scares me."

"I'm not asking for love. It's just that I really like you, Evie."

"And I like you," I said, feeling awkward.

"Well, that's a start, isn't it? We can be friends. Love doesn't have to be painful, Evie. It doesn't have to be this big, tormented passion. It can be easy and simple, like sunshine in the morning, or like walking on the beach and listening to the waves."

There was a lump in my throat. Sebastian and I had never made it to that beach, to that place of warmth and sunshine. We would never see the dawn rise over the ocean. Sebastian had given himself to the night, but he had finally escaped from the darkness, and I could too.

"I'd like . . . I'd like to be friends."

"Then let's be the best of friends," Josh answered. "Let's live one day, and then another and another. And maybe in time, the sun will smile on us."

I pressed his hand gratefully. "You're so good, Josh."

"No, I'm not. I'm just crazy about you." He lifted my hand and kissed it gently, then stepped back and smiled up at me. "There. That wasn't so terrifying, was it?"

I looked into his face, full of life and hope and courage. I had no idea what the future held, but I realized that I was no longer frightened. No, I wasn't frightened at all.

Fifty

There were still a few weeks left before the end of term. We had exams to look forward to, and concerts and the handing out of class prizes and awards. But first there was one other ritual we had to get through.

The funeral was a rather grand, pompous affair. Students, parents, mistresses and school governors, the local mayor, and other dignitaries were all crammed into the little stone church to bid farewell to Mrs. Celia Hartle, the High Mistress of Wyldcliffe. I sat at the back with Sarah. I didn't want to look at the coffin, piled high with costly lilies. Instead I focused on where Helen sat with her head bowed at the front of the church, flanked on one side by Miss Scratton, and on the other by a tall, blond man, who kept glancing down at Helen's pale face in wonder. Every ending was also a beginning. . . .

The vicar spoke of loss, and of hope. The words rolled over me like a cleansing wave.

"'I am the resurrection and the life,' saith the Lord; 'he that believeth in me, though he were dead, yet shall he live: and whosoever liveth and believeth in me shall never die . . .'"

I stood up quietly and slipped unnoticed out of the church. It was still early in the morning and there was somewhere I had to go. As I climbed above the sleepy village on the familiar path over the hills, someone came to join me. We walked in silence, stopping only to collect a few early wildflowers that were growing in the shelter of the hedgerows. A bird sang high overhead, and the lambs called for their mothers.

As we walked over the brow of the ridge toward the old hall, I knew I would never be that innocent young girl who had arrived in Wyldcliffe so many months ago. I had seen the darkness and I would never be able to forget it. But I had also known love, and it had taught me that knowing another person's heart was the greatest adventure life had to offer. I had known what it was like to get up in the morning and rejoice, simply because Sebastian walked upon the earth. I had looked up at the wide blue sky and seen the sun shining especially for me, because I loved him.

And now, finally, I was ready to say good-bye.

I knelt at Sebastian's grave. Soon, the mound by the headstone would be no longer bare, but threaded with tender green roots and moss. I gently traced the outline of his name on the stone with my fingers. *In Memory of a Beloved Son, Sebastian James Fairfax . . .*

My beloved.

I would always love him. My first, my dearest love.

The wind whistled over the hills like the distant echo of the sea. I placed my simple flowers against the headstone and stood up. There was no need to say anything, no need for words or promises. I had been true to Sebastian. There had been no betrayal between us. When I saw him again—and I knew that one day I would—we would meet as creatures of eternal light. There would be no trace of shadow left. The darkness was over. He was free.

And I was free too. Free to grieve and free to live. I had to live, for Sebastian's sake as well as my own. My heart had to be big enough for whatever was waiting; I couldn't allow it to be broken. I was Evie Johnson, I was sixteen years old, and life hadn't finished for me yet. It was just beginning.

"Time to go, Evie," said Josh quietly.

I turned to him and smiled.

"Yes," I said. "Let's go."

We walked down the hill together, back to the school where my sisters would be waiting for me. It was a new day, and our faces were toward the sun, and we didn't look back.

The magic and romance continue in

Prologue

I am not like Evie. I don't belong in some great romance. I'm just the best friend in the background. Always there, always reliable, down-to-earth. Good old Sarah. That's how it's always been. Until now.

Now I have to make the hardest decision of my life. To go on or to go back.

I am standing on the hillside above Wyldcliffe. The sun is setting over the wide, wild land. I love this place. I love the wind on my face, and the high call of the birds, and the deep life and history of these ancient hills. The rocks that lie like bones underneath the heather and gorse speak to me of power and strength and eternity.

When all this began, I thought I could be like those rocks: a backbone of strength for everyone else. "Good old Sarah, she can cope with anything." I have discovered, though, that I am weak. It turns out that I don't just want to tend and nurture the needs of others. I have feelings too—and failings. I love. I hate. I feel anger. And what I feel frightens me. It might stop me from doing what I have to do.

The sun has almost gone now. Night begins to spread over the moors. Out there, in the land that I love, Evie is lost. She has been taken by the enemy and is a prisoner in the still and secret earth. Only I can save her. It is my turn to act.

Where is my courage now? Where is my strength? What shall I do?

There are no answers. The day is over. I have to choose. I begin to walk down the hill, under the dark sky, and into the valley that is called Death.

One

I hadn't been expecting this. In all the chaos and uncertainty of the last few months I had learned to accept many strange things, and I guess I had thought that nothing would ever surprise me again.

But this was something else.

Velvet Romaine.

I'd heard of her, of course. Everyone's heard of Velvet Romaine. The lurid details of her first sixteen years have been splashed across every tabloid newspaper. It's just that I didn't expect her to turn up at Wyldcliffe Abbey School for Young Ladies. Wyldcliffe isn't the kind of school that attracts the daughters of rock stars. The daughters of duchesses, maybe, but not a flashy wild-child rebel like Velvet. But there she was, when I arrived at the school on the first day of the summer term, and she was making a sensation. Her huge limo had pulled up outside the school's imposing Gothic building, and as she stepped out she was surrounded by a crowd of excited students and a gaggle of paparazzi. The photographers snapped away eagerly and Velvet stood there lapping up the attention, dressed as though she was ready for a hot date in some sleazy nightclub.

But I don't want to sound judgmental. Hey, this is me, Sarah Fitzalan, the earth mother type, got a kind word for everyone, always looking for the positive, always ready to defend the underdog. That's what they say, anyway.

I had been so desperate to get back to school. Not that I'm some academic genius or anything. It wasn't my studies that were pulling me back to the remote valley where Wyldcliffe lies hidden. It wasn't the spell of the wild moors either, where the gorse and cowslips would be in bloom. The awakening earth called to me, but I turned my face from the hills and thought of nothing but seeing Evie and Helen again.

You know how people say about their friends, oh, we're so close we could be sisters? Well, Evie and Helen and I really are sisters. Not related by blood, but by deeper ties. Mystic, elemental forces bind us together, in this life and the next. Sounds stupid, but I've always believed there are things in life that we don't understand, that maybe we can't see, but they exist all the same. The feel of a place, an atmosphere, premonitions, and prophecies—I think all that means something. I believe that the soul is eternal and that the spirits of the dead can speak to us. And so when Evie first arrived at Wyldcliffe as a lonely scholarship student and started seeing visions of a girl from the past, I didn't call her crazy. I believed her. I accepted what was going on, and everything that followed.

How the girl was Lady Agnes Templeton, Evie's distant ancestor. How, more than a hundred years ago, Agnes had discovered the secrets of the Mystic Way and had become a servant of the sacred fire. How Agnes's former admirer, Sebastian Fairfax, was the same person as the mysterious young man that Evie was secretly seeing. How Sebastian had become trapped in a futile quest for immortality. How we had discovered our own elemental powers—water for Evie, air for Helen, earth for me—and used them to save Sebastian's soul. And how, finally, Sebastian had passed from this life and left Evie grieving for an impossible love.

All things considered, we had a lot to talk about. We had faced death together. Evie had lost her first love and Helen had lost her mother, and I had been desperately

Perhaps it was simply a reaction to everything I had been through with Evie and Helen, but I believed it was an omen, a sign of more danger to come. Whatever the truth of it, dreams and darkness were pulling me back to Wyldcliffe, and I was longing to see my friends. So I really wasn't too pleased when the circus surrounding Velvet Romaine seemed to be bringing the whole place to a grinding halt.

There she was, posing next to her over-the-top car as the photographers screamed, "Velvet! This way! Give us a smile!" She wasn't smiling, though. She looked furious. Her hair was jet black, cut into a Louise Brooks–style bob, and she exuded the same kind of dangerous sexiness as the classic screen star. Her short skirt showed off slim legs, torn fishnet stockings, and expensive-looking black lace-up boots. All the other Wyldcliffe girls, who were staring with disbelief, were wearing the old-fashioned red and gray school uniform. I wondered what Velvet would look like when the Wyldcliffe teachers, or mistresses, made her get rid of her designer clothes and her heavy eyeliner and goth lipstick. But right now she was making the most of her grand entrance as she pouted for the photographers, sultry and rebellious. Whatever Wyldcliffe's past secrets were, it had never seen anything like this before.

As I watched Velvet, she reminded me of a cornered animal putting up a defiant last stand, ready to lash out at anything and anyone who got in her way.

"Is that really her?" a girl from my class, Camilla Willoughby-Stuart, whispered excitedly at my side. "Velvet Romaine?"

"It looks like it."

"What is she doing here? Doesn't she live in L.A. or somewhere like that? She'll be bored to death at Wyldcliffe. I mean, she goes to these amazing parties with actors and musicians and rock stars. I've read about her in all the magazines. Didn't she go to rehab when she was only thirteen? And last year she ran off with some guy twice her age. . . ."

Other stories about Velvet Romaine flashed into my mind. Despite her money and glamour, she'd already met with tragedy in her short life. I recalled that she'd been in a car crash where her younger sister had been killed, and then there had been some incident about a fire at her last boarding school—I couldn't quite remember what had happened. I usually read magazines about horse riding, not celebrity gossip. But Camilla seemed to know all about her.

"Ooh, it must have been awful for Velvet at L'École des

Montagnes," she rattled on. "It's a fantastic school in the Swiss Alps—all the European royals go there—but her best friend was scarred for life after that fire they had. No wonder she didn't want to stay there. But why come to Wyldcliffe? It's far too quiet for someone like Velvet Romaine!"

"Perhaps that's why her parents want her to come here," I said. "You know—order, purpose, discipline, and all the rest. Old-fashioned values."

Camilla grimaced. "She's going to hate it. Have you seen her clothes? She looks so amazing. I wish my mom would let me have some boots like that. . . ."

As Camilla chattered away, a woman with a plain face and scraped-back hairstyle opened the school's massive oak door and came out to stand on the step next to Velvet. It was Miss Scratton, our history teacher. She addressed the photographers coldly.

"This is private property. If you don't leave immediately, I shall call the police. Please respect the fact that this is a school and a place of learning." She turned to Velvet. "I am Miss Scratton, the new High Mistress of Wyldcliffe. I want to welcome you to the Abbey, but let's go somewhere more private. Girls, what are you all doing hanging about here with your mouths open like goldfish?

Most undignified. I'm sure you all have plenty to do to unpack and settle down before classes start tomorrow." The gaping students reluctantly moved away, and Miss Scratton beckoned me over. "Sarah, could you please stay a moment?" She smiled faintly. "You are just the person I was looking for. You can help show Velvet around."

Velvet flicked a snooty stare at me, as though I were some kind of servant. My heart sank. Normally I was only too happy to help new students, but she was giving off such a hostile attitude, like she could read my thoughts and didn't think much of them. If Miss Scratton wanted me to be friendly with Velvet Romaine, I would try my best, but I was desperate to see my real friends as soon as I could. I looked around uneasily. "Um . . . I was looking for—"

"For Evie and Helen?" Again there was a faint gleam of sympathy in Miss Scratton's sharp black eyes. "They haven't arrived yet. I believe they are traveling to Wyldcliffe together on the train. You'll see them soon enough. Come, both of you. Follow me!"

There was more clamor and flurry from the photographers as we followed Miss Scratton through the heavy door. She closed it firmly behind us, and I found myself in the familiar entrance hall. The somber black-and-white tiles, the grand marble staircase, and the stone hearth were exactly as they had always been, but then I gasped in surprise. For a moment I thought that Evie was staring at me across the hallway like a ghost. The face of a girl with starry gray eyes and long red hair seemed to float in front of my eyes in the gloomy light.

"I see you're admiring the portrait of Lady Agnes, Sarah," Miss Scratton said. "I had it moved here during the vacation. It looks very well in the entrance hall, don't you think?"

For a moment I couldn't speak, but Velvet glanced at the painting and said insolently, "She looks as crazy as the rest of this place. Who is she anyway?"

"Lady Agnes was the daughter of Lord Charles Templeton, who built the present house in the nineteenth century," Miss Scratton replied in calm, measured tones. "She was an extraordinarily gifted young woman who sadly died young. I feel it is only right that we should remember her." Then she swept across the hallway and down a windowless corridor, paneled in dark wood. Our feet echoed on the polished floor as we followed her. Velvet slouched along behind Miss Scratton, and I tried to look as though I hadn't a care in the world. But seeing Agnes's picture unexpectedly like that had unnerved me.

To me, she wasn't just someone from history to

remember and wonder about. To me, she was real. Agnes was Evie's link with the past, but she was also our Mystic Sister of the fire element. And her sea-gray eyes had seemed to hold a clear warning for me that, despite the victories of the term before, our struggles weren't yet over.